A
BURIAL AT SEA

Also by Charles Finch

A Beautiful Blue Death

The September Society

The Fleet Street Murders

A Stranger in Mayfair

A
BURIAL AT SEA

Charles Finch

Minotaur Books ✖ New York

A BURIAL AT SEA. Copyright © 2011 by Charles Finch. All rights reserved. Printed in the United States of America. For information, address St. Martin's Press, 175 Fifth Avenue, New York, N.Y. 10010.

www.minotaurbooks.com

The Library of Congress has cataloged the hardcover edition as follows:

Finch, Charles (Charles B.)
    A burial at sea / Charles Finch.—1st ed.
        p. cm.
    ISBN 978-0-312-62508-5
    1. Lenox, Charles (Fictitious character)—Fiction.   2. Murder—
Investigation—Fiction.   I. Title.
    PS3606.I526B87 2011
    813'.6—dc23

                                                      2011026214

ISBN 978-1-250-00814-5 (trade paperback)

First Minotaur Books Paperback Edition: August 2012

10 9 8 7 6 5 4 3 2 1

This book is dedicated with love to my grandmother, Anne Truitt, who was fond of sea stories. In memory.

Acknowledgments

A *Burial at Sea* required perhaps more research than the previous four Lenox books combined, and correspondingly there are a large number of people to thank. Chief among these is Jeremiah Dancy, naval historian at Lady Margaret Hall, Oxford, who patiently answered dozens of my questions, small and large, and offered me an excellent bibliography. The most useful of the books he recommended to me were *The Navy in Transition* by Michael Lewis and *The Royal Navy: An Illustrated Social History, 1870–1982.* by Captain John Wells. I also want to mention the two writers who inspired this book's setting, C. S. Forester and the incomparable Patrick O'Brian.

As usual, the team at St. Martin's Press, from Charlie Spicer to Yaniv Soha to Andy Martin, was wonderfully generous and helpful. So was my agent, Kate Lee.

Thank you to Dennis Popp and Linda Bock. I owe them gratitude beyond reckoning for all their loyal support and friendship in recent years, and it seems appropriate that I completed this book in their beautiful sunroom.

Emily Popp and Mary Truitt each read early drafts, and each changed the final manuscript considerably for the better with their suggestions. Thanks and love to both of them.

For the name of the *Bootle*, thanks to Gerald Durrell, and for the name of the *Lucy*, thanks to Lucy.

Because I had so much help this time around, I must insist with more than the usual vehemence that all the book's mistakes are my own.

A
BURIAL AT SEA

CHAPTER ONE

He gazed out at the sunfall from an open second-floor window, breathing deeply of the cool salt air, and felt it was the first calm moment he had known in days. Between the outfitting, the packing, the political conversations with his brother, and a succession of formal meals that had served as shipboard introductions to the officers of the *Lucy*, his week in Plymouth had been a daze of action and information.

Now, though, Charles Lenox could be still for a moment. As he looked out over the maze of thin streets that crossed the short path to the harbor, and then over the gray, calm water itself—smudged brown with half-a-dozen large ships and any number of small craft—he bent forward slightly over the hip-high window rail, hands in pockets. He was past forty now, forty-two, and his frame, always thin and strong, had started to fill out some at the waist. His trim brown hair, however, was still untouched by gray. On his face was a slight, careworn smile, matched by his tired, happy, and curious hazel eyes. He had been for much of his life a detective, more lately a member of Parliament for the district of Stirrington, and now for the first time, he would be something else: something very like a diplomat.

Or even a spy.

It had begun two months before, in early March. Lenox had been at home on Hampden Lane. This was the small street just off Grosvenor Square, lined with pleasant houses and innocuous shops—a bookseller, a tobacconist—where he had lived nearly his whole adult life. For much of that time his best friend had lived next door to him, a widow named Lady Jane Grey whose family was also from Sussex: they had grown up riding together, fidgeting through church together: together. Just three years before, to his own confused and happy surprise, Lenox had realized how very much he loved her. It had taken some time to gather the courage to ask her to marry him. But he had. Now, in the winter of 1873, they were just getting used to the upside-down tumble their lives had taken. Their houses, side by side as they were, had been rebuilt to connect, and now they lived within a sprawling mishmash of rooms that matched their joined-up lives. They were a couple.

Lenox had been in his study that evening in March, making notes for a speech he hoped to give the following day in the House of Commons about India. There was a gentle snow outside the high windows near his desk, and the gaslights cast a dim and romantic light over the white, freshened streets.

There was a knock at the door.

Lenox put down his pen and flexed his sore hand, opening and closing it, as he waited for their butler, Kirk, to show the guest in.

"Sir Edmund Lenox," Kirk announced, and to his delight Charles saw his older brother's cheerful and ruddy face pop around the doorway.

"Ed!" he said, and stood. They clasped hands. "Come, sit

by the fire—you must be nigh on frozen. Well, it's been two weeks nearly, hasn't it? You're in the country too often for my taste, I tell you that frankly."

Edmund smiled widely but he looked exhausted. "In fact I wasn't at the house, so you can't lay that charge against me," he said. The house being the one they had grown up in together, Lenox House.

"No? But you said you were going to see Molly and the—"

The baronet waved a hand. "Security reasons, they say, but whatever it is we were at Lord Axmouth's place in Kent, five of us, holed up with the admiralty, the chaps from the army, a rotating cast of ministers . . . with Gladstone."

The prime minister. Charles furrowed his brow. "What can it have been about?"

In person Edmund Lenox looked very much like his younger brother, but he was perhaps less shrewd in the eyes, more open-faced. He served in Parliament out of a sense, not of ambition, but of duty, inherited from their father, and indeed preferred the country to London. Perhaps as a result he had a countryish air. He seemed heartier than his brother Charles.

This innocent, candid mien, however, concealed a more intelligent mind than one might immediately have suspected. It had been to Lenox's great shock when he first learned, five or six years before, that Edmund wasn't the stolid backbencher he had always appeared to be, but in fact a leading member of his party who had declined important posts again and again, preferring to work behind the scenes.

Now he surprised Charles again.

"You know something of my purview?" Edmund said.

"Something." Lenox himself was still a backbencher, but could say without undue immodesty that he was a rising man; long hours of work had seen to that. "You advise the ministers, consult with the prime minister on occasion, find votes—that sort of thing."

Edmund smiled again, an unhappy smile this time. "First of all, let me say that I come to ask a favor. I hope you'll agree to do it."

"With all my heart."

"Not so quickly, for love's sake, Charles."

"Well?"

Edmund sighed and stood up from the armchair, staring for a moment at the low, crackling glow in the hearth. "Might I have a drink?" he asked.

"The usual?" Lenox stood and walked over to a small, square, lacquered table crowded with crystal decanters. He poured them each a glass of Scotch whisky. "Here you are."

"There are other parts of my job, that I haven't mentioned to you before," said Edmund after a sip. "A role I play that you might call more—more secret."

Lenox understood instantly, and felt well inside him some mixture of excitement, tension, surprise, and even a slight hurt that he hadn't heard of this before. "Intelligence?" he said gravely.

"Yes."

"What branch?"

Edmund considered the question. "You might call me an overseer, of sorts."

"All of it, then."

"Since the new prime minister came in, yes. I report to him. These weeks we have been—"

"You might have told me," said Charles, his tone full of forced jocularity.

With comprehension in his eyes Edmund said, "I would have, believe me—I would have come to you first were I permitted to speak of it."

"And why can you now? This favor?"

"Yes."

"Well?"

"It's France," said Edmund. "We're worried about France."

"That doesn't make sense. Everything has been cordial, hasn't it? Uneasily so, I suppose, but—"

Edmund sat down. "Charles," he said with a hard look, "will you go to Egypt for us?"

Taken aback, Charles returned his brother's stare. "Why—I suppose I could," he said at last. "If you needed me to."

So that spark had burst into this conflagration; Lenox would set sail twelve hours from now aboard the *Lucy*, a corvette bound for the Suez.

A cool breeze fluttered the thin white curtains on either side of him. He felt his nerves shake slightly, his stomach tighten, as he contemplated the idea of leaving, of all his fresh responsibility. This Plymouth house—a cream-colored old Georgian in a row, let by the week or month to officers and their families—had in just two weeks come to feel almost like home, and he realized with a feeling of surprise that he would be sorry to leave it, even though he had looked forward to nothing else for two months but his voyage. Then he understood that it wasn't the house he would miss, but the home that his wife had made of it.

He heard the door open downstairs.

"Charles?" a voice rang from the bottom of the stairs. It was Lady Jane.

Before he answered he hesitated for a brief moment and looked out again at Plymouth Harbor, under its falling golden sun, savoring the idea, every boy's dream, of being out at sea.

"Up here!" he cried then. "Let me give you a hand."

But she was clambering up the stairs. "Nonsense! I'm already halfway there."

She came in, pink-faced, dark-haired, smallish, pretty in a rather plain way, dressed all in blue and gray—and holding her belly, which, though her dress hid it, had begun to round out.

For after hesitation and dispute, something wonderful had

happened to them, that daily miracle of the world that nevertheless always manages to catch us off guard, no matter our planning, no matter our dreams, no matter our circumstances: she was pregnant.

CHAPTER TWO

The next morning was bright, and now the harbor shifted and glittered brilliantly. Anchored some way out, close enough that one could see men moving aboard her but far enough that their faces were indistinct, lay the *Lucy*, bobbing up and down.

She had come into dry dock some six weeks before, after a two-year tour in distant waters, and had since then been refitted: her old and tattered sails, mended so often they were three-quarters patch, replaced with snow-white new ones, the dented copper below her waterline smoothed and reinforced, her old bolts refitted, her formerly bare engine room again coaled. She looked young once more.

Lucy had come off the same dockyards as Her Majesty's ship *Challenger* in the same year, 1858, and both were corvettes, ships designed not for firing power, like a frigate, or quick jaunts out, like a brig, but for speed and maneuverability. She carried three masts; from stem to stern she measured about two hundred feet; as for men, she held roughly two hundred and twenty bluejackets—common seamen—and twenty-five or so more, from the rank of midshipman to captain, who belonged to the officer ranks. The *Challenger*, which was well known because of its long scientific mission to Australia and the surrounding seas, was quicker than the *Lucy*, but the *Lucy* was thought to be more agile and better in a fight.

In her means of propulsion she embodied perfectly the uncertain present state of the navy's technology. She was not steam-powered but rather steam-*assisted*, which is to say that she used the power of coal to leave and enter harbor and during battle, but the rest of the time moved under sail, not all that differently than her forebears in the Napoleonic Wars sixty years earlier might have. Using coal added several knots to the *Lucy*'s speed, but it was a problematic fuel source: coaling stations were few and far between and the burners were thin-walled and had to be spared too much taxation lest they falter in an important situation. (New, thicker burners were being manufactured now, but even in her Plymouth refitting the *Lucy* didn't receive one of them.)

Lenox had learned all of this information three nights before from the captain, Jacob Martin, a stern, youngish fellow, perhaps thirty-five, extremely religious, prematurely gray but physically very strong. Edmund said that he was much respected within the admiralty and destined for great things, perhaps even the command of a large warship within the next few months. Martin politely did his duty by welcoming Lenox to the ship and describing her outlines to him, but all the same didn't quite seem to relish the prospect of a civilian passenger.

"Still," he had said, "we must try to prove our worth now, the navy. It's not like it was in my grandfather's day. He was an admiral, Mr. Lenox, raised his flag at Trafalgar. Those chaps were heroes to the common Englishman. Now we must stretch ourselves in every new direction—diplomacy, science, trade—so that you mathematical fellows in Parliament will continue to see the use of us. Peacetime, you see."

"Surely peace is the most desirable state of affairs for an officer of the navy?"

"Oh, yes!" said Martin, but in a slightly wistful tone, as if he weren't entirely in agreement but couldn't tactfully say as much.

They were in a private room at a public house near the water, where many officers regularly took supper. It was called the Yardarm. "I realize there must be fewer men afloat than during war," said Lenox, trying to be sympathetic.

Martin nodded vehemently. "Yes, too many of my peers are on shore, eking out a life on half-pay. Dozens of children, all of them. Meanwhile the French have started to outpace us."

"Our navy is much larger," said Lenox. He spoke with authority—he had read the world's driest blue book (or parliamentary report) on the subject.

"To be sure, but their ships are sound and fast and big, Mr. Lenox." Martin swirled his wine in his glass, looking into it. "They were ahead of us on coal. Our *Warrior* was based on her *Gloire*. Who knows what they're doing now. Meanwhile we're all at sixes and sevens."

"The navy?"

"It's a period of transition."

"Coal and steam, you mean, Captain? I know."

"Do you?"

"I thought so, at any rate. Please enlighten me."

"It's not as it was," said Martin. "We must now train our men to sail a full-rigged vessel, as we always have, and at the same time to coal a ship to fourteen knots under steam even as we fire a broadside. Because she's built for speed the *Lucy* is very light in guns, of course—only twenty-one four-pounders, which would scarcely trouble a serious ship—but still, to be worried at once about sail, steam, and shooting is no easy task for a captain or a crew. And the Lord forbid you find yourself without coal." He laughed bitterly and drank off the last of his wine.

"I understand the depots are few and far between."

"You might say that. I think it's more likely we'll see three mermaids between here and Egypt than three proper depots where we can take our fill."

Lenox tried good cheer. "Still, to be at sea! It's stale to you, but for me I confess it's a thrill."

Martin smiled. "I apologize for sounding so negative, Mr. Lenox. I've been afloat since I was twelve, and I wouldn't be anywhere else for money. But a captain's job is a difficult one. When I'm on the water all of my problems are soluble, you see, but on land I can think over them and fret and worry myself half to oblivion. Before we leave, for instance, I must meet with the admiralty to discuss the prospects of my lieutenants. I'm bound to break one of their hearts. Well, but let us speak of other things. You'll have a child soon, as I hear it? Might we drink to your wife's health?"

"Oh, yes," said Lenox fervently, and signaled to the waiter at the door for another bottle.

If supper at the Yardarm had been morose in stretches, due to Martin's heavyhearted fears over the future of his service, Lenox's visit to the wardroom of the *Lucy* had been entirely different.

It was in the wardroom where the rest of the officers took their meals. They were a far more rollicking, jovial set of men than their captain, and they had insisted Lenox actually visit the ship by way of introduction.

In the wardroom itself—a low-slung, long chamber at the stern of the ship with a row of very handsome curved windows, where lanterns swung gently from their moorings in the roof, casting a flickering light over the wineglasses and silver—Lenox met a bewildering array of men. All were seated at a single long table that ran fore-to-aft through the entire room. There were the ship's five lieutenants, each of whom hoped one day to take on the responsibilities that Martin bemoaned; two marines, dressed in lobster-red, a captain and lieutenant, who commanded a squadron of twenty fighting men in the ship, and were thus part of the navy and not quite part of it at all; and finally the civil officers, each with a different responsibility, from the surgeon to the chaplain to the purser. Each of the fifteen or so people present sat in a dark mahogany chair, upholstered in navy blue, and as Lenox had learned from the rather rough quarterdeckman who had fetched him from shore, none could speak out of rank until the Queen was toasted.

When at last this happened the fierce decorum of the first glasses of wine fell off and people began to converse companionably. Lenox had already forgotten half the names he had heard, but to his pleasure he discovered that the person seated to his left, a second lieutenant called Halifax, was an agreeable sort.

"How long have you been with the *Lucy?*" Lenox asked him.

"About five months," said Halifax. He was a plump fellow with a face slick and red from the warmth and wine. He seemed somehow gentle, though—not the card-playing, hard-drinking type Lenox might have expected. His voice was soft and melodious and his face was more than anything a kind one.

"What brought you on board?"

"Captain Martin's previous second lieutenant had been lost at sea just before, and I met the ship at Port Mahon to replace him."

"Poor chap."

A troubled look passed over Halifax's face, and his eyes ran along the faces at the table. "Yes. Unfortunately the navy can be unkind. Not all men get their wishes—not all lieutenants are made captain, for instance, however much they may feel they deserve it. Or take my case: nobody likes getting work at another man's expense, of course, but I admit that I'm happy for the time at sea. Shore is dull, don't you find?"

"I don't," said Lenox, "but then I've nothing to compare it to."

"Very true. Do you fish, at least?"

"When I was a boy I did. Not since then."

"I've a spare rod—you must come with me to the quarter-deck some time." Halifax smiled to himself, his eyes fixed somewhere in the middle distance. "Watching your line bob along the water as the sun goes down and the ship is quiet—a mild wind, leaning over the rail, cool breeze, perhaps a cigar—it's the only way to live, Mr. Lenox."

"What do you catch?"

"It depends where you are. My last ship, the *Defiant*, was broken up, but I sailed with her to the northern waters with Captain Robertson. There you found char, sculpins, cods, gunnels. Any number of things. We raked over a fair few hundred jellyfish. Have you ever seen one?"

"I haven't, except in pictures."

"They're enormous, several feet long. Harmless, though their sting hurts like the dickens. Rather beautiful. Translucent."

"And on our way to Egypt what will you find?"

A delighted look came into Halifax's face. "The Mediterranean is a treat, from all I hear, enormous tuna fish, bream, mullet, marlins, swordfish. A velvet-belly shark, if we're very lucky."

"I must strike off my plans to go for a swim."

"Nonsense—most refreshing thing in the world! If you're sincerely afraid of sharks the captain will put a net out alongside of the ship, which you may swim in. Oh, but wait—a toast."

The white-haired chaplain was rising, wildly inebriated, and when he had (not without difficulty) attained a standing position, proclaimed in a loud voice, "To a woman's leg, sirs! Nothing could be finer in the world! And to my wife Edwina!"

There was a raucous cheer at this, and as anyone might have predicted who witnessed that moment, the wardroom's supper went on very late into the night.

CHAPTER THREE

E at this," said Lady Jane, and thrust out an orange at him.
"For the fiftieth time, dear heart, I'm not likely to come
down with scurvy."

They were walking down to the docks now. Behind them
were two sailors from the *Lucy*, carrying Lenox's effects: a large
steamer trunk and two smaller bags. Lenox himself carried a
small leather case full of documents that he thought it best to
keep in his possession at all times. They were from his brother.

"Indulge me, won't you?"

With a not unhappy sigh he took the piece of fruit she held
out and began to peel it with his thumb. "I make this the six-
teenth orange I've eaten in the last fortnight, and I'm not even
counting the lemons you sneak onto every piece of fish I put in
my mouth or those lime-flavored sherbets you plied me with at
the admiral's supper. I'm heartily sick of citrus fruits, you
know. If I do get scurvy that will be the reason."

"I would prefer you to return with all of your teeth, Charles.
You can't blame me for that."

"I knew I was marrying a noblewoman. Such discrimination!"

She laughed. "I've packed a few more oranges in your trunk—eat them, will you?"

"I'll make you a deal. I promise to choke down these oranges you give me if you promise in return to stay off your feet after I leave."

"Oh, I shall," she said. "Shake my hand—there, the deal is finished. I'm ahead of you anyhow—I told Toto I would let her read to me in the afternoons while I stayed in my bed."

"Dr. Chavasse's book?"

"I threw that away. *Advice to a Mother on the Management of Her Children*, indeed—that man knew no more about real mothering than Kirk does, or a bear in the woods. It's more a book to frighten women than help them."

"But he's a doctor, Jane, and—"

"And what sort of name is Pye Henry Chavasse, too? I don't trust a person who can't have an honest name. Just call yourself Henry if your parents were foolish enough to burden you with 'Pye,' I say."

"I'm not sure anyone related by blood to a man called Galahad Albion Lancelot Houghton can cast such aspersions."

"He has the humility to go by Uncle Albert, doesn't he? Pye Henry—for shame. At any rate I don't need a book to tell me about what our child will be like. I have friends, oh, and cousins, all sorts of people who have been through it before."

"That's true enough."

They turned into a small street that led straight down to the water. It was swarmed with bluejackets in the last minutes of their shore leave, some wildly drunk, others buying shipboard provisions at the general store, and still others kissing women who might equally be sweethearts from home or prostitutes working out of the coaching houses. As he was taking it all in he felt Jane clutch his arm.

"Stop a moment, will you?" she said softly.

He stopped and turned to look at her. "What's wrong?"

There were tears standing unfallen in her gray eyes. "Must you go?" she said. Her bantering tone had vanished.

His heart fell. "I promised that I would."

"I wish you hadn't."

She put her face to his chest and started to cry. Embarrassed, the two sailors carrying Lenox's trunk and bags both studied a bill of goods in the window of the grocer's they had stopped by, though Lenox knew for a fact that the smaller one, LeMoyne, couldn't read.

"We'll meet you by the water," he said to the men, and shepherded Jane toward a tea shop next door. "Call it twenty minutes."

He knew there to be a private room in the back, and as they entered he handed over half a crown to the landlady that they might take it. She obliged them by leaving them alone.

It was a small room, with Toby jugs—old clay mugs from Staffordshire, brown salt glazed and molded into human figures—lining a shelf on one wall. They sat opposite each other in the low wooden chairs.

"What's happened to make you change your mind?" he asked Jane gently, taking her hand in his.

She wiped her eyes and tried to calm herself. "I'm so sorry," she said. "I know you have to go. It's only—it's only—" She burst into fresh tears.

"Darling," he said.

"I know I'm foolish!"

"You're not. Shall I stay with you? We can go back to London this evening if you prefer."

"No! No, you must go. I know it's important, oh, in every sort of way. And I know you want to go! But it will be hard to be alone for two months, and just when I'm with child."

The landlady came in now, carrying a tray laden with tea cakes, biscuits, sandwiches, mugs, a milk jug, a sugar pot, and a teakettle. She avoided looking at them as she transferred the tray's contents to their small table with rapid precision. "And take your time," she said before she hurried out.

When they had discovered Jane was pregnant, a week or so after Lenox had committed to this trip for his brother, both had been immensely happy. Strangely it wasn't the chattering, social sort of happiness their marriage had been: both found in the next days that more than anything they would prefer to sit on the sofa together, not even talking much, perhaps reading, eating now and then, holding hands. It was a joy both of them preferred to experience almost silently, perhaps because it was so overwhelming.

When it occurred to Lenox that leaving might mean missing two months of that joy, he had immediately decided that he wouldn't do it. In fact it had been she who convinced him he still must, after he told her the reason Edmund had asked. Since then she had always been staunchly in favor of the voyage. This was the first hint to Lenox that she felt otherwise.

Sitting at the table, looking despondent, not touching the steaming cup of tea in front of her, Jane said, "This is silly—we'll be late. We should go."

"I'd rather sit here," he answered. "Will you eat something?"

"No."

"I should, then."

He picked up a sandwich with butter and tomato on it, no crusts, and took a bite. He found that he was hungry—the orange was still in his jacket pocket, half peeled—and when he had finished the sandwich he took a tea cake too and started to butter it.

Through her tears she smiled. "You can always eat, can't you?"

He stopped chewing his cake in the middle of a bite and, with a look of surprised innocence, said, "Me?"

"You, Charles Lenox. I remember you as a seven-year-old,

stuffing your face with slices of cold cottage pie when you thought nobody was looking, on hunt days."

They laughed. Tenderly, he put his hand to her stomach. "I'll be back soon, you know."

"I worry you won't come back at all. What do you know about a ship, Charles?"

"Ever so much now. How many sails it has, what it's made of, who all the officers are, what the midshipmen do, where one sleeps and eats . . ."

"I don't mean that. I mean you're liable to fall off and vanish into the ocean because you thought you could lean on the railing . . ." She trailed off and gave him a miserable look.

"You can't think how careful I'll be, Jane," he said, and again grasped her hand.

"I'll worry myself sick, is all I know."

"I'll write to you."

She rolled her eyes. "That will do me no good—you'll beat your letters home, I'm sure."

"It's not a far sail, and the weather is calm. Captain Martin has a great deal of experience. She's a good ship."

"Oh, I know all that! Am I not allowed to be irrational once in a while?"

"You are, to be sure you are."

To his sorrow their conversation progressed this way and ended inconclusively, as he promised again and again to be safe and avowed his disappointment at missing two months of her company, and as she said again and again that well, it was all right, even though plainly it wasn't.

Just as they absolutely had to leave, however, she reached up for his cheek and gave him a swift kiss. "It's only because I love you, Charles," she whispered.

"And I you."

They went out and walked the final street that slanted

sharply down to the docks, which were loud with bickering voices and smelled of heat, fish, salt, wood, and rope.

He took some mild solace in thinking of the letter he had left behind on her pillow in London: it was a very good sort of letter, long and full of thoughts and declarations of love and speculation about what their child would be like and ideas for what they might do when he returned to London. She would be comforted by that at least. He hoped.

They found the sailors with Lenox's effects, and then Lady Jane pointed off to the right.

"Look, there they are—your brother and Teddy. The poor boy looks green with fear." She looked up at him. "I still find it difficult to believe you and your nephew will be novices aboard the same ship, don't you?"

CHAPTER FOUR

This was indeed the case. Lenox had discovered it during the course of his fateful conversation with Edmund two months before. On that snowy evening the older brother had offered the younger an explanation of his request.

"We've had a disaster, Charles. That's why I've been in these meetings with the prime minister."

"What happened?"

Edmund sighed and rubbed his eyes, weary from long days and worry. He took a deep sup of whisky. "What do you know of our intelligence systems?"

"Very little. What they say in the papers, perhaps a bit more."

"Our officers are all across Europe, of course, Charles," said Edmund, "and despite this peace—this tenuous peace—many of them are still concentrated in and around France. The prospect of another war is very real, you should know.

"Eight days ago an Englishman named Harold Rucks, resident in Marseille, was found dead in a bedroom above a brothel near the docks. He had been stabbed in the heart, and the woman who

worked from that room—a new recruit to her work, you'll note—
was nowhere to be found."

"I take it he was one of your men?" said Charles.

"Yes. In Marseille he was considered a simple expatriate
drunk, but that was merely the façade he had adopted. He was
quite a competent man, if violent-tempered. At first we considered the possibility that he had died in an argument over something personal—money, let's say, or indeed what he was paying
for—but the next day another Englishman died, this time in
Nîmes. His name was Arthur Archer. He was garroted in an
alleyway. Nasty death."

"I see."

"You can guess what happened then. Three more men, two
in Paris, one in Nice. All dead. Five of ours."

"How were their identities discovered?"

Edmund sighed and stroked his cheek pensively, looking for
all the world like a farmer anxious over crops. But these were
higher stakes.

"A list went missing from our ministry. Eight names on it.
The three who weren't killed were fortunate: two were back in
England, one who just managed to get out of Paris with his life,
though he left all of his possessions behind. He was fired upon
as he got into the ferry."

"The French mean business."

"You can see that the peace is . . . a complex one," said Edmund with a wry smile. He took another sip of his drink. "What's
fortunate is that none of them were tortured for information.
There's some evidence that Archer was to be kidnapped, but
struggled enough that they simply killed him. The same may be
true of one of our men in Paris, Franklin King."

"Does this mean that someone in our government is working for the French?"

"I fear it does. We're looking into it, you may rely on that."

"Treason."

"Yes. We haven't found the man yet, but we will, and in the meantime all of our activities—our intelligence activities—have been suspended." Edmund looked uneasy then. "Well. Except for one."

"Egypt."

The brothers sat in silence for a moment. Charles, for his part, was knocked backwards, though through some ancient childhood wish to seem strong to his older brother, he acted calm. But he had had no idea that such arcane and troubling matters fell within his brother's bailiwick. Edmund had been a good member of the party, but devoted his time (as far as anyone knew at least) to broader public issues like voting or the colonies.

Worse still, he saw that it was taking a toll on Edmund, who looked tired and dogged with worry.

As if sensing Charles's thoughts, Edmund said, "I didn't ask for the responsibility, but I couldn't decline it, could I?"

"No. Of course not."

"You see the problem."

"Well, tell me," said Charles.

"We don't know how much information the French have. Is it everything, every name? Are they sticking to this list of eight men to make it seem that they know less than they do? Or do they really know nothing beyond those eight names?"

"We need to find out what they have, then."

Edmund rolled his eyes. "They need ice water in hell, too, but I doubt they get much of it."

"Tell me about Egypt."

"In our disarray we've accepted that we must sacrifice certain knowledge we had hoped to acquire about the French munitions, their navy, so forth and so on. Rucks was particularly well placed to study their navy, being in a port city, but so be it. Still, there's one thing we must know."

"Yes?"

"Whether the French mean to strike at us preemptively. To start another war."

"They wouldn't. It wouldn't be in their interests, would it?" said Charles.

As Edmund pondered how to answer this question the fire shifted, a log breaking in half. Both men stood up and started to fiddle with it, one with the poker and the other with a sort of long iron claw that could pick up bits of wood.

"We've still the finest navy that has ever gone afloat," Edmund said at last, "but the margin is shrinking, I can tell you frankly, and on land they may be just as strong as we are. The colonies have spread us a bit thin. If they have any ambitions of greater power . . . let's say it's not impossible."

"I see."

"Making matters worse, of course, is that we still don't know quite where we are with this government. Napoleon the Third has been gone for three years now—and for that matter died in January—and this third republic is unpredictable. We can never be sure whose voice matters there. We had thought these *boule-versements* might cease, but the deaths of our men . . . this is where we need you to step in."

"How?"

"We have a man in place in the French Ministry of War, working directly under Cissey, their secrétaire d'état de la guerre. This fellow is very high up, very clever, but rather poor. Despite the death of the empire it's mostly the aristocrats who work in their government as I understand."

"How unfamiliar," said Lenox.

Edmund laughed. "Well, quite so. Not all that different from here, I suppose. This chap is no aristocrat. He's clever, though, and he's a mercenary. For money he'll tell us all we need to know about the new government's intentions."

"How much?"

Edmund quoted a figure that made Charles whistle. "It's not

ideal. A man you have to pay is much less reliable than a man who burns with patriotic fervor, but so be it."

"How do you know he's not acting under orders, Ed? Playing a double game?"

"We have other informants, men who would know if that were the case. But they're not at so high a level as this gentleman."

Charles sat down again and for a moment brooded over all this. "You're in disarray, then," he said at last, "and need someone the French couldn't possibly have on any . . . any list of names?"

"Precisely. We need someone who can go to Egypt in a public guise."

"Why Egypt?"

"We don't dare send anyone to France, because of course they'll be on guard at such a tense, decisive moment. But this French gentleman, the one who can pass us information, has business he may plausibly conduct in Suez."

Charles saw all now. "And you thought you would send me to the canal as a member of Parliament—but in fact to meet this gentleman?"

Edmund nodded, and then, with a look of eagerness that made his younger brother nearly smile, said, "What do you think?"

"I'll do it, of course."

"Excellent. What a relief that is."

This puzzled Charles. "Why?"

"Well—because we need someone we trust."

"There are other men in Parliament who would do it, I imagine."

"But we don't want a man without any special loyalty to Gladstone and the current government to have this information—this power over the leadership of the party, you see. You're my brother, and it's our luck that on top of that you're a clever and discreet member."

"Thank you, then."

A brief pause. "There one thing I've omitted, however."

Lenox had felt it coming. "Oh?"

"We would ask that you go on the *Lucy*. Does the name ring a bell?"

"Vaguely."

Edmund looked uncomfortable now. "It will be Teddy's first ship, you see."

Indignation filled Lenox.

Teddy was his—very beloved—nephew, Edmund's second son, who had been groomed, like many of his mother's clan, which had seemingly a hundred admirals lurking in its family tree, to enter the navy at a young age. He had recently turned fourteen, and was just now ready to become a midshipman.

"So there's no special task," said Charles. "You don't need me. You simply want a babysitter."

"No, no!" Edmund, to his credit, looked horribly unhappy. "I feared you would take it this way."

"I don't mind, of course. I'll do it. But I wish you had been honest."

"Charles, no! I view this as nothing more than a lucky coincidence. Your primary job will be to meet our French contact in Egypt, and make some sort of trumped-up speech we give you as cover for that job."

"Oh, is that to be my 'primary' job?" Charles said, hearing the bitterness in his own voice.

"Listen, Charles—if this doesn't convince you nothing will. It wasn't I who brought your name up. Gladstone did."

This gave Lenox pause. "The prime minister? Asked for me?"

"Yes. And he had no idea that Teddy would be on our next ship to Egypt, either." Edmund looked hopefully up at Charles, who was pacing toward the snow-covered window. "He likes you. And to be certain, it helped that you were my brother—someone we could trust. But he wouldn't send an incompetent for loyalty's sake."

"Hmm."

"Charles, listen to reason. England needs you. This may be the most important thing you do, you know."

"A lucky coincidence?"

"I swear," said Edmund.

"Well, I would have done it either way," Charles said ruminatively. Then, pouring two more glasses of whisky, he added, "By name, the prime minister asked for me?"

CHAPTER FIVE

L ady Jane waved a hand and called out to her brother-in-law. "Edmund! Teddy!"

The father and son turned around and when they saw Lenox and Lady Jane, both smiled. Edmund's grin was broad and happy; Teddy's less enthused. He did look greenish.

"Hello, Uncle Charles," he said when they were in earshot. "And Aunt Jane."

Everyone shook hands. Edmund really was beaming, but in a low voice he said to Charles, "Remind me to speak to you for a moment before you go."

"Are you ready to ship out?" Lady Jane asked Teddy, tapping him on the shoulder in what she must have imagined to be a hearty fashion.

He clearly longed to say that he wasn't, but instead choked out the word, "Yes," with something less than perfect zeal.

"And are you, Charles?" said Edmund.

"I am. I'm also ready to be back in London, strangely enough."

Lady Jane squeezed his hand.

The men who had been carrying Lenox's things had touched their caps and then vanished back into the streets of Plymouth (and, suspiciously, given that they were due on the *Lucy* soon, in the direction of a public house). The family stood alone over two trunks and four or so bags, waiting.

Off to their right was the massive, shamrock-green field where Sir Francis Drake had with famous tranquility played bowls while the Spanish armada loomed offshore, on the way to the rollicking Drake ultimately bestowed upon them. Lenox had walked over it several times in the past two weeks, twice with Lady Jane, and in the twilight of evening contemplated all sorts of things: seafaring, wives left at home, children, French spies. To the left was the dock that the famous settlers of America had left from, aboard the *Mayflower*.

Closer at hand was the intense activity of the docks. Every day Plymouth handled naval ships, commercial freighters, and several unsavory varieties of black-market transaction that just about managed to avoid the observation of the local constabulary. Men swarmed around them, voices rose in the middle distances, wood smacked against wood. It suddenly felt much more real, this sea voyage, than it had half an hour before.

The two brothers, Teddy, and Lady Jane waited by slip nineteen, and about five hundred yards out they saw the men who were coming to fetch them. They were easy to spot, these two, because their jolly boat (belonging to the *Lucy*, pitched up sideways alongside deck during voyages) was a vividly striped yellow and black, with its name, *The Bumblebee*, scrawled in large letters on one side. It certainly stood out among the dozen odd brownish boats near it. Idly Lenox wondered whether it attracted attention when the *Lucy* wanted to be stealthy, but perhaps she was too fast a ship, designed for speed as she was, to worry much about that: nothing with very heavy guns would be able to catch her in a fair race.

"Not long now," said Edmund.

Charles felt his stomach turn over. "Perhaps Jane and I will take a short walk," he said.

"Of course, of course."

They went toward Drake's lawns, and managed to escape in some small degree the din of the docks. As they walked they spoke to each other in low, earnest voices, saying nothing much and repeating it over and over, all of it tending toward the incontrovertible truth that they loved each other; that they loved the child they would have; that all would be well, even if it seemed bleak at the moment.

Feeling slightly better, they returned to find the *Bumblebee* tied on to shore and two able seamen transferring trunks and bags into its deep middle section. (Captain Martin had permitted Teddy Lenox to come on board with his uncle, but with the caveat that once the boy stepped on the deck of the *Lucy* all such preferential treatment would be terminated.) Not long now.

At the last moment Edmund pulled his brother aside, producing a thin sheaf of documents from some inner pocket of his jacket. "Here they are—your orders. Secure them somewhere in your cabin that nobody can find, even your servant, if it's possible."

"I thought I had the information already?" said Lenox, puzzled.

Edmund shook his head. "Those pages were a dummy. We wanted to leave off committing any facts to paper until the last possible moment. You can get rid of those."

"Very well."

"Be safe, Charles. On board and on land." A pained look came into Edmund's eyes. "And if you could—if it's not trouble—not that I would ever ask you . . ."

Lenox laughed. "I'll look after Teddy, Edmund. I swear."

Edmund laughed too, but looked colossally relieved. "Good. Excellent. I want to see you both back safe, soon."

"You shall."

Before either of them knew it, Charles and his nephew were in the *Bumblebee*, and while Lenox could still feel Lady Jane's final kiss on his cheek, they cast off. Both Lenoxes sat at the rear of the boat gazing back at Edmund and Jane, who stood on shore and waved them off. With the two powerful men rowing the *Bumblebee* Charles's wife and his brother were soon indistinct among the hordes on the dock, and then it was impossible to see whether they had even remained by the slip where they had said good-bye. But only when there was really no possibility of making out who was who, or who was waving, or even whether any figure on land was a man or a woman or a shaved ape, did the two turn and look at their ship.

Teddy was a creature Lenox had always loved—a good-spirited, mischievous, endearingly freckled blond boy—but now Lenox realized that his nephew had come at least partially into manhood, and in that alchemical process become a mystery.

"Well," he said, "are you ready? Or were you being brave?"

Teddy, looking queasy, said with winning honesty, "Being brave."

Lenox clapped a hand on the boy's shoulder. "In a day's time you won't be able to remember feeling frightened."

Teddy nodded but didn't look as if he believed a word of it. "William says the food will be terrible."

This was Teddy's older brother, a pupil at Harrow now. "I have some provisions," Lenox answered in a mild way. "You shan't go hungry while I'm on board. But no word of it to the captain, d'you hear?"

The boy managed a smile. It was wiped off when they came up alongside the ship, and a row of men leaning on the railing cackled and shouted.

"This little white-faced beggar won't see much more of the world, I reckon," one called out, to general merriment.

Charles and Teddy climbed the rigging and as they neared the deck rough hands took them under the arms and pulled each up over the gunwale in turn, and onto the *Lucy*'s main deck. To Lenox they were courteous, and he even heard one murmur to another, "Which he's the member of Parlyment," but Teddy received no such deference. There were exaggerated sweeps of the cap to greet him, and an equally exaggerated, "Hello, *sir*," followed by laughter.

Two sorts of midshipmen went to sea: college boys and practicals. The practicals were often from a slightly lower segment of the upper and middle classes, but they had the advantage of knowing the sea and the navy backward and forward, having been in it for many years: since the age of ten, say. They all displayed a deep reluctance to admit the college lads, who had a great deal of classroom learning but very little practical training, and that all done on a battered-up old frigate in the harbor of Portsmouth, as their peers. Yet it was the college boys who would ultimately ascend the highest, through their superior education and interest at the admiralty. This was considered unfair. Teddy, who was fourteen, could speak French, navigate by the stars, do math, and tie any sort of hitch or knot you pleased—the Matthew Walker, the Turk's head—but his experience at sea was almost nil. Like the men in his mother's family he would likely be an admiral one day; for now he was almost certainly bound to be an object of scorn.

All this Lenox had heard from Edmund, whom it quite clearly pained, but the truth of it hadn't been clear until now. The quicker-witted bluejackets made flippant, ostensibly respectful remarks to the boy, and Lenox spotted another midshipman some yards off, laughing into his sleeve.

"Enough!" a voice barked out. It was the captain. "Mr. Lenox, you are very welcome on board. Mr. Midshipman, report to the gun room immediately. As for you lot, back to work."

Without any grumbling the men dispersed across the ship, and Teddy, whose trunk and bag preceded him, went off obediently to find his way below deck.

"You know the way to your quarters, I believe?" the captain asked Lenox. "I would show you myself, but there's a great deal to be done before we may ship. Your man should be there, unpacking your things."

"Thank you, Captain."

When he was alone, Lenox had a chance to look over the *Lucy*. It was in a wondrously clean and tight-rigged state; he had thought on his previous visit that the ship had been well maintained but saw now that he had actually witnessed her in a state of almost unprecedented laxity. There wasn't a rope out of place, nor a blemish on the great polished quarterdeck. The sails were either aloft or furled tightly to the masts. Everything was in faultless order, and for the second time that day he thought that traveling to Egypt by sea might be not any kind of ordeal, as he had feared, but a real pleasure.

What he couldn't know, of course, was that the first murder was less than a day away.

CHAPTER SIX

The *Lucy* left Plymouth Harbor under steam (somewhere below deck—Lenox suspected it was in the orlop, but couldn't feel sure—men were shoveling coal as if their lives depended on it) about an hour later. It was nearly five in the afternoon, and in a cloudless sky the great yellow sun had just begun to mellow into orange and broaden toward the curve of the earth.

When they reached open water Captain Martin ordered the jibs and staysails set. This request precipitated a profound flurry of action and movement among the men at the fore of the ship, and a somewhat stupefied Lenox, ignorant of shipboard terminology, managed to ask his friend Halifax what the directive meant.

They were on the quarterdeck, that deck of the ship, six steep steps up from the main deck, that was reserved for officers. (It was the sole privilege of the midshipman's life on board that he could walk on the exalted planks of the quarterdeck; otherwise he slept in a hammock like a common bluejacket and took rather worse food.) Captain Martin had, as was common when dignitaries sailed with the navy, invited Lenox to use it, though he had advised Lenox that the poop deck, one level higher up, was, while not technically off-limits, a place in which he might make mischief among men at work.

"Quite without meaning to, of course," Martin had said over that supper of theirs at the Yardarm.

"I understand, of course. I should never like to be underfoot."

When Lenox asked Halifax what it meant to set the jibs and staysails, the officer pointed toward the fore of the *Lucy*. "If you look toward the bowsprit—"

"The bowsprit?" said Lenox.

Halifax laughed his melodious laugh. "I had forgotten there were men who didn't know what a bowsprit was," he said, and then, seeing Lenox redden, said, "No, my dear man, I value you for it! The navy can be a confinement, if you let yourself fall oblivious to its limitations. But listen: I imagine you saw the great spar—the great pole—that extends off the prow of the ship?"

"Of course," said Lenox, still stung.

"That is the bowsprit. There are three sails that may be run up from it, all of them triangular—the flying jib, which is farthest out, and two staysails. Can you see?"

"Oh, yes, now I can."

Of course he could, and felt stupid that he hadn't been able to locate the object of so many men's attention. Two sailors were all the way out along the bowsprit, hung upside down over the water in a way that looked extremely dangerous. Neither kept more than a casual hand on the spar, however, instead primarily using the strength of their legs to hang on.

"What are they for, these sails?" Lenox asked.

"In a medium wind like this—"

"Medium!"

"What would you have called it?"

"A stiff wind—very stiff indeed."

"Oh, dear," said Halifax feelingly, and Lenox could see that he had committed another solecism. "No, this is quite a medium wind—even a light one, you might say. In such a wind the jib and staysails give you a bit of a pick-up, and better still they make you more maneuverable. The captain will want to be able to catch the wind again quickly if it shifts, you see."

"Thank you," said Lenox. "I fear I shall have more questions—if you find them importunate—"

"Never!" said Halifax, his plump face animated. "It's a pleasure to have you aboard, Mr. Lenox."

There was a deep sensory pleasure that Lenox found in these first hours on board the *Lucy*. There was the salted wind, the flecks of water that occasionally caught his hands or face, the orange and purple sunset, and always the mesmerizing, muscular gray-blue water. Land had vanished some time since. Then, too, he discovered how much he enjoyed watching the sailors at work. At the very top of the rigging (which acted as a kind of ladder), some fifty feet up, a small number of men were hard at work with the same apparently casual attitude toward danger as the men on the spar had had. For one terrifying moment, in fact, Lenox thought one would die: a man in a blue serge frock and blue trousers who flung himself off the mainmast and for a brief, paralyzing moment was in the open air, only at the last possible moment to grasp safely a rope that led to the foremast.

"Skylarking," said a thin, rather dour lieutenant on the quarterdeck, Carrow by name, but Lenox perceived that this disapproval was almost unwillingly mingled with a faint but detectable dash of admiration. Even joyfulness. Everyone on board, it seemed, was happy to be out of harbor.

He only left the busy quarterdeck at nearly seven in the evening, knowing that he had to dress for dinner in the wardroom; the first lieutenant, a fellow called Billings, had extended him a standing invitation to supper. Martin had done the same but with considerably less enthusiasm, which made sense when

Lenox learned from Halifax over their meal aboard the *Lucy* that the captain preferred to dine with a book in his private stateroom.

He had been very fortunate in the cabin he received, which his steward informed him had generally belonged to the chaplain on previous voyages, and which he had seen before his supper earlier that week with the officers. It was ranged alongside the wardroom, like several other officers' cabins, toward the larboard side of the ship. He could only just stand up straight inside it, but it was nevertheless much larger than he had expected.

Immediately to the right of the door (which swung out, thankfully) was a narrow bunk lying over a nest of drawers, while farther back there were a desk that looked out through the cabin's two small windows and a row of bookshelves built into the curved wall. Opposite the bed, just far enough for the drawers underneath the bunk to extend all the way out, were a washstand and a small but eminently serviceable bathtub, circular and made of copper.

While he had been on deck Lenox's steward had unpacked for him, and he arrived to find his drawers full of clothes, his bookcases quarter-filled with the twelve or so volumes he had brought, a leather satchel full of papers on the desk, a cup of pens with an inkstand by it, and, best of all, beside the windows, the framed pen drawing of Jane he had brought. It had been done by Edmund's wife, who was an accomplished sketcher, and given to Lenox the previous Christmas. It captured beautifully the prettiness of Jane's eyes and nose and also, more difficult, her innate mildness, her gentleness.

This steward (who would bring Lenox his meals, stand behind his chair in the wardroom, fetch him water, clean his clothes, and perform a hundred other minor offices) was a Scot called McEwan. He slept in the tiny hallway between Lenox's door and the wardroom, where apparently he strung up his hammock. It must have been a strong hammock, too, for he was perfectly enormous.

Better still he had the astonishing ability, it seemed to Lenox, never not to be eating. During their initial encounter McEwan had been holding a cold chicken wing that he glanced at longingly from time to time while Lenox tried to make conversation, and since then McEwan had consumed, at various moments, a piece of salt beef, some buttered brown toast, a large slab of cake, and a wing from the same unfortunate bird. Halifax had mentioned, confidingly, that McEwan was one of the few men on board who didn't drink or carouse on land, saving his pay packets instead for the various delicacies he stowed in secrecy about his living quarters. Little wonder that he weighed twenty stone.

As Lenox walked through the wardroom he heard a voice, and stopped just shy of the corridor that would have led him to his cabin.

"These political gennlemen," the voice said with deep disdain, "don't know their arses from their foreheads—"

"Elbows," McEwan interjected.

"Or elbows," said the voice triumphantly, "and what's worse I bet you six to one he's a bad luck and'll get us sunk from some ship hearing we have treasures and the like, or worse yet papers. They all want papers, don't they."

"He has some, too," McEwan whispered.

A dissatisfied grunt. "Wish he weren't aboard, the bugger, and I don't care who knows it. Joe Meddoes reckons he's an albatross, like."

"He brought a fair bulk of food, though, I will say as much as that for him."

Lenox swung the door open. Both men looked at him in surprise, and then each took their cap off. The one he didn't know, who was a very large, strong-looking fellow with black hair and a dark complexion, spat his tobacco into the cap. This was custom when speaking to an officer, Lenox had seen that afternoon. Otherwise he would have been disgusted.

"Hello, McEwan," he said. "Who is this?"

"Only Evers, sir," said McEwan. In his cap was not a plug of tobacco but a single hard-boiled egg. "Which he got turned the wrong way and lost, like."

"By the wardroom."

"Oh—yes," said McEwan.

Lenox tried to look severe. "Since he has seen it once he shan't get lost here again. Good day, Mr. Evers."

"Sir."

Evers stalked out past him, his face black, and Lenox, doing his best not to seem perturbed, asked McEwan to lay out his evening wear.

CHAPTER SEVEN

The meal they had that night passed in a haze of goodwill and excitement over the new voyage, with many toasts being proposed to the continued health and florescence of the Queen and various other gentlewomen.

Lenox still hadn't seen Teddy since they came over the gunwales together, but during supper Billings, the first lieutenant, assured him that his nephew was doing well. This Billings was a willowy, straw-haired chap with a great deal of native intelligence in his face, in contrast to the kinder mien of Halifax, his immediate subordinate and close friend.

Billings told Lenox, "He'll take the middle watch, being a youngster and the new boy. The oldsters—that is to say, the sixteen- and seventeen- and eighteen-year-old boys—are the day men."

"Forgive my ignorance, Lieutenant, but when is the middle watch?"

"From midnight to four, Mr. Lenox. It's fearfully unpopular,

of course. Primarily because the midshipmen take their lessons
in math and navigation in the forenoon."

"What will he do during his watch?"

"Practically speaking, nothing. As he gets to know the ship
better he will spend his watch time keeping men in line, giving
orders, and performing whichever tasks the officer of the watch
might want him to."

"How many men are on deck at night, if I might ask?"

"Not many—one officer, one midshipman, and a few dozen
seamen, who will be relatively inactive bar some change in the
wind or the sighting of an enemy or land. Of course the helms-
man will be steering the ship and watching the course."

"It sounds rather desolate."

"On the contrary, I find it peaceful. If I could only have a
glass of my favorite whisky and a stout cigar during the watch
it would be my favorite time of the day."

"Not too frightening, then?"

"Oh, not at all," said Billings, and smiled kindly.

"I'm relieved to hear it."

He hoped Teddy would no longer be afraid; if he were, a
watch in the dark, with the ship pitching and rolling in the
wind, with men awaiting orders from his inexperienced lips,
might be a dread thing to him. Even as this thought occurred
to Lenox, however, he realized that it was a mistake to assume
that he knew what would be good for Teddy and what would
not. If nothing else that day had proved to him his own ignorance. He perceived that it would be dangerous to offer his
nephew any sort of aid or comfort that might interfere with his
progress on the ship, however kindly intended it might be.

McEwan stood behind Lenox's chair at dinner, refilling his
wineglass, running to the galley to clear dishes and silverware,
alert if Lenox needed a snuffbox or cigar or glass of port after
supper. All the officers had their servants behind them, too,
though McEwan was notable for being swathed in an enor-

mous, perfectly shipshape uniform with its brass buttons nearly popping off because the cloth of his shirt was so taut over his stomach.

After supper he fetched warm water for Lenox to shave and wash in, and then a glass of water to drink.

Shaving, Lenox asked McEwan, "Out of curiosity, where do you get the water? Fresh water? From barrels, I know, but . . ."

The assistant was scrubbing the floor in Lenox's tiny hallway with a stiff bristle brush, in a place where he had evidently spilled a small bit of his own food. From his girth Lenox would have guessed McEwan to be lazy, but nothing could have been farther from the truth; like all the men on the *Lucy* he seemed to spend an almost preposterous amount of time cleaning things that were already clean. Lenox's shirt from dinner had gone straight into a basin of warm water and his cabin had been swept twice in the five hours since they had left harbor.

"It's in the hold, Mr. Lenox."

"That's farthest down."

"Yes, sir, below the waterline."

Lenox pondered this. "For fear of sounding stupid—"

"Oh, no, sir."

"Doesn't it change the weight of the ship? Emptying out the barrels of water? I mean to say, if we leave Plymouth with a hundred tons of water and return with none, won't she sail differently?"

"Why," said McEwan with some of the same astonishment Halifax had betrayed when Lenox hadn't known what the bowsprit was, "we fill 'em up, of course."

"With what?"

McEwan laughed. "What's most out there, of course." In his amazement he evidently had forgotten all about saying "sir."

"Water."

"Oh, seawater."

"Yes!" McEwan, so surprised that anyone might not have

known this that he had stopped scrubbing, went on to say, as if speaking to an infant, "It's called ballast, sir."

"I knew there was a word for it. Well, I've learned more today than I have in a while, at least."

McEwan, shaking his head and muttering to himself—and somehow also chewing—returned to his task.

Over dinner Lenox had had a chance to round out his circle of acquaintance, all of the people he had met in the wardroom before without fully remembering. He had a better idea of the ship's hierarchy now.

There was the captain, of course, who in this floating world was more akin to a king than anything. Then there were his lieutenants: Billings, who must have been about thirty and, it was obvious from the way he carried himself, longed for a command of his own, and as his second, Halifax, red-faced and gentle. There was also Carrow, the dour lad who had nevertheless taken pleasure in the "skylarking" the mainmast men had done among the sails that afternoon; he was the navigating lieutenant, who had particular skill in navigation by compass and the stars, and who knew the waters they were to sail for, from the Atlantic through the Mediterranean. Two more lieutenants—young men, just graduated from the rank of midshipman—stayed quiet, so Lenox didn't learn their names from Halifax, who had been seated to his right.

As for the civil officers, the chaplain of the Church of England was named Rogers. Based on their two suppers together Lenox concluded without much hesitation that he was a drunkard— but then a harmless one, jolly and foul-mouthed. ("Much better than a nervous teetotaler—at sea at least," Halifax had said of him, still somehow respectfully.) The surgeon was a silent, smallish man, quite old, named Tradescant ("not entirely a gentleman," Halifax said without malice, "but a fine medical man"), who spoke only with the engineer, a similarly aged and quiet soul, though instead of Tradescant's white hair he had a bright red top. His name was Quirke. Finally there was the purser. He was a pale and harried-looking man who had risen from the position of captain's clerk to command all of the ship's provisions. He didn't even merit "not entirely a gentleman" as a description, for he was quite clearly of lower stock. For this reason, perhaps, he was deferential in the extreme, though Lenox sensed in him some bitterness or maybe ambition that would bridle against any admission of inferiority to his nominal superiors. He was named Pettegree.

In addition to all of these the wardroom had one other occupant, who was easily the most beloved among the men of the *Lucy*, however much they might favor their captain or their first lieutenant. This was a dog, named Fizz. He was small, probably not more than nine pounds, but he was, Lenox would come to learn, a noble beast. He was a black-and-tan terrier of mixed origins, with bright brown eyes, a black nose, and two sharply pointed ears. He never barked, and slept on a rug under the dining-room table; as for food he ate like a king, for every man on board had a soft spot for him. If you told him to roll over he would do it, or if you asked him to dance he would do a little pirouette. The men fought over who got to haul him up the rigging, for he loved to visit the perches along the mast.

At any rate these were the men of the wardroom: Billings, Halifax, the grim Carrow, Rogers the drinker, quiet Tradescant and Quirke, and Pettegree, plus the two other lieutenants. By the next afternoon all but one of them would be a suspect.

"Could you tell us, Mr. Lenox," said Billings after their desserts had been cleared away, "what your purpose in visiting Egypt is?"

"With pleasure. As seafaring men you have all heard of the canal in that country, I hope, the Suez?" All of them nodded their affirmation that they had. "Then you will understand its great importance is linking the Mediterranean Sea with the Red Sea, and therefore the Indian Ocean. A few hundred miles

of digging have opened up tens of thousands of miles of water-
ways to Europe. Rather than going overland or around the
southern tip of the continent, for instance, goods may come
from East Africa—from Kenya, from Tanganyika, from Abys-
sinia, from Sudan—by water. I scarcely need to tell you how
financially significant that is."

They looked suitably awed now, and Lenox went on, "For
much of its life the canal has been primarily a French concern."

General and humorous hissing at this. "Not for long," said
Billings, which led to an inevitable toast in the Queen's honor.

"Be that as it may," said Lenox after he had drunk his wine
along with the rest of them, "Britain is only now coming to
hold a stake in the region. When they started digging fifteen
years ago, only the French had the foresight to see how dra-
matically it would change the world's commercial ventures."

"I had understood that we didn't approve the use of slave
labor there," said Halifax.

"Very true," Lenox said. "But since it's already been dug . . .
at any rate, it's crucial that we catch up with the French. I'm an
emissary of the prime minister, officially, sent to affirm our
rather weak alliance with Egypt. Fortunately the governor
there, a chap called Ismail, is open to our use of the channel.
I'll take him presents, flatter him, attend an audience with him,
impress his friends . . ."

"All this over a canal," Billings said. It wasn't a disrespectful
statement, exactly, but it seemed to reflect the mood of the room.

"It could be worth ten million pounds one day, this meeting. A hundred million."

To men who would have felt themselves quite rich on eight
hundred pounds a year this number was nearly unfathomable,
but it effectively undercut whatever unvoiced dissatisfaction
they had collectively felt with Lenox's mission. Worth sailing
to Egypt a hundred times for *that* sort of meeting, they would
say to each other confidentially, out of his hearing.

To his explanation there was in fact some truth. His trip to Suez would help British interests there. But of course it was secondary to his true purpose in making this voyage.

"And you? Why were you sailing for Egypt?"

"In part to take you," said Billings. "The navy has orders to prove itself useful."

"A friend in Parliament wouldn't go amiss." Halifax chuckled as he said this but Lenox felt stares of evaluation directed at him.

Billings went on. "We also like to patrol the trade waters. The prevention of piracy is still essential, though it's not the old swashbuckling sort of the last century."

Then Quirke spoke, the redheaded engineer. "They also like to give a ship like the *Lucy* a short mission after they give her a long one. Bless the Lord, for we've been afloat a very long time."

"That's sensible."

"Mr. Lenox, by traveling with us won't you miss your time in Parliament?" asked Carrow, the third lieutenant. "Votes— meetings—that sort of thing?"

"Yes, although we're close to recess. I suppose this is more important."

"Parliament," said one of the anonymous young lieutenants with some wonderment, almost as if he were speaking a magic word. "What is it like?"

"It took some getting used to," Lenox said. "But now I wouldn't trade it for anything. There's a great deal of shouting, there are many long, tedious meetings, but with that said there's more camaraderie and excitement than I expected."

"You know the lads—the midshipmen—are eager to ask you about murders and all that," said Halifax, smiling. "They say you were a detective."

"Once. A long while ago, it seems now. I don't do anything in that direction nowadays."

In his cabin later (after he had finished his ablutions and

McEwan had finished scrubbing) he stretched out in bed feeling some queer emotion that was neither sadness nor quite melancholy. For the longest time he couldn't think what it was, until it hit him: homesickness. It had been so many years, thirty perhaps, since he had felt it.

But almost as if by magic the diagnosis cleared the sensation itself away, and immediately after promising himself that he would write Lady Jane a long letter in the morning, he fell into a heavy and dreamless sleep.

CHAPTER EIGHT

An urgent hand shook him from it.

"Mr. Lenox!" a man's voice said. "Mr. Lenox! Come, wake up!"

It wasn't McEwan, Lenox knew even in that bewildered state of half wakefulness that follows a startle from rest. But who then?

A yellow light that had seemed to be emanating dimly from the floor of the cabin rose, and as he came into self-possession Lenox saw that it was a lantern. It illuminated the face of the ship's captain.

"Mr. Martin?" said Lenox in surprise.

Martin spoke in his usual dry, imperturbable voice, but there was a tremor beneath it that Lenox hadn't yet heard. "I would ask you to come to my mess, Mr. Lenox. Please, be quick about it if you will."

"What time is it?"

"Running on four in the morning. It's through the last door

in the wardroom and along a corridor. Hurry, if you please. I'll leave you this lantern."

"Is it Teddy? My nephew, rather, Edmund?"

"No, no, he's well. He'll be asleep in the gun room now."

There had been enough middle-of-the-night visitors in Lenox's past life that he was quick to get ready. He threw on a shirt and braced himself with a splash of water to the face, taken from the small pool left in his washstand. McEwan, in his hammock, slumbered on apace—or seemed to at any rate—and Lenox just managed to squeeze past his bulk and through to the darkened wardroom.

By contrast the captain's spacious and well-appointed mess was a blaze of light, with lanterns on their chains swinging from the beam over the dining table. There were two men besides Martin seated at the far end of the table. One was Tradescant, the surgeon, who had a vinegary look on his face. The other was the slender Billings, Martin's first lieutenant.

"There you are," said Martin. "Please, come sit. Take a glass of brandy."

"I thank you, no," said Lenox.

"You had better," said Billings, and Lenox saw that his face looked haunted.

"If you prefer it, then."

"There you are." Billings, who seemed relieved to have some duty, poured Lenox a crystal tumbler full of brandy and slid it down the table to where he was sitting.

"Plainly something has occurred, gentlemen," Lenox said, his drink untouched, hands folded before him. "What is it?"

"You were a detective once?" said Martin.

"Once."

"I mean to say that you retain the . . . the faculties of an amateur detective."

"An intermittently professional one, in fact. But they are corroded by disuse, I assure you. Why do you ask? Mr. Tradescant,

I can see the various spots of blood on your cuff—they are fresh, not darkened by washing—I presume you do not wear your nightshirt to see your patients. You have roused me from sleep—from all this I conclude that somebody has been wounded unexpectedly. It only remains to ask whether the person is dead or not."

There was a long pause.

"They are," said Martin at last. "He is."

"Who?"

"Lieutenant Halifax."

After his short speech the onetime detective had felt in control of this tense congregation, but this name knocked the wind out of him. His only friend aboard the *Lucy*, really. And a good man—kindly hearted—gentle. A gentleman in the old sense of the word. A thought strayed across Lenox's mind: he hadn't had time to fish, Halifax, on this last voyage of his life. What a pity. Now he took a sip of that brandy before speaking.

"When did it happen?"

Billings answered. "His body was discovered on the quarterdeck fifteen minutes ago."

"Discovered!" said Lenox. "Surely it would be impossible to shift a body around—to kill someone—without others knowing about it, on a ship this small? Why, there are two hundred and twenty men aboard the *Lucy*!"

Martin gave him a dry glance, as if to indicate that this piece of information was already in his possession, but said nothing.

It was Billings who spoke again. "It's the dead of night. Very few men are on deck, and those that are would have been on the poop or about the main deck. He could have been brought from below, I suppose."

"Leave the conclusions out," said Martin. "Mr. Lenox, I'm afraid we must call upon your skills."

Rather than acknowledging this request, Lenox said, "Mr. Tradescant, you attempted to resuscitate him, I take it?"

"I did, after a fashion. That is to say I checked his pulse, though a dunce in medical college could have spotted from fifty yards off there wouldn't be one, and then checked his breath."

Impatiently, Martin said, "Mr. Lenox, we have agreed that you should look into this. I feel certain that whoever did it will come forward—before morning, I would lay odds—but on the off chance that they don't . . ."

"Did Mr. Halifax have any disagreements with the sailors?"

"Mr. Billings, perhaps you can answer that."

"On the contrary, though he had only been here for several months he seemed quite popular. Occasionally they'll take advantage of someone—someone—well, Faxxie wasn't soft, exactly, but he wasn't the martinet that some lieutenants might be. He had a reputation as a very capable gentleman at sea, though, which the men seemed to understand and value. I would have called him beloved, in fact. Certainly more than Carrow or I."

"That squares with what I observed," said Martin.

"Then there's nobody likely to have borne him ill will?"

"Not for more than a passing moment. No."

Lenox pondered this. "And of course," he said, half to himself, "if someone bore a grudge why not kill him in Plymouth?"

"What can that mean?" asked Martin sharply

"On shore they would have had six weeks to do the job. The ship is in effect a closed room. Impossible to flee, should you be discovered. It's peculiar, I'll say that. Did you take many new men on board for this voyage? Someone who might be violent?"

"Only two."

"Two! Is that all? Out of two hundred odd?"

"Yes. A new lieutenant, our fifth, Lee, and a new forecastle-man, Hardy. Both, I can assure you, came with unimpeachable references."

"I thought there was tremendous turnover on a ship of this sort."

"In others, perhaps, but there is no war on at the moment," said Martin, "which means there are more men than places, and the *Lucy* is a remarkably steady sailor. And then, I have something of a reputation for taking prizes."

This made sense: to take a prize, an enemy ship, meant that everyone on board got in various proportions some reward of the prize money. It was an incentive to courage, and indeed an incentive to sail with the navy. A good prize for a common sailor might have meant enough money to buy a small cottage or open a public house, while for a captain it would be enough money to buy a splendid estate on a hundred acres in the countryside.

Lenox forced himself to focus.

"Who found the body?"

"Carrow. He was on duty."

With a lurch in his stomach Lenox remembered that Teddy would have been, too. "Were there any witnesses?"

"From what Carrow says, no. There was a loud thump on the quarterdeck, which might have been the murder itself, and he went to look at what had caused it after several moments. The quarterdeck would have been hidden from his view, you see. When he went to look he found the body."

"And so it was Carrow who came to fetch you, Captain?"

"He came to me first," said Tradescant. "I ran up on deck. The captain followed shortly thereafter."

Martin nodded his confirmation of this sequence of events. "I called for Billings, then. We agreed to find you."

"Mr. Tradescant, how long had Halifax been dead when you saw him? You said a dunce in medical college could have spotted that he was?"

"Five minutes, I would say, just to hazard a guess. Not more than ten or twelve. His skin was still as warm as yours or mine. And his heart was still hot to the touch."

There was a moment of quiet at this news.

"But how on earth could you know that, about his heart?" said Lenox. "Did you perform an autopsy so soon?"

The three men—Martin, Billings, and Tradescant—exchanged looks.

"No," said the captain at last. "We found him on his back, cut open straight down the middle from his throat to his stomach, and the skin pulled back so that you could see his entrails."

CHAPTER NINE

To have a preference among types of murder was absurd, of course—grotesque even—but Lenox had always had a particular distaste for death by the knife. Gunshot, strangulation, poisoning: for reasons hidden even to him, none of these seemed quite as grim as a stabbing or a cutting. Somehow the image of Halifax meeting such an end made everything worse.

He stood. "Good Christ. Let me see him then. Is his body alone? We must go at once if it is, before anyone can interfere with it."

"No, no, Carrow is standing over him," said Billings. "Nobody else has been permitted close to the body—Halifax's body—or indeed the quarterdeck, besides the three of us and Carrow. Though I'm afraid several seamen saw the body."

Martin stood. "You'll do it then, Mr. Lenox? If nobody comes forward, you'll find the man who did this?"

"I could scarcely do anything else."

They climbed up to the main deck. A cool breeze there just ruffled the otherwise slack sails.

"Why aren't we sailing?" he asked.

"We need to beat to windward," said Martin, "but that takes men, and I wanted to keep the deck as clear of people as possible. We're simply drifting at the moment."

"I see. Out of curiosity, what's the nearest port?"

"London, I would imagine, perhaps Whistable. Why?"

"In case we need to seek help on land."

The captain shook his head. "No. We have our own ways in the navy, sir, and we may try and convict a man of a crime as legitimately here as they might in the assizes."

"Hm."

"We're not putting into port, with all due respect. I won't go back there tail-tucked, a man who can't control his own ship."

"Very well. Let's see poor Halifax, then."

The quarterdeck of the *Lucy* (domain solely of officers) was one level up from the main deck and the poop deck was one level up from that, but each had a separate set of stairs leading to it from the main deck. This left the quarterdeck invisible in parts from the others, just as Martin had said, particularly where the poop deck's rail blocked off from sight the back half of the quarterdeck. It would be just possible, then, to do something out of sight of both the main deck and the poop deck at once. Still, it seemed improbable somehow that a man could be murdered within ten feet of a half-dozen other men without attracting attention.

"When was Halifax's watch?" said Lenox as they walked single file up the quarterdeck.

"First watch," said Billings.

"Eight in the evening until midnight, I take it?"

"Yes."

"It's past four now," Martin added, "but we're letting the next watch stay down. The fewer people see this the better."

Lenox nodded. "What I was asking, though—Halifax wouldn't

have had any reason to be outside of his cabin at the hour he was killed?"

Billings and Martin both shook their heads. No.

They came to the body; it was under a smallish piece of spare white sailcloth, presumably out of respect, though Lenox would have preferred the scene to rest untouched. Uneven splotches of red had started to seep into the canvas. Worse still, Halifax's shins and knees protruded from the covering. It seemed somehow undignified.

"Carrow," said Martin, "any activity?"

"Nobody has been on deck, sir, but I've heard the men speaking. They know Halifax is dead."

"Inevitably," said Martin. "Mr. Lenox, what shall we do?"

"Perhaps you and I, Mr. Tradescant, could take a look."

They stepped up toward the body, Lenox treading carefully so that neither man put his foot on any piece of evidence, and removed the sailcloth. There he was. The moon was just waning, but it was still full enough to cast in a brilliant white light every gory detail of Halifax's death.

"Unfortunate sod," murmured Martin.

Billings took off his cap and soon all four men besides Lenox had done the same. He was bareheaded.

Halifax's face was unmarked, but his torso was mangled out of all recognition, soaked in blood. Still, it was evident what the murderer had done; Halifax was indeed sliced open from his throat to his navel, and the skin had been pulled neatly back into flaps, revealing an exposed rectangle of his insides.

"Jesus," said Carrow, and both Martin and Billings looked as if they might be ill. Only Tradescant, a medical man, remained phlegmatic. And of course Lenox, who had seen this kind of thing before.

"Well, Mr. Lenox?"

The detective didn't answer. He was stooped down by the

body. Very gingerly he turned Halifax's head one way and then the other, looking for any signs of violence upon it.

"He's bare-chested," said Lenox.

"Yes," said Billings.

"Well, and that's your most important detail. Would he have come onto deck bare-chested?"

"Certainly not."

"Then where is his shirt? You see?" Lenox thought for a moment. "Mr. Tradescant, you observed the repeated stab wounds around Mr. Halifax's heart?"

"Yes."

"The stabbing and the subsequent—well, dissection—were different acts."

"Yes, I thought the same."

"If he was stabbed with his shirt on, there will be fibers of cloth in the wounds. I suspect that's what we'll find." Kneeling still, he turned to Martin. "Captain, if you find that shirt you'll find your murderer. Unless it's gone overboard."

Martin whirled around and looked down at the main deck, where a few sailors leaned against the gunwales. "We can still check every damned inch of this ship. You, Harding—yes, you—spread word among each mess that nothing is to be shipped out through the portholes or over the sides of the ship, hey?"

"Yes, sir," said Harding, a strong man of middle age, and went below deck.

"There are a million places aboard a ship to hide such a thing," said Lenox. "It's a shame."

"You would be surprised," said Martin. "If it's here we'll find it."

"What color would it be?"

"His light blue shirt, I imagine," said Billings. "A rough old thing—he wore it when he was off duty."

There was a pause as all five men contemplated Halifax's corpse. The ship pitched slightly.

"Mr. Tradescant, is there somewhere you and I could examine the body in greater detail?" said Lenox.

The captain spoke up. "How many are resident in the surgery?" he asked.

"Only one, sir. An able seamen named Costigan took a smack to the head from a flying spar. He's sleeping it off under sedation."

"Then clear a table there. We'll bring the body down."

"If the three of you could do that," said Lenox, "I might inspect the area and then follow you down. Where is the surgery?"

Tradescant told him, and then hurried down to ready a table. Carrow, Billings, and Martin—to his credit—all helped wrap Halifax's body in the sailcloth and begin the arduous work of transferring its bulk down below deck.

Lenox stood in the moonlight for a moment after they had gone, looking out at the water.

It was strange. Though his primary feelings were of sorrow for his friend Halifax and alarm at the nature of the murder, he had to admit to himself that in some recess of his mind he was excited by the prospect of a proper case. It was one of those facts he would never have told a soul, but which it was useless to deny to himself.

He missed this work. Had missed it every day at first, when he entered Parliament three years before, and then every other day, and finally once a week, once a month . . .

Much of his work he had passed onto his protégé, Lord John Dallington. Their weekly meetings about those cases, often held over supper in some public house or gentlemen's club, full of animated speculation and intense parsing of clues, comprised Lenox's favorite hours of the week. How he missed the chase! Life in politics was absorbing, remarkably absorbing, but it never inspired in him the same feeling of vocation that being a detective had: that this was his purpose on earth not from sense of duty and ambition, like Parliament, but from instinct and preference. He knew he would never be as good at anything as he had been at being a detective. Sacrificing that had been painful. The profession had brought him no honor—had in fact discredited him in the eyes of many of his caste as a fool—but what pleasure it had given him! To be on the trail!

So part of him couldn't help but revel in this opportunity. No doubt someone would come forward, but if they didn't . . . well, it was impossible to call in Dallington or the Yard here. This was a chance to live again what had once given him such keen happiness and focus, and which he thought he had given up for good.

CHAPTER TEN

He stooped down to look at the spot where Halifax's body had lain.

There was a great deal of blood that had spilled out from him, but it had left unmarked a patch of the deck that roughly conformed to the man's shape. Lenox stepped into this area so that he could survey the deck more easily.

As he stepped over the blood and into this clearing he heard a creak underfoot. He looked down and realized that the board he had stepped onto had a deep crack through its middle. The exposed wood looked to Lenox's eye raw and unweathered, unvarnished by time—newly splintered—and knowing that the ship had just come out of repairs he felt sure that it was a fresh fissure. But from what?

A first puzzle.

The blood was coagulating thickly on the quarterdeck. He took a small ebony stick out of his pocket, roughly the size of a twig, like a smaller version of a conductor's baton. It was intended to be a line marker for use while reading, but in fact

Lenox had never used it after its proper fashion. He only carried it because Lady Jane had bought it for him, many years before.

Now he used it to drag through the blood, looking for any objects that might have been left behind, hidden in that maroon murk. Nothing was apparent to the naked eye, and on his first trawl he found nothing. Still, he decided to try it again and the second time came upon a small object he had missed before. It was roughly the size and shape of a coin.

He took his handkerchief out of his pocket and deposited the object in its center, then folded it carefully and put it in his pocket for later inspection. Then he spent ten minutes or so looking over the area very carefully again, though without finding anything.

He broadened his search, moving in concentric circles around the entire quarterdeck and looking for anything out of place or unusual. But his efforts went unrewarded: besides the crack in the wood of the deck and the coin-shaped object, nothing out of the ordinary presented itself to his (keen, he hoped) eye.

He went downstairs, following the surgeon and the officers by some fifteen minutes.

They were all stood around Halifax's body, which was on a table roughly waist-high. In a dim corner of the long, low-ceilinged room Tradescant's sole patient slumbered on. There was plenty of light around the cadaver, however.

Tradescant had a bucket of water and a sponge and was very carefully sluicing Halifax's wounds, then drying them with a cloth. When he saw Lenox he plucked something from the table and held it up: several blue threads.

"From the wounds around his heart. No doubt from his nightshirt."

"Have you found anything else?"

"Not yet. We were correct in our surmise that the . . . surgery on Lieutenant Halifax's body came after his death, whose cause was this flurry of stabs to the heart." Tradescant pointed to an area cleansed now of blood but still brutal-looking. "At the moment I'm only trying to wash him."

Lenox approached the table. Martin and Billings were some feet off, staring impassively on; Billings had a handkerchief over his nose.

"I wonder if all of his organs are intact," the detective said.

"Sir?"

"Or if an organ might be missing altogether—liver, spleen, stomach."

Tradescant peered into the body. "That will take a moment or two. Why do you ask?"

"The peculiar nature of these cuts to his torso—that they're not random or angry, like the initial stab wounds, but surgical. It makes me wonder if the murderer had some specific aim."

"I see."

"Such a method isn't unknown. Burke and Hare were surgeons in Edinburgh, though they preferred smothering, which is why we call it burking now. Then there was the American killer Ranet in 1851, working around Chicago. He extracted the livers of his victims."

"Why?"

"He was a cannibal, I'm afraid."

Billings, already looking pale, rushed out of the room.

Tradescant nodded. "I'll do a thorough examination of the abdominal region, then," he said.

"The heart is still there?"

"Yes—that I can say with certainty. For the rest, give me a moment."

Lenox found that he liked Tradescant; the man was admirably calm despite his advancing age, steady-handed, and frank.

"In that case, Captain, perhaps we might have a word?" said Lenox.

"I was just about to suggest the same. First I must attend to the ship, however, since Halifax cannot. Come on deck with me if you like."

It was past five in the morning now, and the vast black sky had begun to show the pale blue light, at first almost like lavender against the black of night, that comes at dawn. Martin, with creditable energy, ran briskly up to the poop deck, gave several orders there, and then dismissed Carrow, ordering him to send up the next watch before he went to sleep.

"And get this quarterdeck swabbed and holystoned," he added, then disappeared below deck, holding up a finger to Lenox to tell him to wait.

New men arrived on deck as the exhausted men of the middle watch strung up their hammocks in between the cannons on the gun deck and fell asleep. Soon these awakened sailors were cleaning: the broad slap of the swabs, mixed with hot water, diluting and then vanishing Halifax's blood. Groggy at first, they exchanged quiet words about what might have happened, and then, rumor quickening, spurred on by the strange state of the sails, the level of the chatter rose. A midshipman Lenox hadn't seen, quite old, told them to keep it down, but still it was only five minutes before everyone on deck understood, somehow, that it was Halifax who had been wounded. Leaning against the rail of the quarterdeck Lenox listened to theories fly; it was a duel, it was a fistfight, it was a pistol shot from a French ship. He was pleased in a glum way to hear the men speak affectionately of the dead lieutenant.

At last Martin came back on deck.

"Apologies," he said. "I was having a word with Billings. We're going to have all the men on deck in the forenoon and identify whatever fiend did this to Halifax. Unless you object?"

"No. In fact I think it's wise—such social pressure often brings someone feeling guilt to confess. Though I wonder whether someone capable of this sort of murder feels much compunction."

"What are your initial impressions of the matter, Mr. Lenox? I don't know how long we can sail with this over our heads. The men already know."

"I heard."

"Well?" said Martin. "Give me some good news, would you?"

"I haven't drawn any conclusions, unfortunately. There are clues however."

"Yes?"

"Firstly, let us discuss how the body might have reached the quarterdeck. There are three ways that I can see."

"What are they?"

"First, that the murder was carried out there."

"Unlikely," said Martin.

"Why?"

"Noise, for a start. Everyone would have heard an argument or, more likely still, a fight."

"True. And even if he had been taken by surprise, Halifax would have shouted before the knife struck him, I imagine—the stabbing came from the front, not from behind. Would the quarterdeck have been empty?"

"For short periods, but even in the dead of night someone or other is generally there every few minutes, one of the midshipmen or lieutenants on duty who circulates through the ship."

"Just as I thought—after all, the body was discovered almost instantly. We'll count that as possible, but not probable."

"Yes," said Martin. Because of his premature gray hair it was easy to mark him as old or weary, but there had been a steeliness in him all night that showed why he had a ship full of sailors who had chosen to stay on with him. He was responsible, resourceful, energetic: a good captain.

"The second option is that someone killed him below deck and brought him up. It would have been insanely chancy, of course. And then, where to kill him? I suppose an officer's cabin—perhaps even Halifax's cabin, which I would like to inspect soon—but I doubt that too."

"What is the third option?"

Lenox sighed and looked up among the masts. "Was there a crack—a splinter—in one of the boards on the quarterdeck, before we left Plymouth?"

"Certainly not."

"Are there men aloft—among the riggings and those platforms I see at intervals going up each mast—during the middle watch?"

"Rarely. At war or near land perhaps someone in the crow's nest. But visibility is nil."

"And might a man go up there at that time without being seen?"

"Very easily. But can you mean—"

"Yes. I think Halifax was lured up this back mast—"

"That one, Mr. Lenox? From fore to aft the three masts are called the foremast, the mainmast, and the mizzenmast. You are pointing in the direction of the mizzenmast."

"That platform halfway up—you see it?"

"Yes."

"I would bet any fellow in Piccadilly that Halifax met his killer there, under some pretense, and died there too."

"Their voices would have carried, surely."

"Not if the murderer stressed the need for secrecy and quiet. A knife can appear very quickly in someone's hand, and the stabbing may have been so violent because the murderer wanted to silence Halifax immediately. Hence the contrast with the later cuts . . ."

"But you mean to say, then, Mr. Lenox, that in this hypothetical scenario a man carried Halifax, a large gentleman, halfway down the mizzenmast and onto the quarterdeck, without being spied?"

"No. I think he was murdered there, and then tossed down

onto the quarterdeck. It would be a straight fall down, and from there the murderer could have done his work deliberately and thrown the body down when he saw, from above, that those on deck weren't looking. The weight of Halifax's body falling from such a height cracked a board beneath his body."

"Jesus. Like a sack of flour."

"That's the loud thump Carrow reported, I daresay, which compelled him to go down to the quarterdeck in the first place."

CHAPTER ELEVEN

I f nothing else, Martin was decisive. He ran straight up to the quarterdeck to look at the crack in the board that had been underneath Halifax's body.

"You," he called out to the midshipman who was sitting on the rail, looking out at the water, "go and fetch me Mr. Carrow and Midshipman Lenox. They were the only two officers on duty during the middle watch, I believe?"

"Yes, sir."

"Then go. I see you hesitating—yes, you have permission to wake Carrow up. Lenox it goes without saying."

The boy ran off downstairs.

Martin went over to the plank—the whole deck was now innocent of blood, though Halifax's body had lain there scarcely an hour before—and looked at the crack.

"New?" Lenox asked.

"Unquestionably. You need only look at the wood."

"Quite so."

Martin stood up. "Where is that blasted Carrow?" he said,

though there had barely been time for the midshipman to get below deck. "Well—no matter—up we go, Mr. Lenox."

"Both of us?"

"It's no climb at all—thirty feet—children do it. Old Joe Coffey goes to the crow's nest for his cup of grog every evening, and he must be seventy."

Lenox was in fair physical condition—he often took his scull out on the Thames to row—but suddenly doubted whether he could make it up the taut, unyielding rigging without falling and smacking his head. On land it would have been a simple task, but the pitch and roll of the ship made everything unsteady.

Still, the tale of Old Joe Coffey (whom Lenox suddenly rather despised as a show-off) goaded him on. "You first, then," he said.

"Remember you're on my ship, Mr. Lenox." A hint of a smile came into Martin's face. "You mustn't give me orders."

"Of course. Shall I go first?"

"No, no." He paused. "I've just thought—it's a damn good sight I've left the sails slack—otherwise the platform would have been trampled on no end as the men set sail, and the whole area might have been contaminated."

Martin leaped onto the rigging, shouting a man out of the way, and began to climb like a monkey. Lenox followed—much more slowly, not at all like a monkey, in fact, unless it was some tremulous old monkey who had never been much for climbing anyway. At first the rigging felt solid enough, but as he got higher the small waves that smacked the ship began to vibrate in the ropes. Halfway up he made the mistake of looking down and concluded the fall would probably kill him, not least because of the uneven surfaces below.

(Was it possible the fall *had* killed Halifax, and that the wounds—some of them, all of them—were postmortem? But why? No, it was a silly thought.)

Eventually, with much deliberation and care, he reached the perch where Martin had now been for some time. The captain's face made clear what he had found. After Lenox had pulled himself through the hole he steadied himself, then looked down.

There was blood spattered across the low railing and a great slick swath of it, drying into a darker color, at their feet.

"This is our spot, then," said Martin. He didn't speak for a moment. "Look at this blood. Halifax—he was the most placid of men. Of officers in this service. I can't conceive of anyone wanting to kill him."

"My question is how it was done."

"Isn't that plain enough?"

"I suppose—only this area is barely big enough for the two of us to stand. Wouldn't a fight spill one or the other over?"

"Maybe it spilled Halifax over."

"No, because he had been very precisely prepared before he fell to the quarterdeck, I believe. The real question is whether the man who killed Halifax has any marks on him."

"We shall see when all the men are piped up to the main deck for inspection."

Lenox shook his head. "I still wonder whether he would have gotten out of bed for a common sailor . . . met them here . . . I suppose there are circumstances under which it might have been possible."

"A false name, for instance—saying that I or one of the lieutenants wanted to see him there, perhaps a midshipman," said Martin, "but I think it exceedingly doubtful."

"Or perhaps one of the sailors provoked him into coming there, with a threat or a piece of gossip. Mutiny, say."

Martin's face went deadly serious. "No, sir," he said.

"I don't mean that it would have been true. A ruse."

Still, the captain didn't seem to like it. "Well."

"Listen—while we have a moment to ourselves—do you know what this might be?"

Lenox pulled his handkerchief from his pocket and unfolded it, stained red but dry. The object he had found, coin-shaped and -sized, lay in the middle.

"A large coin, I would have said. A crown?"

"No, look closer." He rubbed some more blood off of it, though it was still hard to make out the writing on it. "I'll need to wash it, but for the moment . . ."

"It's a medal, isn't it?"

"I thought so too. Can you identify it?"

Martin picked it up and turned it over twice, looking much more painstakingly now. "Maybe, once you soak it and the lettering comes clean. It's naval, I can say that much. Silver. An officer's medal."

"Possibly Halifax's?"

"Possibly."

"But he wouldn't have carried a medal with him to such an assignation, would he have?"

"No, I highly doubt it. It would have been in a box, the sort you keep for cuff links, and worn with his best uniform."

"Ceremonial occasions, then. Not pinned to his nightshirt."

"Never."

Lenox thought for a moment and then sighed. "I suppose we had better go look at his cabin. If I weren't out of practice I would have done it before. Now someone may have been in it already. Stupid."

"Let's hurry, then."

Going down the rigging was considerably easier than going up, so easy that Lenox was fooled into false confidence and nearly slipped a quarter of the way down before he caught himself. On deck Martin barked an order at someone to clean the perch straightaway.

Carrow and Teddy Lenox were waiting for them on the main deck.

"Sir?" said Carrow.

"Mr. Lenox," said Martin, "would you go to Halifax's cabin or hear their story?"

Lenox sighed. "We must hear their story while it is fresh in their minds," he said. "Perhaps a sentry could be posted—"

"Very well, it shall be done. Come down to the wardroom," said the captain to Carrow and Teddy. "We'll speak there."

In the wardroom Carrow told their story. Teddy Lenox, looking in uniform perhaps more suited to his new role, stood by silently. They had both been on the poop deck when they heard a thump. After a moment or two Carrow, curious to see if perhaps a bird had smacked into the ship or some piece of equipment had fallen, went down and discovered Halifax's body.

"Did you see it?" Martin asked Teddy.

"Yes, sir."

"You went down after Carrow?"

"Yes, sir."

"And then he dismissed you."

"Yes, sir."

Lenox badly wanted a word with his nephew, but knew this wasn't the moment to have it.

"Did you see anyone in the rigging of the mizzenmast at around the same time?" he asked.

"No, sir," said Carrow. "It was dark, of course, and beyond that you wouldn't expect anyone to be up skylarking in the middle watch, barring, I don't know, a squall or some enemy action."

"Quite right," said Martin.

"How many men would have been on deck during your watch, Lieutenant?" asked Lenox.

"A few more than twenty."

"Where would they have congregated?"

"Sir?"

"Are they at work the whole while?"

"Oh—no, sir. Unless they have orders they would be on the

main deck, or perhaps up at the fore of the ship, sitting along the bowsprit."

"At the other end of the ship from the quarterdeck, in other words."

"Yes, sir."

"I see. Another question, if you don't mind—which of the men on this ship are capable of violence, in your opinion?" he asked both the young lieutenant and Martin.

"Difficult to say," Martin answered. "In the right circumstance, all of them."

McEwan chose this moment to lumber through the door with a biscuit in his hand. He retreated to his hallway, bowing as he left, when he saw that the room was occupied.

"Except him, perhaps," said Martin. "But of course the men will all fight. Carrow? You deal with the sailors more from day to day."

"There are a few bad tempers, sir."

Lenox shook his head. "No—a planned meeting, the surgical nature of Halifax's wounds—I don't think this was a moment of bad temper, but rather one of planned and executed malice. Still, Mr. Carrow, if you would put a list together of men you don't trust, it would be useful."

Carrow looked unhappy, but nodded when he saw in Martin's face a stern confirmation of this request. "They're good men, sir," he added, as if to formally express his unhappiness with the request.

"One of them is not," Lenox said. "Now, would one of you show me Lieutenant Halifax's cabin? Then we shall see how Mr. Tradescant has progressed. With your permission, of course, Captain."

CHAPTER TWELVE

Halifax's cabin was a good deal smaller than Lenox's. The detective—for the last few hours had made him such a creature again, which he knew because he felt that peculiar vibrant alertness in his mind that this work had always galvanized in him—visited it alone.

"I'll leave you to it. I've got to start us sailing again," Martin had said. He looked tired but showed no signs of slacking energy. "You can find me on deck if you like. Tell me, first, what you think happened."

"I don't know," said Lenox, and Martin, perhaps used to his directives being followed and his questions answered frankly and fully, looked unhappy with the answer.

"We can't have a murderer roaming freely aboard the ship."

"At the very least—if we cannot rout out this murderer—everyone will be far more aware and cautious now. This is not a large place for hiding."

"Nothing could be worse for the mood of the men, though,"

said Martin. "Suspicion everywhere—rumors, arguments, accusations. Still, it's a short voyage, bless the Lord."

Halifax's cabin (also off of the wardroom) felt personal in a way Lenox's didn't yet, the result of many months' habitation. It was tidy but crammed: notes and sketches pinned on the wall over his tiny desk, clothes hung up on the back of his chair and the bed's short posts, fishing tackle in the corner. Lenox searched through this assortment of items methodically, but ultimately without recompense. There was no note lying about—or indeed in any pocket or drawer Lenox could find—inviting Halifax to a rendezvous during the middle watch. Nor was there any object that didn't seem natural in its place. On the contrary, the cabin looked as if the lieutenant might walk into it at any moment and carry on living his life there.

One detail, however: the porthole at the far end of the cabin was swung open, though it was ship's policy to keep the portholes closed. It would have been the quickest way to jettison such a note, or indeed a murder weapon—a knife, say.

After he had concluded his inspection of Halifax's cabin, Lenox made his way down to the surgery. The corpse of the officer lay on the table at the center of the room still, rinsed clean of blood now, but Tradescant wasn't there.

Lenox found him on deck, smoking a small cigar and looking out over the water. The sun was up.

"You finished examining the body, Mr. Tradescant?"

"Yes, not five minutes since. I can show you what I found—come along." The surgeon threw his cigar overboard, though the ship was now moving at a sufficient clip, with new sails set, that they didn't hear the hiss of it being extinguished. "There was one interesting discovery I made."

Standing over Halifax's body a few moments later, Tradescant described in clear language each wound the dead man had sustained.

"These here are not very precise," he said, pointing to the incisions along Halifax's torso, "and the wounds that killed him—these, around his heart—are not very deep or strong. I suspect he died of blood loss rather than a deadly blow to his heart, in fact. His artery was nicked here."

"What conclusion can you draw about the murder weapon, then?"

"I have the murder weapon."

Lenox paused, dumbstruck, for a moment. "You've—how have you got it?" The wild thought that Tradescant might be the murderer crossed his mind, and he even stepped backward slightly.

This produced a bark of laughter from the surgeon. "It wasn't I, Mr. Lenox. Here it is."

Tradescant went into the pocket of his vest and produced a gleaming silver pocketknife. He held it out and Lenox took it.

It was about five inches long, on the larger side for these sorts of knives, and had three blades of different lengths that folded out and locked into place. There was also a fourth implement that folded out of the knife: a minute compass on the end of a metal rod.

"Useful for a man at sea, that," said Tradescant. "Specially made, perhaps."

"Are you certain this is the weapon? How did you find it?"

He gestured toward the body on the table. "You asked me to check that Lieutenant Halifax's organs were intact. They were, but this was tucked underneath the stomach, hidden from immediate view but not at all tricky to find."

"It couldn't have been this clean."

"Oh, no. I washed it. I wanted to see if it had any distinctive markings."

"And you feel that this matches his cuts?"

"There's very little doubt in my mind. As I say, the wounds are too ragged in the one case and shallow in the other to have been the result of anything as precise as a scalpel or as big as a kitchen knife. A pocketknife such as this fits the bill."

"Sterling silver," murmured Lenox.

Tradescant nodded. "Well beyond the reach of any common bluejacket, I would have thought."

"Easily thieved, however."

"Perhaps, yes."

"Wouldn't the blade have folded back into the knife if you attempted to stab someone with it?"

"As you'll observe, if I may show you—the blade locks out into place, and only pressing this button allows it to be folded back in."

"Ah, I see. Well done, Mr. Tradescant. May I ask, to change the subject only for a moment—did you look at his back? Halifax's?"

"I didn't, no. Why? Surely the wounds are frontal?"

"If he fell from a good height to the quarterdeck, as I believe, there might have been bruising on the back."

Tradescant nodded. "Yes, and in fact I did find a bloody cut on the back of his head. That might have been inflicted by the fall. Here—help me turn the body onto its side, so we may see."

They performed this operation with what delicacy they could manage, and as Lenox had suspected found great red welts on Halifax's back.

"These swellings would still have appeared postmortem?" Lenox asked as they laid the body back down flat.

"Immediately postmortem, yes, it's certainly possible. I would be inclined to accept your theory."

It was a relief to have confirmation of at least one fact.

"Did the body tell you anything else?"

"Not in particular. He was a healthy man. As you predicted, there were blue fibers in the wounds around his heart—the shirt must have been removed or at a minimum unbuttoned before the incisions in the abdomen were made."

"Any wounds on the hands?"

Tradescant frowned. "I don't know, why?"

Lenox lifted one of Halifax's hands. It was easy to forget how valuable his friend Thomas McConnell's medical expertise had been when Lenox was working as a detective every day. "From his hands we may observe whether he defended himself."

"I see."

"But both hands appear to be unhurt. It must mean that Halifax wouldn't have expected to be stabbed—or that it came quickly."

"Yes," said Tradescant. "Sensible."

"I suppose that covers the facts, then," said Lenox. "Thank you, Mr. Tradescant."

"I'm for bed, then, even though I spy daylight. It's been a long night."

Suddenly Lenox felt overwhelmingly tired. "Yes," he said. "I'll go on deck to tell Martin we're going to steal some sleep. There's nothing we could do now that can't be achieved in four hours' time."

"Or ten hours, if I have my way," said Tradescant.

They both looked down at the body of Halifax then, and a strange moment of frustration and dazed bafflement seemed to pass among the three of them. How had they ended up this way, two of them alive, one dead, when not twenty hours before they had been on land, and not twelve hours before they had been dining together?

It had all happened so fast. And poor Halifax! Lenox thought of the fishing again. He would have to try out the dead man's fishing pole one day soon. A minor—and insufficient—tribute to what might have been a real friendship, had they both made it through the journey together.

As he lay in bed fifteen minutes later, Lenox's mind muddled through the facts—the medal, the knife, the incisions on

Halifax's torso—but without any constructive result. It was merely a whirl of thoughts. Fruitless.

He also thought of the comfortable green baize benches in Parliament, the cups of tea and hot wine rushed in by young secretaries when discussion went late into the night, his comfortable office in Westminster . . . and of course he thought of Jane, of leaving Parliament for home and finding her there, waiting for him long after she ought to have been in bed. Had he softened? Or merely changed? He was past forty now, definitely middle-aged. It had been three years since he had regularly taken cases. He had a child on the way. The exhilaration of late nights in the Seven Dials, chasing down some gin-soaked murderer, of being in on the hunt as a forger fled to Surrey, of those old cases, was now some years in the past. Did they belong to a different part of his life? Of himself?

Could he still do this?

CHAPTER THIRTEEN

The naval day began properly at noon.

Of course in the forenoon there was sailing to be done, an officer on watch, and men up among the rigging and down on deck doing their work. (In particular the forenoon was when the entire deck, regardless of its cleanliness, was soaked, cleaned, and beaten dry in preparation for the day.) It was in the forenoon as well that the midshipmen received their instruction.

But it was at noon when the officers took a sighting of the sun to help establish their position, the captain there to hear it. Immediately afterward all the men were piped for dinner. This was the main meal of the day: the purser's mate issued the men salted beef, dried peas, and beer or grog depending on the ship's stores. They ate where they had slept the watch before, in what they called their mess—the narrow area between two great guns that they shared with seven other men. This day there was a steady hum of gossip; they had been ordered to appear in full uniform on deck after dinner, something usually reserved for Sundays, when church was rigged.

Lenox woke up a bit before noon. When he called for Mc-Ewan, the assistant, with a note of genuine sympathy in his voice, said, "Which you must be starving, sir. Would eggs in toast do you?"

"And tea, if you please."

"And tea, of course, and you'll be needing biscuits, and I think I saw some marmalade, and . . ."

Lenox was still tired—and his mind still racing—but the strong, dark tea refreshed him. Better still, McEwan could cook. The eggs, cracked into an oval hole in the middle of two pieces of toast, cooked until brown on either side, and served with the cut-out ovals toasted on the side, were wonderfully flavorsome.

"Chickens laid 'em this morning," said McEwan when Lenox complimented the breakfast. "We call it a spit in the ocean."

"What other animals do you keep on board?"

"Why, I don't rightly know, sir, leastways on this voyage." McEwan chewed an edge of toast himself, ruminating. "Though I imagine there's a goat, sir, and a mess of chickens, and it might be as there's a lamb."

As was customary among men with the means to do so, Lenox had brought his own provisions on board: hams, cheeses, wine, biscuits, and whatever else Jane had thought he might need. They were stowed in locked hampers outside his cabin, where McEwan had taken to lovingly stroking them every time he passed.

Lenox took a second cup of tea, reading from a copy of *The Voyage of the Beagle* he had brought on board. When he heard the men being piped to dinner he went to his cabin and, with a smile, took an orange Jane had packed for him. This he ate while leaning over the rail of the quarterdeck, thinking of Halifax and Halifax's murderer, tossing the rind over the side but savoring the fruit both for its taste and the person it recalled to mind.

Soon all the officers and all the men—everyone afloat on the *Lucy*, from McEwan to Martin—stood on deck, all dressed ceremonially. A drummer played a short burst of formal rhythm and then the captain spoke.

He had come to Lenox only a moment before the drummer began.

"Is there anything you can tell me? Anything to draw out the murderer? Anything I should omit?"

"I wouldn't mention the murder weapon." Lenox had told Martin about the pocketknife that morning, just before he had gone to sleep. "You might mention that we have a strong suspicion of whom the murderer is—it would make us seem as if we have the situation in hand."

"Which we don't," the captain said flatly.

"It might also induce a confession."

In the end Martin followed this advice. His voice booming over the brisk sounds of the water and the wind, the sails, he said, "For three years now I have been proud to call the *Lucy* my command. I say with complete confidence that there is no finer ship in Her Majesty's navy. She is a taut ship; a fast one; a friendly one; a dangerous one. She can outsail and outmaneuver anyone in the ocean, and though she has fewer guns than most she can outshoot many of them, too. That's down to her crew.

"Perhaps that is why I am doubly downcast at what occurred during the middle watch last night. You may as well know what many of you will have heard in differing accounts: Lieutenant Thomas Halifax was murdered. And, after a fashion, was the *Lucy*. She cannot be the same ship now."

It was clever, thought Lenox, to appeal to their pride in the ship they sailed. But futile, too, he expected. Whoever murdered Halifax had too cool a head to succumb to such manipulation.

"I ask the man who committed this foul deed to step forward now," Martin said. He took a deep breath. "If he does so, his family and friends on land will think he died during a storm. There is no need for such a stain to extend to a wife or a son.

The name can remain good. I don't think you could reckon a fairer bargain than that."

The men evidently agreed. A murmur of assent rippled through the multitude, and they all turned their heads back and forth and round to see if anyone would rise.

But nobody did, and Martin, nodding as if it was only in confirmation of his expectation, said, "Very well. I see this murderer—one of you—is every bit as cowardly as I anticipated he would be. Let it fall on your own head, then. Stand in three lines now, bare-chested, and Mr. Lenox, Mr. Tradescant, and I will inspect you all. The midshipmen shall divide the groups by mess, that no man may go unaccounted for."

The surgeon, the captain, and the member of Parliament briefly huddled and agreed to send anyone with a suspicious wound into the surgery. This was Lenox's thought, one last gambit to encourage guilt: the suspects would be standing over Halifax's body.

"Consider particularly the forearms and the faces," he added before they split into groups.

Privately he wondered whether they should be making a similar examination of the officers. It was a point to raise to Martin later.

If the sailors had thought Lenox was bad luck previously, this murder was, it seemed, all the verification they required. Each man he inspected gave him a dirtier look than the last.

He noticed Evers—the man who had told McEwan Lenox was an albatross—standing back several places in line. When their eyes met Evers spat into his cap and turned away.

McEwan himself was in Lenox's grouping. His hands, arms, face, and chest were all free of suspicious markings, and he somberly nodded to Lenox when dismissed. As he left he appeared to pluck a small parcel from his own cap (pockets were forbidden in the navy, by tradition if not written rule) that looked suspiciously biscuit-shaped.

In the end nine sailors assembled in the surgery, not counting the patient who slumbered peacefully on, deep in coma, in the corner of the room.

Halifax's body was beginning to decay; Tradescant uncovered it as the sailors filed into the room. Each crossed himself when he saw it.

The review was thorough but inconclusive. The first man they interviewed had a great scrape across his right forearm, but claimed—and in the captain's opinion it seemed probable—that a rush of rope from a slack sail had given him the burn. Two or three more had such shipboard injuries. Evers had a great welt on his chest, which he said came from a drunken stumble down the streets of Plymouth.

"What did you land on?" Lenox asked.

"Dunno. Sir. I woke up with it."

"It looks fresh."

"It's only from yesterday."

Two more men had injuries that looked older than eight hours. In the end Martin, Tradescant, and Lenox dismissed the men; Lenox marked two in his mind for continued observation, but felt relatively sure that he had ended up down another blind alley.

"Back to work for me, then," said Martin.

"Have you slept?" asked Lenox.

"Tonight. You'll continue to look into this?"

"Yes."

Lenox took to the quarterdeck. In the early afternoon the sky was hot and brilliant, cloudless.

Idly he examined the pocketknife Halifax had been killed with, as if it might unfold not just three knives and a compass, but, more useful than any of these, some kind of answer to this puzzle.

Suddenly he spotted something he hadn't seen before.

Along the broad side of the smallest knife was a faint inscription. He had believed Tradescant's statement as true, that the pocketknife had been unmarked, but then these words were all but faded from wear and would have been easy to miss in the wrong light. The white sun helped Lenox read them now.

For my son, Aloysius Billings, they said, *July 1861*.

CHAPTER FOURTEEN

So the knife that had killed Halifax belonged to the first lieutenant of the *Lucy*.

Lenox retracted the blade into its groove and considered what he ought to do. After several unhurried moments of reflection, he went down to the wardroom and sought out McEwan.

"Which of these is Lieutenant Billings's cabin?" he asked.

"The one three to the left of yours, sir."

"What is his servant's name?"

"Mr. Butterworth, sir."

"Thank you."

Lenox counted three doors and knocked on the third. There were footsteps within it and Butterworth came to the door, a jaundiced man, too tall to be aboard a ship. Even answering the knock he was stooped over, nearly brushing the beams of the ceiling with his head.

"Sir?"

"Is Lieutenant Billings within?"

"No, sir. He's on duty."

"I didn't see him on the quarterdeck."

"Indeed, sir? He should be off shortly."

"I'll check back."

Lenox returned to his own cabin and made a provisional list of clues, simply to organize his own mind: the penknife, the surgical incisions in Halifax's torso, the missing blue shirt, the unusual fact that Halifax was not on duty but nevertheless on deck, and finally the medallion.

This he pulled from the handkerchief he had been keeping it in. (Pockets might be unloved within the navy, but Lenox retained his own.)

"McEwan, could you bring me a basin of warm water here at my desk?" he called out.

The warm water came, McEwan trotting it to Lenox. With a bit of rag and a sliver of grayish hand soap, Lenox set about cleaning the medallion.

It was, as the captain had initially observed, roughly the size of a large coin, a crown, say, but made entirely of sterling silver. When the blood was gone from the object's surface it sparkled again as if newly polished, which perhaps it recently had been, in particular if it were a treasured element of one officer's formal dress.

Lenox pulled out the magnifying glass to look at the object more closely. (This magnifying glass was one of his favorite objects, a present from his friend Lord Cabot, which had an ivory handle and gold rim, small enough to fit into a breast pocket.) Just as he was about to do so, however, there were footsteps in the wardroom and he abandoned the medallion and the magnifying glass to discover whose they were.

It was Billings, as he had hoped.

"Hello, Mr. Lenox," said the lieutenant.

Lenox scanned the man's face for guilt, an action that he had never found particularly edifying, given the variety of men's demeanors and the basic inscrutableness of the brains behind them, but nonetheless performed out of habit.

"I hoped it would be someone I might ask a favor of. Lieutenant, do you carry a penknife, or a pocketknife, about your person?"

Billings's reaction, which Lenox carefully watched, was one of seemingly legitimate surprise. "No," he said, "aboard ship I only have a compass and a short telescope with me, in general, as you may see."

He motioned to where these two objects, the second a brass tube no bigger than a half-burned candle, hung from a cord around his waist. Now that he thought of it Lenox perceived that both were worn as Martin wore his, perhaps in imitation.

"Ah, of course."

"Why do you ask?"

"Do you have a penknife at all?"

"I do, in my cabin."

"Could I borrow it, by any chance?"

Billings frowned. "You may, of course—but is it possible that you don't carry one, or that McEwan doesn't?"

"Oh, yes," said Lenox, rather lamely. It was a barefaced lie. "And just when I want to shave my pen down, to write a letter home, you know."

"Come into my cabin and I'll fetch it for you."

They went into Billings's roomy cabin, which was unadorned to the point of austerity. On the desk, set in a slight circular depression in the wood so that it wouldn't rock, was a silver christening cup, much battered and dented but lovingly polished. Poking up from it was a quill and a short length of string spilled over the side.

"Should be in here," said the officer, and started to root around in the cup. When he didn't find it he actually picked the cup up and turned it over on his desk, fluttering chits of paper and old bits of rubber out with the quill and the string.

"Mr. Billings?" said Lenox.

"How strange. It doesn't seem to be here. I say, Butterworth!" he cried out toward the galley.

Lenox opened his palm and extended it out. "Lieutenant, is this it?"

"Why—and so it is! Where did you find it?"

"This was the weapon that killed Lieutenant Halifax."

Billings was struck silent by this information. Only after a moment did he manage to ask if Lenox could repeat what he had said.

"This was the weapon that killed Halifax, I'm afraid. Tradescant believes it to be such, at any rate, and his reasoning is sound so far as I can see."

"That cannot be."

"It was in the corpse, underneath the stomach."

Billings, who had been close to vomiting when they inspected Halfax's body, inhaled sharply as if to steady himself, and for good measure took two deep breaths. "I suppose it might have been stolen from my cabin," he said.

"Who would have had the opportunity?"

"Sailors are in here occasionally, on errands. Any officer, of course, and their servants, might have slipped into any of the wardroom cabins."

"The purser's mate, for instance, or the surgeon's?"

"Yes. Our cook. There must be twenty people, thirty. More." Now something occurred to Billings. "But look here—why did you go through that foolery of asking whether I had a penknife?"

"It was a shabby trick, and I apologize. Will you shake my hand?" Lenox asked. "In my profession—I suppose I should say my former profession—it is necessary occasionally to be deceitful. I didn't believe that you killed Halifax, but I wanted to judge your reaction."

Billings was perhaps too honest to make a diplomatic reply, but he shook hands and said, "Yes, I see."

"If you don't mind, I'll just keep the knife—not for long."

"It was given me by my father," said Billings, "when I first sailed. I hold a great attachment to the object, foolish though that may be."

"I shall take good care of it."

"Well, if the situation requires it, I can scarcely refuse."

"Thank you."

"Am I a suspect?"

"Everyone must be," said Lenox. "But I don't think you killed Halifax, no. Nor do I suspect Carrow, for he was on watch, and among men. Nor the surgeon, nor the captain if it comes to it. Everyone else is fair game at the moment."

"What will you do?"

"Begin interviewing people."

CHAPTER FIFTEEN

In his mind Lenox was all but persuaded that someone of the wardroom—a neighbor of his, in other words—had committed this deed. He was open to the possibility that a sailor had murdered Halifax, but didn't the theft of Billings's penknife at least suggest proximity to his cabin? Moreover, didn't Halifax's midnight rendezvous with his murderer suggest an equal, rather than a subordinate relationship—in other words a gentleman of the wardroom, who might reasonably have asked a second lieutenant to meet him in secret?

For this reason Lenox decided to begin his interviews with the two lieutenants whose names he did not know—now the third and fourth lieutenants, with Carrow assuming Halifax's role as second, at any rate for the duration of the *Lucy's* present voyage. One of them, a lad not past twenty named Amos Lee, was on duty, so with Martin's permission Lenox asked the other one if they might meet. The wardroom being occupied, in these daylight hours, in much the way a gentleman's club on Pall Mall might have been, with the master sprawled in a chair reading and the purser whittling with his boots up on the table, Lenox decided that they might meet more discreetly if they sat in the quiet area at the aft of the *Lucy*.

The fourth lieutenant was called Mitchell, a very short, very sturdy chap, rather dark-complected, and possibly even surlier than Carrow. He had been quiet at both of the officers' dinners Lenox had attended.

He met Lenox by the long, hip-high taffrail that curved off the back of the ship, where one could lean on one's arms and watch the ship's wake furl back white and die again into its metallic blue. "The captain said you wanted to see me, Mr. Lenox?"

"Yes, thank you. I hope I didn't interrupt your rest."

"No," said the lieutenant, his intonation terse.

"I was wondering what you might tell me about this murder."

"Nothing, I'm afraid."

"Where were you at the time?"

"Asleep in my cabin. I didn't hear anything about it until the morning."

"Only Carrow was awake, among you officers?"

"And Halifax."

"Yes, of course. But you and Lieutenant Lee kip together, I understand?"

"Yes, we have bunks in the same cabin."

"Was he asleep?"

"As far as I know. I didn't observe it firsthand because, as I may have mentioned, I myself was asleep."

Lenox paused. "Is this conversation a matter of inconvenience to you, Mr. Mitchell?"

"Yes, as a matter of fact."

"You don't care to help discover who murdered Halifax?"

"Oh, the murderer ought to be caught."

"Is your issue with me, then?"

Mitchell was silent.

"Well?" said Lenox.

"May I speak freely?"

"I should hope you would."

"It's a ridiculous use of a good ship, hauling you to Egypt."

"I understood that the ship was bound for Egypt already."

"Faugh!"

In other circumstances Lenox might have tried to conciliate him, but the truth was that whether he recognized it or not his time in Parliament—in power—had, perhaps inevitably, made him less tolerant of disrespect, less quick to amicability. Besides, it was worth seeing if this Mitchell had a bad temper.

"And you think you know enough of state, enough of our position in the world, enough of Her Majesty's government, to pass judgment on what I plan to do in Egypt?"

"No, sir," said Mitchell—not removing his gaze from Lenox's, however.

"Then who do you think you are?"

"I asked if I might speak freely, sir."

"Given which I hope you don't mind that I shall, too. Your judgments are a fool's, taken in haste and for clumsy pride's sake not withdrawn. I would scarcely inform you of how to set a spinnaker, and I advise you that your ignorance of politics is as severe as mine of sailing. Now, answer my questions before I'm forced to see the captain about you—how long had you known Halifax?"

Mitchell's face was venomous, but he choked out a reply. "Only a few weeks. I was called into the *Lucy* while she was in dry dock. The captain is a friend of my father's. *Sir*," he spat out.

"Did you kill Halifax?"

This knocked Mitchell down. "No!" he said. "What—no!"

"The newest man on board must be a suspect, of course."

"I didn't do it, and I resent the question."

"It's shabby to go around stealing penknives, too."

Mitchell looked genuinely baffled at that. "Excuse me?" he said.

"Never mind. Tell me, what do you think happened?"

"I don't know. I suppose one of the sailors got angry and took his revenge. They're a coarse lot—devils on land."

"Why not kill him in Plymouth?" said Lenox. "Why wait until they were on board the ship?"

"I can't say, sir."

Lenox stared at the younger man for a moment. "Thank you," he said, and turned on his heel abruptly to walk away.

"I didn't do it," Mitchell called after him.

Lenox wanted to speak to more of the wardroom officers now, but before he did he stopped into his own cabin: it was time to inspect this medallion once and for all.

To his astonishment, however, his desk was empty. The medallion was gone.

"McEwan!" he shouted.

The steward lumbered in, not surprisingly working a bit of food in his jaw. The whole cabin smelled like cinnamon toast, and Lenox felt a pang of hunger in his stomach.

"Did you take away the basin that was on my desk?"

"Yes, sir."

"Then you have the medallion that I was cleaning? The one that was in the basin?"

"No, sir. The basin was empty—even the water had been thrown out the porthole, sir."

"The porthole was open?"

"Yes, sir."

Lenox felt sick—how amateurish of him to be distracted from a tangible clue. No doubt the water and the medallion had been splashed through the porthole together. By the murderer.

"Lord."

McEwan looked confused. "I figgered you'd come back and took it away, so I cleaned the basin."

"This damn naval obsession with cleaning. Listen to me now: Did you look at the medallion, when I left it here earlier? I know you must have been in to sweep."

McEwan gulped. "No."

"Deal honestly with me and I won't be angry." Lenox paused. "I'm sorry to have spoken sharply, but it's important."

"Well, I may have *glanced* at it, is all, sir, to make sure it didn't need . . . cleaning, or polishing, I suppose, the way things do, which is only right," he concluded, rather lamely.

"Yes, I'm sure. Tell me, then—what did it say?"

"It was a medal given out for service in the Second Opium War. On the front was a picture of the HMS *Chesapeake* as well as the date, and on the back was the name of the midshipman who received it. And a very little nipper he must have been, too, not past ten or eleven."

"Who was it?"

"Lieutenant Carrow, sir."

"Carrow!"

"Yes, sir."

Lenox went deep into thought for a moment, as McEwan looked anxiously on.

Something strange was happening now; inside and near the body of a murdered lieutenant had been objects that belonged to two of his fellow officers, both presumably stolen, neither there, it would seem, for any particular reason. After all, another knife would have killed Halifax just as well, and in all probability with more efficiency. As for the medallion, it wouldn't have been torn from Carrow's breast in a struggle—Lenox's first thought— because he wouldn't have worn it on deck.

He would have to have a word with Carrow, to be sure.

"Interesting," Lenox said at length. "Well, keep it to yourself, please, no talk of it to that Evers chap."

"No, sir."

"And don't look at my things again, please. I know it's your job to tidy my cabin, but there must be some proper expectation of privacy."

"Yes, sir."

Lenox paused. "Incidentally, could you go to the galley and sort me out a piece of that cinnamon toast? And maybe a cup of that Chinese tea I brought, the dark stuff?"

"Oh, of course, sir."

CHAPTER SIXTEEN

The body of Lieutenant Thomas St. James Halifax having been thoroughly examined and, of course, confirmed dead, that night the men of the *Lucy* made preparation for its burial at sea.

As the hour of the ceremony marched closer—all men on board knew from their superiors, down to the purser's third assistant, that it was to be at half past five—a deep melancholy took hold of the ship. The men were quiet in their preparations. Lenox observed them, two sailors letting the starboard gangway out, a group of others clearing the main deck and furling the mainmast's sails tight around it, four more bringing a long mess table onto the deck and setting it beside the open gangway.

Martin himself supervised them, and also ordered the sails set in counterpoise to each other, so that the ship would be as perfectly still as possible. Then he called out, "Top gallant yards, acock bill," an order that sent men scurrying up the rigging.

As soon as the gangway was folded out and the *Lucy* was as

near motionless as the rocking of the ocean would permit, men began to head below deck, the officers, the warrant officers, the midshipmen, the bluejackets, the marines, all in a great drove, to change into their best dress.

Lenox, already in a black suit, stayed above, and found himself nearly the only person there.

Downstairs, he knew from Tradescant, the sailmaker was sewing Halifax's body into a snow-white sheet, with two cannonballs at his feet to weigh him down. The last stitch would go through his nose, by old naval custom, as a final confirmation that he was dead.

At five fifteen the men began to assemble on deck in long, tidy rows, all dressed in their white duck trousers, blue shirts, and blue caps. Usually a gathering of this variety on ship was loud, but nobody spoke now. Then the officers came on board; each, Lenox saw, was carrying a white flower.

"You will stand with us, Mr. Lenox?" said Martin, coming up from behind him with his tricorn hat tucked under his arm.

"I should be honored."

When several minutes later they were all assembled and the body in its white sailcloth had been hauled onto the deck and laid out on the long mess table, the bosun—a sort of head sailor, in charge of various small crews of seamen, generally the soundest naval mind at a captain's disposal—piped, and then called out "Ship's company, off hats!" in a loud voice that seemed to carry unnaturally in that great void of ocean.

The men removed their hats.

The chaplain stepped forward before the men and began to speak. In their short acquaintance he had been a figure of fun, of comedy, to Lenox, but in his vestments now he looked terribly grave, and his booming voice seemed free of the slur it took when he drank spirits.

"We come here today to bury at sea a good and God-fearing man, Lieutenant Thomas Halifax. May he rest in peace.

"I shall read from the book of Job, and from the book of John." The chaplain sighed heavily, and then spoke. "'He brought nothing into this world, and it is certain we can carry nothing out. The Lord gave, and the Lord hath taken away; blessed be the name of the Lord.'"

"Blessed be the name of the Lord," the ship's company chanted back.

The chaplain went on. "'I am the resurrection and the life, saith the Lord: he that believeth in me, though he were dead, yet shall he live: and whosoever liveth and believeth in me shall never die.' Amen."

"Amen."

Now the chaplain began to read from Lamentations, following them with two psalms, the thirtieth and the ninetieth. Lenox listened to them more as music than as words, and found himself staring into the soft golden twilight, the birds wheeling through it, the ocean mapping the light, the sky clear and more white than blue. A great hollow feeling came into his chest, almost like tears, of something inarticulate and enormous, something he only vaguely understood.

The chaplain finished and motioned the four remaining lieutenants, Billings, Carrow, Lee, and Mitchell, forward. Each took one corner of the mess table upon which Halifax, sewn into his sail, was laid. As the chaplain spoke again they walked the table down the starboard gangway and slowly, agonizingly slowly, began to tip the body into the sea.

"We therefore commit the body of our brother and shipmate Thomas Halifax to the deep, looking for general resurrection in the last day, and the life of the world to come, through our Lord Jesus Christ; at whose Second Coming in glorious majesty to judge the world, the sea shall give up her dead; and the corruptible bodies of those who sleep in him shall be changed, and made like unto his glorious body; according to the mighty working whereby he is able to subdue all things unto himself.

"Ashes to ashes, dust to dust. The Lord bless and keep him. The Lord make his face to shine upon him and be gracious unto him. The Lord lift his countenance upon him, and give him peace. Amen."

"Amen," the ship's company called back.

The body slid heavily from the table and for a brief moment seemed to hang in the air, then broke the water's surface with a tremendous crash. For a moment, not longer, a white ghost lingered in the sea, but before anyone could be sure they had seen a final glimpse of the ensheeted body it was already speeding toward the depths.

The officers and the captain now went to the rail and each threw his flower onto the water. *Full fathom five thy father lies,* went through Lenox's head, an old schooldays' memorization, *of his bones are coral made: Those are pearls that were his eyes; nothing of him that doth fade, But doth suffer a sea-change into something rich and strange. Sea-nymphs hourly ring his bell: Hark, now I hear them, ding-dong bell.* There was something far worse about a body going into the water than into the ground; far worse.

Now the captain stepped forward and gazed out over the men he commanded. He was such a very religious man that Lenox expected words of Christian emphasis, but apparently that role had been filled by the chaplain. For his part, Martin spoke of Halifax as a naval man.

"This is an unhappy burial, I know—but refuse to believe, for to be buried at sea is a great honor for a proper man of Her Majesty's navy, as Thomas Halifax was, and though his virtues would have well adorned a longer life, though his service to our Queen was too brief in duration, though his death was an unfair and bitterly hard-fought one, at the hands of a peasant and coward, nevertheless he goes to the same deeps Drake did, the same deeps to which his grandfather's body fell. And in that there must be great honor. He is numbered among us, a man of our ship the *Lucy*. May none of you forget that, until the last who stands among us on this deck draws his final breath. Whomever it shall be."

The bosun stepped forward again. "Ship's company, on hats!" he cried. The men put their blue cloth caps back on and started, with a low murmur of conversation, to go back below deck to change, and many of them soon to eat.

The officers watched them go and then Martin, his face flushed red—though it was impossible to say whether with emotion or cold, for the sun had all but gone—turned and said, "I invite you all to my dining room for supper. The midshipmen will be with us too. In honor of Halifax."

The officers murmured their assent, and began to go below deck themselves.

This supper was a downhearted affair despite the captain's excellent food and wine, although for Lenox the affair was somewhat enlivened because he was able to snatch a few moments of conversation with his nephew.

"How has your first day been?"

Teddy shrugged. "Well, Lieutenant Halifax . . ."

"Aside from that? Are you settled in?"

"Oh, yes. I know one of the chaps from the college, and they all seem decent enough. In fact they asked me to invite you for supper in the gun room."

"I should be delighted."

"If you might bring provisions, Uncle Charles . . ." Teddy's earnest face was screwed up in concentration, trying to phrase his request with some measure of delicacy. "The lads themselves don't have much aboard, and by the end of the last trip out they were roasting rats."

"Say no more—it shall be a feast."

Slowly people began to tell stories of Halifax, beginning with the captain and then to Carrow—whom Lenox thought perhaps he might manage a word with after supper—and the engineer Quirke, who spoke amusingly about his own attempts to fish off the side of the *Lucy* with Halifax.

As they were drinking their port, however, something arrived out of the sky—which had been clear all day—that would distract them all from their stories and, indeed, from Halifax's murder: a storm.

CHAPTER SEVENTEEN

It was Mitchell, Lenox's antagonist of that afternoon, who drew their attention to the situation. He had stayed on deck, being the duty officer, while the others ate, and had taken the ship back on course after it had fallen still for Halifax's burial. Now he came into Martin's cabin.

"With pardon, sir, there's weather above," he said to the captain.

Martin's brow furrowed. "It was clear not an hour ago."

"Yes, sir."

Martin stood. "Only a passing squall, I imagine, but I had better go upstairs. Gentlemen, please finish your port."

Lenox turned to Carrow after the captain had gone. "What will you do in a squall?" he asked.

"Would you care to see? It shouldn't be too bad yet. You might come up on deck."

"With pleasure."

It looked ominous outside to Lenox's eyes, but he had learned enough of his own lack of comprehension of naval matters to keep quiet. There were huge clifflike black clouds toward the east, and the air carried a peculiar salt tang.

"More than a squall," Carrow murmured as they reached the quarterdeck.

"Do you think?"

The captain was on the main deck delivering orders. "Reef the topsails!" his voice boomed out. "Prepare for heavy wind, gentlemen!"

The crew were in action even before he had finished speaking, moving in a kind of symphony of coordination. Soon the masts looked barer than they had when Lenox and Carrow came on deck.

For his part Carrow was watching not the men but the clouds. "This is an overnighter," he said. To Lenox's surprise the young man, usually so stern and pinched-looking, was now beaming.

"Might we not outrun it, using coal?"

"We might," said Carrow, not taking his eyes off of the storm clouds, "but then again we might not. And if we did not, we would have used half our coal and worn our men to the bone just before a storm, just when everyone must be at their sharpest."

"I see."

Now he turned to Lenox. "You needn't worry. A storm is the best fun in the world, I promise you—once you make it out alive, at any rate."

The other officers evidently agreed, for they were drifting onto deck now, giving orders along with the bosun—lash down this, ship that below deck—and soon the sailors came above too. Those who didn't work chewed their tobacco and leant on the railings, looking out at the black clouds just as Carrow had.

One man was unhappy, however: the purser, Pettegree, who tailed the captain, occasionally offering a comment when his superior's attention was less than fully occupied.

"Why does he look so anxious?" Lenox asked Carrow.

"A purser always hates a storm—and since they were never proper sailors, but always purser's mates, they never shall grow to love them, either."

"He rose to the position of officer?"

"Oh, yes, he would have started out in hammocks with the rest of them. Now he's a warrant officer, but still—" Carrow made a gesture that seemed to indicate this wasn't worth much count.

"And why does he hate a storm?"

"Water is terrible for the purser's stores, you see. It gets the flour wet, or rolls crates around and destroys them . . . he'll be asking Captain Martin for help. To give him his due, he'll have a difficult night."

Indeed, Martin finally gave Pettegree his full attention, and once he had heard—with no great measure of patience—the purser's request, he detached four stout-looking men from their work and sent them below deck.

It was clear now that no amount of coal would have pushed the *Lucy*, fast as she might be under sail and steam, beyond the reach of the storm. Fat drops of rain started to dot the deck dark.

"Reef the mainsails!" cried Martin.

When this was accomplished the masts looked all but bare—there were a few small, tough-looking sails at the center of the ship, presumably to guide the ship without encouraging her to too great a speed.

"Had I better go below deck?" Lenox asked Carrow.

"If you prefer."

Martin came charging past them toward aft, stopping long enough to say, "Now you will see my men at their best, Mr. Lenox. Tell the boys in Parliament. Tell Her Majesty, for that matter."

"I shall." When he was gone, Lenox went on, "I say, Lieutenant Carrow, why are we running into the wind now?"

"It's the best way to keep the ship from capsizing," Carrow answered with a dry smile, "and so I deduce that such is the captain's desire."

Lenox went rather pale. "Is there a chance of that—of us capsizing?"

Carrow laughed. "Oh, no. A chance in a thousand, perhaps, but no. This is only a bad storm, from the look of it, not what we call a survival storm. The wind will run us along at eight or nine knots—stiffly enough, mind you!—but not more than that. If it were more we couldn't sail. In a nine-knot wind you have the great advantage of still being able to use your sails."

"I see."

"Even if we couldn't, however, no, I shouldn't imagine we'd capsize. And now I really might go below deck, Mr. Lenox," said Carrow, "or else look sharply about yourself—one hand for you and one for the *Lucy*, you know!"

Carrow tipped his hat good-bye and went to the aft of the ship, where several men were preparing a line with a drag—or a drogue, as Lenox would learn it was called—to hurl behind the ship, slowing them down, in case they caught the wind fully.

When Carrow had recommended that he go below deck, the weather had been relatively consistent, wetter now, slightly windier, but not bad. Suddenly, though, as if from nothing, the wind went from a heavy breeze to a force so powerful and un-relenting that it nearly lifted Lenox from his feet. As it was he lost his hat, and did well to grab on to a lifeline running down the boat, which he used to retreat below deck.

When he put up his head a few moments later there was a tor-rential rain; there were great crashes of whitecap onto the deck; brilliant flashes of lightning in a sunless, midnight sky; and that wind, always that wind. Martin's voice was the only audible one. Everywhere else men worked in grim, silent concentration, always keeping one hand along a lifeline that they might not be swept overboard.

The ship looked in utter disarray. Strips of canvas were streaming out to leeward, sails were running from their boat ropes. He had seen enough, and ducked below the main hatchway and below deck.

"McEwan!" Lenox said when he reached his cabin and found the steward in his tiny hallway outside it, seated on a stool and polishing Lenox's boots. "Have you ever seen such a storm?"

McEwan considered the question seriously and then responded, "Oh, only seventy or seventy-five times in all, sir."

"Is it so common? I've never seen its like, I swear to you!"

"Here, take a towel, sir, and I'll find you a fresh shirt. This is a fair storm, I'll grant you that, but in the Mediterranean we had a twelve-knotter once. That, I can tell you, sir, was fearful. We hove to it and just barely managed to keep our masts upright. This was when I was a younger man, sir. We lost nine."

"Nine men? How?"

"It was so dark and the rain was so thick that you couldn't see a foot in front of your face. Men would take their hands off of the lifeline for a fraction of a second and be gone forever. Now then—a towel. And you'll be wanting something warm to drink."

McEwan trotted off to start a pot of tea.

If his speech had been designed to reassure Lenox, it failed. With a heavy feeling in the pit of his stomach he patted himself dry, keeping one ear bent toward the deck. Occasional claps of thunder seemed to shiver every board and plank of the ship. Suddenly it seemed the most insane chanciness, a madness, to be afloat on a man-made vessel out here in the middle of nothingness. Why should he have the slightest faith that the mast was well constructed? Or the sails? It was well-on impossible to find a decent carpenter in London, he had learned when he and Jane rebuilt their houses together, and yet here they were in a ship that hundreds of men had worked on, each capable of any of a multitude of small mistakes that might see them all dead.

This panic lasted in Lenox's breast for some half an hour, and only subsided when he recalled the slapping of the swabs on the deck that morning, and the great cleanliness McEwan kept in his cabin. Perhaps that was the secret to it: in the navy one was always far too careful, to the point of absurdity, because when it mattered lives were staked to that precision and effort. Not in matters of cleanliness, perhaps. But the cleanliness was simply in keeping with the rest of the service's fastidious care. Thank God.

Glumly he followed his cup of tea with half an orange. He would have traded the storm for scurvy in a heartbeat.

CHAPTER EIGHTEEN

Each man at sea endures his first storm differently. Lenox knew he was lucky not to be seasick, and in fact when he lay still upon his bunk the pitching of the ship and the lashing rain had more of a somnolent than a terrifying effect on him. Just as he was actually dozing off, however, he remembered Teddy.

This woke him up, and, putting on a warm jacket, he lurched through the soaked middle deck toward the gun room. He prayed for Edmund's sake that the boy wasn't on deck. Better to start, surely, with a storm that wasn't so immense. If it had been a squall, perhaps . . .

He needn't have worried. When he reached the gun room and knocked on the door there was a pause, and then the door cracked slightly.

"How do you do?" said an older boy, perhaps seventeen, with terribly red, inflamed skin.

"Whosit, Pimples?" a voice called out.

"May I come in?" Lenox said.

It was a snug room, rounded with a blue leather bench that

ringed the entire room, including the back of the door. At the center of this circle was a large, very rough table. Beneath the bright orange glow of two swinging lanterns five boys sat there, with hands of cards out, bottles of (no doubt contraband) ale on the table, and cigars crooked in their fingers. Their noisy chatter quieted when Lenox entered.

He spotted Teddy at one corner of the table, looking very young but also very definitely a part of the group.

"I'm Charles Lenox, gentlemen. I was just coming to see—"

As he was about to say Teddy's name, however, he saw a desperate plea on the boy's face not to do it. He didn't want babysitting, apparently.

"Sir?" said Pimples.

"I was just coming to see Lieutenant Billings. But I appear to have been turned around. He'll be nearer the wardroom, I expect."

To Lenox's slight disappointment they evidently found it entirely plausible that he would commit such an immense stupidity as mistaking the gun room, halfway across the *Lucy*, for a cabin next door. What a landsman he must have seemed to them!

"He'll be on deck," said a senior-looking midshipman gently. "Perhaps you might wait until the morning?"

"Just so," said Lenox. "Thank you."

As he closed the door laughter exploded behind him. It didn't aggrieve him to hear it, however—it delighted him.

He returned to his cabin then, to wait out the storm.

It lasted throughout the night, and maybe longer, for Lenox couldn't see from his cabin what was the darkness of night and what was the darkness of the storm. The rain fell torrentially the entire time, though the wind would occasionally subside. When this happened the waves gentled down too, only to rise in great heaving motion when the wind, seemingly without reason, erupted back into life.

He slept only fitfully, and in between sleeping he rolled off of his bunk and down to his desk, where by the light of a candle stub he wrote a long letter to Lady Jane, telling her of the storm and Teddy's progress. Only in a postscript did he mention Halifax's death, and concede that he was looking into the matter on the captain's behalf.

What he wanted most of all was a word on that medallion with Carrow. It would have to wait until the storm was over, of course, but even through the worst weather it rankled in Lenox's mind. What was the significance of two objects belonging to other officers being found in or near the murdered body of a third? And why would anyone other than Carrow, for whom it might have had sentimental reasons, take the risk of stealing it back?

It was puzzling, and Lenox worried that the part of his brain that had once sprung to life when it met this sort of clue was atrophied now, flabby with disuse. Suddenly he wished Dallington were aboard too. The way the young man had handled the poisoning in Clerkenwell that January, for instance . . . exemplary. He still made errors, but these were fewer and farther in between now. And—somewhat to Lenox's unhappiness, he found—fewer and fewer cases came to Dallington through his mentor. The boy was building a reputation that wasn't contingent on Lenox's. As for Lenox's own reputation: it was more exalted now, but he wondered whether people even remembered what he had once been.

All of this he considered writing to Jane, but in the end he decided not to trouble her with it. And so as to end on a happy note he wrote a second postscript:

Incidentally, you may be wondering why I haven't written anything about what the child shall be named, which in Plymouth seemed at times like our only subject of conversation, other perhaps than the dangers of scurvy and pirates (neither of which, you will be pleased to learn, has beset the *Lucy* as of yet). This is because I have alighted in my mind on the perfect name for our daughter, should the child be a girl—as I feel convinced she will be—and as I well know your taste in these matters we may both consider the question as answered and put to rest.

What is this name? That you shall hear from my own lips, not four weeks hence, in London. Until then I remain, as above, your most loving Charles.

He signed and sealed this letter and put it between two pages of *The Voyage of the Beagle*. Then, feeling much better for it, he extinguished the candle with his thumb and forefinger and climbed his bunk again to fall to sleep.

When he woke the storm was gone—indeed, might never have been at all, but for the demeanor of the sailors: the sky was a motionless pale blue, glittering at one end with brilliant white sunlight. Lenox ate an apple on the quarterdeck and watched the men work. They appeased every single one of them at once exhausted and blissful. Even Lenox, though he might have been an albatross, received warm looks from some of the sailors.

Martin, too, was still on deck, and he came to the detective after fifteen minutes, looking pale and unshaven but as happy as everyone else aboard the *Lucy*.

"The storm has passed."

"So I had observed," said the captain. "The crew came through it beautifully."

"But what of the purser?"

Martin frowned. "What do you mean?"

"Mr. Carrow told me that these pursers dislike storms."

Now Martin laughed. "Oh, yes—well, I daresay he lost some dry biscuit, and he won't be happy that I've ordered double rations of grog for the men when they have their dinners at midday. Nevertheless they deserve it."

"I congratulate you," said Lenox. "No injuries?"

"Oh, a host of them! Tradescant has been up all night—eight or twelve of them down there, every kind of scrape and contusion and concussion you can imagine. Still, we may count ourselves lucky in such a storm that nobody died."

"Will you go to sleep now?"

A stern look. "No. Not until the last man has gone off duty, and all have rested. There is work to be done—bilging, repair work—and of course we are fearfully off course, and must make up time. My steward should be bringing me coffee, however."

The steward appeared as if on cue, carrying a tin mug letting off fragrant steam from the top. Martin took it down in three gulps and then set off for the orlop. As for Lenox, he went down to fetch a cup of coffee, too, and drank it as he gazed over the becalmed sea.

When the captain passed the quarterdeck again, Lenox waved him down.

"Yes?" said Martin.

"I need to interview Amos Lee, your fourth lieutenant. And I might as well have a word with the warrant officers, too."

"Lee will be awake in an hour, I daresay—could you leave him to then? He put in a hard shift overnight. In fact I must think of raising up one of the oldsters to acting lieutenant, just for this voyage." This put more to himself than his interlocutor.

"Oh, of course," said Lenox.

"Who do you think killed Halifax?"

"I don't know. But there are enough clues that it shouldn't be long before I do, I hope. I simply need a more complete picture of the suspects."

"The suspects?"

Lenox described his suspicion that someone living in the wardroom had done the murder, enhanced now by the theft of the medallion. For a common bluejacket to be wandering around the wardroom would have been uncommon in the extreme, Martin agreed.

A steely look came into his eye. "When he is found out there will be no mercy, you may be sure of that," he said. "A four-bag and a hanging."

Lenox had to find out some minutes later from McEwan, who was eating about six breakfasts, that a four-bag meant forty-eight lashes on the back.

CHAPTER NINETEEN

Amos Lee was almost completely different than Mitchell, his fellow officer: tall and fair where the other was small and dark, placid where the other bristled, of excellent manners where the other was rude. Of course Lenox had watched men who had seemed the gentlest of souls in his acquaintance swing from the gallows, for crimes that would have made thugs from the East End widen their eyes.

They spoke in the wardroom. Lee had an accent that Lenox had noticed among the younger generation of aristocratic public school graduates, which elongated every vowel, so that the word *rather* sounded like "raaawther" and *London* had about six *o*'s in it. The accent seemed to match Lee's somewhat tired, heavy-lidded eyes. There was an air of boredom to him despite his polite attention to Lenox's questions.

"How did you discover that Halifax was dead?"

"Mr. Mitchell told me the following morning."

"May I ask how long you've been on the ship?"

"Certainly. I think it's twenty-six months now, or thereabouts."

"You must have been friends with Halifax, then."

"Friendly, to be sure—there's no way around that in the wardroom."

"Do you have any inkling of who might have killed him?"

"No. I wish I had. Perhaps it was one of his men?" Lee ventured.

"I had heard he was quite popular among them?"

"It may be so, he and I carry—carried—different watches. He seemed perfectly competent from what I did observe of him, however."

"Do you know anyone aboard ship who has a . . ." Lenox paused, searching for the right word. "A morbid air? Anyone who seems a little too cold-blooded?"

He thought for a moment. "I don't think so."

"Among the officers, perhaps?"

Lee looked troubled now. "I wouldn't like to say."

"Please, it might be important."

"Well, if it is in the strictest confidence—"

"That goes without saying."

"Lieutenant Carrow has always struck me as a cold fish. An able officer, exceedingly able, but not endowed too plentifully with warmth or happiness."

Lenox had observed Carrow's demeanor now more than once, and agreed. Then there was the medallion. "It may simply be reserve," he said.

Hastily Lee agreed. "I've no doubt of it. I wouldn't for a second accuse him of killing poor Halifax. But you asked me."

"I did—thank you for answering. May I ask, have any of the stewards struck you similarly?"

Again Lee thought. "I suppose Mr. Butterworth is never overly friendly. I don't know that I would call him cold-blooded, however."

"You surprise me—Lieutenant Billings being so amiable."

"Yes, I know. They seem like a mismatch."

Lenox paused, and then said, "How often have you borrowed Billings's penknife?"

"Sorry?"

He decided to lie. "His penknife—he said you had borrowed it now and then."

"I shouldn't like to call him a liar, but I can't remember ever seeing the thing, much less borrowing it."

"I must have misheard. Thank you, Mr. Lee."

"Of course."

A thought occurred to Lenox now and he went to the surgery to speak to Tradescant, who was treating the casualties of the storm. One sailor had a particularly nasty blue and green bruise across half of his face. Tradescant ordered a cold salt compress for it, and then stepped into the galley with Lenox.

"I wondered in passing," said Lenox, "whether either of your assistants in surgery strikes you as a likely suspect? The cuts on Halifax seem surgical, don't they?"

"I suppose they do, and yet I should sooner believe that you had done it, or the captain. My first assistant would have been on duty here in the surgery, Wilcox. I suppose he might have left to do it, but it would have been a strange risk—his presence on deck being so much less usual than anyone else's, and there being a whole empty room, the surgery itself, to which he might have invited Halifax."

"What to do with the body, then?"

"True; and yet Wilcox doesn't have that in him, I swear to you. The second assistant I have is little more than a simpleton, Majors he's called, good for fetching things, lifting things. No more knowledge of surgery than a dog has."

Lenox sighed. "It was a shot in the dark, I know."

The problem was the preponderance of suspects. It was strange to think so, given that his cases in the old days had usually taken place in London, with its millions of men and women flung into every corner of every building. Now two hundred and twenty seemed an impossibly large number. Was it a random sailor whose face, much less whose name, Lenox didn't know? Was it an officer, or an officer's steward? The definite clues he had—the penknife, the medallion, the strange nature of Halifax's wounds—seemed to point in every different direction.

Perhaps, he thought, the time has come to search not for the murderer but for the victim. Why had someone wanted to kill the man at all, much less with such brutality?

He went back to his cabin with his mind unpleasantly fuzzy, the specifics of the case receding before him, and realized as he sat down at his desk to think that he was extremely tired. The first night he had spent aboard was interrupted by the murder, and the second by the storm. He would rest.

When he woke up some hours later it was already past the middle of the afternoon.

"McEwan!" he called out.

The steward appeared in the doorway. "Sir?"

"What time is it?"

"It's just gone four, Mr. Lenox."

Lenox groaned. Nearly five hours of daylight wasted. "Could I have some tea, please?"

"Yes, sir. And if it's any consolation the captain has been asleep for ever so long, sir, just as long as you."

Some men could wake up from a nap and spring immediately into action. Lenox had never been one of these. He preferred a gentler awakening, of the sort he had now: teacup encircled in one hand, his book laid flat on his desk, a warm jacket resting loosely over his shoulders against the chill of the oncoming night.

The book was the most important part, and he had chosen the right one. In *The Voyage of the Beagle* Darwin described his youthful trip through the Atlantic to South America, during which he had collected fossils and plants; Lenox had chosen it because it was first and foremost a tale of the sea, written aboard a ship not all that dissimilar from the *Lucy*. Both, in fact, had left from Plymouth. (Darwin himself only ever took a copy of Milton's *Paradise Lost* on his trips, but that was varsity stuff, slightly pale in interest, to Lenox's taste.) And yet the book was an escape, too: Darwin's *Beagle* had been full of interesting men, watercolorists, botanists, naturalists, and a captain, the great Robert FitzRoy, who was himself a pioneering observer of weather phenomena.

The *Lucy*, by contrast, sailed with a murderer and a wide variety of surly officers.

On every page of the book some quotation or another struck Lenox enough that he wrote it in his commonplace book, and now here was another one, just as he poured a second cup of tea and helped himself to a shortbread biscuit: "No one," Darwin wrote of the forests he had visited in Brazil, "can stand in these solitudes unmoved, and not feel that there is more in man than the mere breath of body."

This was precisely how Lenox felt about the quarterdeck of the *Lucy*, and the great solitude of the ocean. Though it had been a fraught few days, he was beginning to love the ship, to internalize and comprehend her pitch and roll. For instance she had just met a great wind and was running very close to it, very quickly. He watched the sun-dappled water pass by at an astonishing speed through his porthole and felt at one with the vessel.

After sitting in silence for some time, having forgotten even about his book, Lenox came back to himself. "McEwan," he called out, "please lay out a suit of clothes and parcel out some of my food. I'm due at the gun room for supper in an hour. I'm just going to look around on deck for a moment first."

CHAPTER TWENTY

At five minutes before seven o'clock Teddy Lenox, bound up like a mummy in his stiff wool midshipman's uniform, came to the wardroom to fetch his uncle. They stole a few words as they walked toward the gun room.

"How are you?"

"Very well, thanks. I was ever so sick the first night—nerves, I think—but I'm fine now."

"How are you getting along with the other fellows?" Lenox asked.

Teddy seemed much more at ease than he had when they were making their way out to the *Lucy* from the docks at Plymouth. "They're splendid chaps," he said. "Alastair Cresswell—we all call him Alice—will be an admiral one day, if he can keep off the gin, everyone thinks so, Pimples even—Mercer, that is. They're the two older midshipmen."

"I don't know that gin is always an impediment to success in the navy, at that," Lenox said.

"It's ever so different than *school*." He said this word with particular scorn. "The watches are very long, you know, and in the morning you have to learn about, oh, celestial navigation, and shipbuilding, and that sort of thing. But only from the chap."

"The chap?"

"The chaplain—all of us call him the chap." Teddy paused. They were near the gun room. "I say, Uncle Charles. When we're in there you won't mention . . . things about home, will you? Christmas or anything?"

Lenox felt a great swelling of tenderness for the boy then, and thought of his brother Edmund, who lived very close to Lenox's heart indeed. The previous winter the family's old dog, a spaniel named Wellie, had taken himself to a warm and obscure corner of the enormous house and died. It had been Teddy who was closest to him; it had also been Teddy who found him, the others diffident in their searching. And it had been Teddy who wept so bitterly throughout Christmas Eve, while his parents tried to console him with platitudes about old age and good lives.

"I'm much more curious to hear about all of you than to talk about anything like that," Lenox said, and the young midshipman nodded with studied nonchalance.

The gun room looked rather as it had the evening before, though the playing cards were nowhere to be seen and there was a decided absence of wine and cigars, too. The other four midshipmen were ranged around the cabin's blue circular bench, and rose when Lenox entered. Only Fizz, the little black-and-tan terrier, was rude enough to keep his seat on the floor.

"Hello!" he said to the boys. "I'm Charles Lenox."

He met Alastair Cresswell, a very tall, leggy, black-haired lad whom Lenox had seen around ship, and then Mercer, or Pimples, from the night before—these were the two older boys. The two younger ones, slightly older than Teddy, had names he didn't quite catch.

"I'm very pleased to make your acquaintance. And look at this feast!" he added, waving a hand out at the small dish of potatoes, the single roasted chicken (which must have been a scrawny bird when it had walked the earth), and the half-hearted mash of carrots. "Would it insult you if I ventured to append a few small items to it? I could scarcely improve it, of course, but if we had heartier appetites."

Here he took the parcel of food that McEwan, never one to stint, had packed. There were a dozen slices of rich cold ham, a bottle of Pol Roger, a loaf of Plymouth bread, kept fresh in wax paper, and lastly a large, dense fig cake, honeyed on the outside. As these were unpacked the table came to seem much richer in its contents.

The gratitude on the boys' faces gave Lenox a great deal of pleasure, though he had been planning to save the fig cake for the trip back from Egypt. If it was true that the longtime *Lucys*, however, had been eating skinned vermin, they deserved it more than he did. What they did have, perhaps because it was early in the trip, was a fair bit of wine. All at the table drank.

Conversation was formal and limited, as each of the midshipmen fervently scarfed down the ham and the chicken and the bread, but eventually, as the pace slowed, they managed to speak.

"Tell me, each of you, how was it that you first went to sea?" Lenox asked.

Two were college boys, and two were practicals, including Pimples, who had been afloat for nearly a decade. Cresswell had a bit of both in him.

"My father was a vicar in Oxshott," he said, "in Surrey. I doubt anyone in his entire family tree set foot on one of Her Majesty's ships. On my mother's side, however, there was a great naval tradition, and after a tremendous row it was decided that I should be a naval man rather than a vicar. Thank God," he added without apparent irony.

"I went to the college at Portsmouth for a year. I would have gone back, too, but when I was eleven one of my mother's brothers heard of a berth in the *Warrior*, which has been sold out of the service now, but which was at that time a highly reckoned ship."

"Our first ironclad, was she?"

"Just so, Mr. Lenox. At any rate I went into London to see the captain there, he and his first lieutenant. They made me write out the Lord's Prayer, jump over a chair naked, tie a Turk's head knot, and then the first lieutenant gave me a glass of sherry on being in the navy!"

There were titters from the other midshipmen at this tale, and then when Lenox laughed they all did. "A strange examination," he said.

"It was, just—the captain was of the old school, I can promise you. But do you know who the first lieutenant was?"

"Who?"

"Captain Martin! I've sailed with him ever since."

Teddy interjected. "Alice will be a lieutenant on his next ship."

Cresswell frowned. "Well, that's as may be. One can only do one's best."

One of the other smallish boys piped up. "Is it true you were a murder solver?" he said in a high-pitched voice.

Pimples shot the boy a dirty look and, before Lenox could answer, apologized. "Excuse him, sir."

"Not at all. It's true, once upon a time I did that. Now my work is much less exciting, I'm afraid. I sit in an office and read papers all day. But here—did I spy you boys smoking cigars last night?"

"Oh, no, sir," said Pimples. "They're not allowed."

"What a shame that these must go to waste, then," said Lenox, unrolling a soft leather case that held half-a-dozen cigars. "For myself I don't smoke them that often, and I have a dozen more in my cabin."

"Sorry," said Pimples.

All of the boys looked at them longingly, but nobody spoke. Lenox smiled inwardly, trying not to let it show. "Well," he said at last, "what if you *had* to smoke them—orders of a member of Parliament? Who would tell the captain as much?"

They were still silent but Lenox could feel their willpower sapping. At last Teddy said, "Might I hold one?"

He took one, paused, and then, apprehensively, took a candle from the table and lit the cigar.

There was a moment of stillness and then the other four boys nearly leaped at Lenox, their voices bursting out of them at last—"Oh, thank you," "If you insist," "Shame to let them go to waste"—and took the remaining cigars.

After this the formality of the earlier part of the evening vanished, and the boys' formality was replaced by a definite bonhomie born of the late hour, the champagne, and Lenox's cigars. Pimples did an extensive and deadly accurate impression of the chaplain teaching them Scripture every morning, which Lenox laughed at despite himself. Then there were a round of toasts, remarkably similar to the wardroom's, in fact, the Queen, various sweethearts from home, the admiralty—but also, rather touchingly, the boys collectively toasted their mothers. Lenox raised his own glass and thought of his mother, dead now, and felt a stir of emotion within.

When the wine gave out nobody wanted to go to bed, but of course the midshipmen had lessons in the morning. Lenox, thinking perhaps he ought to leave Teddy to bask in the glory of having indirectly provided them cigars and food, thanked them for their hospitality. Each boy in turn shook his hand and clapped him on the shoulder and said with great ardor that he ought to come back any time.

"Why not tomorrow?" one of the younger boys even said, thinking perhaps of further hams and loaves of bread, an invitation that drew a look of disapproval from Cresswell.

"We oughtn't to tax Mr. Lenox with our company, but I hope he will return later in the trip."

"With great pleasure," said Lenox.

He walked through to his cabin somewhat tipsily. It was the end of the first watch, nearly midnight, and he heard the increasingly familiar creaking of the ship as one watch turned into another, a wave of men going downstairs to their rest and another wave rising to the deck to assume their duties.

As he sat at his desk, drinking a glass of cold water to sober himself, he started another letter. This one was to Edmund, a report on Teddy's high spirits and seeming good cheer. He fell asleep over his pen, and so missed the cry that went up on deck some minutes later.

Only the next morning did he hear that the first breath of that most dreaded movement had been whispered on board: mutiny.

CHAPTER TWENTY-ONE

It was midday before he would hear of it. Indeed, he woke up thinking that despite the murder, the ship felt exceedingly affable to him, after his supper in the gun room, and when he went on deck following his eggs and tea the only thing on his mind was the ship's rigging, and a possible ascent of it.

Lenox's trip with Martin to that perch of the mizzenmast where Halifax had died had piqued his interest. The climb had been precarious, but now he felt determined that he would go higher. He wanted to conquer the ship in all of her dimensions. Nobody would be able to lord over him Old Joe Coffey, the seventy-year-old sailor who had his grog in the crow's nest, if he climbed there himself.

The morning was placid, thankfully, the wind nearly still. Carrow was the officer on duty. Lenox was torn between the desire to go up the rigging and the desire to ask him about the medallion. In the end the detective in him won out. The crow's nest would have to wait.

"Is it a bad time to have a word?" he asked Carrow.

"Not an ideal one—but if it's about Halifax?"

"It is, in fact. I understand you served on the *Chesapeake?*"

Carrow turned to him, his somber face filled with surprise. "I did. Who told you?"

"Nobody. I saw a medallion of yours, actually, thanking you for your service. A parting present from the captain, I thought."

"How on earth did you see that?"

"You know the object to which I'm referring?"

"I do, and I wish I knew how you did."

"Do you have the medallion?"

"Yes, I do—I keep it in a box with my watch and my cuff links. As far as I know it hasn't gone missing. I hope you haven't been among my things."

"I haven't. Would you mind if I saw the medallion with my own eyes?"

"You must explain to me, Mr. Lenox—"

"Would you indulge me by showing me the box, before I do?"

Carrow flung an angry word or two at the bosun, who was at the ship's wheel, that he would be available below deck in the event that he was needed. "I'll be gone five minutes."

They went to Carrow's cabin, though when they actually arrived at the door the lieutenant held a hand up. Lenox waited in the wardroom and Carrow came out with the box a moment later.

More than enough time to hide the medallion, if he had been the one to steal it back. Though it was just as likely to be a gesture of resentment at Lenox prying into his life.

"Here is the box," Carrow said.

Lenox watched him open it. "I see your cuff links."

"Yes, they were from my father. My watch, as I said. A personal memento"—this when he hastily palmed a dried rose in his hand—"and here!" he said triumphantly. "My medallion! Now, before another question from you, please tell me how you knew of it!"

Lenox was struck dumb. Carrow passed him the medal.

"Is there a duplicate of this?" he asked.

"No, I received it and have treasured it since then. It hasn't left the box other than once or twice, on full dress occasions. To the best of my knowledge."

"The best of your knowledge is, in this instance, insufficient, I'm afraid. That medallion was in my hands yesterday."

"How?"

"It was found next to Halifax's body."

Now it was Carrow's turn to look startled. "How can that be?" he said. "How is it in my box, if that was the case?"

"I don't know. It was stolen from my cabin yesterday afternoon, after I had been examining it. Did you lend it to Halifax? Would he have taken it?"

"No."

"When was the last time you wore it?"

"Not for some six months at least, when we dined with an Indian pasha in full uniform. Since then it has been in this box. Or had been, I would have said."

"I see."

Lenox was silent for a long while now. Carrow stood by him in a state of increasing consternation. Finally he said, "Well? Have you concluded that I killed Halifax? I know in detective stories it was always the chap who found the body. Only one problem with that, of course—"

"Yes, you were on the poop deck with my nephew, I'm aware. No, I don't suspect you. What puzzles me is how the medallion came to be next to the body. I think it possible that you've been framed."

"I want to give this scoundrel his lashes for myself," he said in a froth of anger, "this, the mutiny . . ."

"It would have been pointless of the criminal to frame an officer on duty during the commission of the murder, however, and that is what puzzles me. I wonder if there was some other motive."

"There could not be. I was—"

Lenox looked up. "Did you say mutiny?"

"Excuse me?"

"Mutiny—I heard you mention the word?"

"Yes. There was shot rolled down the main deck last night, as the first watch gave way to the middle."

"Can you tell me what happened in greater detail?"

"Do you think it might be relevant to the case?"

"Of course!" said Lenox. "An officer is murdered and mutiny against the officers of the middle watch—they may well be linked, yes."

Carrow frowned. "That makes it all the more serious. Perhaps you had better speak to Captain Martin. I need to be on deck, anyhow."

"I'll do that," said Lenox. "Keep a close eye on that medallion. And I'll ask you—as I've asked the only other person I mentioned it to, Captain Martin—to keep its existence quiet."

"I will."

Carrow walked off. What Lenox hadn't mentioned was that Carrow had had the perfect opportunity to steal the medallion back, as good as anyone else in the wardroom, when Lenox and Mitchell had spoken on deck while Billings was on duty. What might Carrow be hiding?

His mind full of questions, Lenox sought out the captain in his quarters. It was nearly noon, meaning that the naval day would begin soon. But there might be time for a quick word still.

He knocked on the door and was called in. The captain was sitting at his desk, writing in a large book of red leather—his log of the voyage, evidently. Normally this contained only measurements of latitude and speed, that sort of thing, but now he was writing, Lenox could see, an account of some sort. A half-empty bottle of spirits was at hand, though there was no glass to be seen, and there were the leavings of three or four cigars in an ebony ashtray.

Martin set down his pencil. "Mr. Lenox, how may I help you?"

"Are you writing in reference to this mutiny?"

"For heaven's sake don't call it that—one disgruntled bastard is all it was."

"Apologies."

"There's absolutely no evidence of a concerted attempt at revolt. This is one of the most contented ships in Her Majesty's navy."

"So it had struck me."

Martin leaned back in his chair, put his pen down, and rubbed an eye. "It's a terrible business."

"I came to see whether it might be connected to Halifax's death."

"The problem with one mutinous sailor," the captain went on without looking at Lenox, "is that every other fool on board begins to wonder why their comrade is aggrieved, and whether they should be too. You hear of one man getting shorted half a ration of grog and leading an entire ship into revolution against the captain for it. They're not all clever men, these sailors—more courage than intelligence."

"May I ask what happened?"

"It was while the first watch gave over to the middle watch, which means there was a hopeless muddle of people on board. Shot was rolled down the main deck."

"You'll have to explain."

"It's rather an old-fashioned method of—well, of warning, I suppose you would say. One of the great iron balls that goes in our guns, weight about a pound, is rolled down the deck toward the officers and midshipmen. If it picks up enough speed it can hurt a man quite badly."

"If so many people were on board someone must have seen who did it."

"It was dark, of course, and the balls aren't very large."

"Do you think whoever rolled the shot killed Halifax?"

Martin sighed. "I hope not. It would be going things backward—an expression of unhappiness preceded by something as violent and inhuman as that murder. Normally you would imagine the events in reverse order. But it may be. It's impossible to say. I spoke with some of the leading seamen, good long-serving *Lucys*, the quartermaster, the captain of the maintop . . . none of them had heard any stirring of discontent."

"And indeed the ship seemed a picture of happiness, after the storm," Lenox said. "Certainly nobody looked likely to disobey orders, and as far as I observed there were no black stares behind the officers' backs."

"Precisely."

"That's what makes me think it's connected to Halifax."

Martin stood. "This trip has been a curse. Shot rolled aboard my *Lucy*! Never once did it happen in the Indias, and now we're four days from Plymouth Harbor and it does. Well, I must be on deck."

CHAPTER TWENTY-TWO

As Lenox walked toward the quarterdeck that afternoon he looked at the faces of the sailors. Though it had been so short a time he felt he could read them already, having seen them sunken in dark suspicion after Halifax's death, then, after that stale mood dissipated under the pressure of the storm, in good spirits. Now they were closed, guarded. He had no doubt whatsoever that the great majority of them were loyal to Martin, and puzzled by the incident (which he was, apparently, the last to hear of). But many of their faces seemed to say: *The captain is a fine gentleman; the officers too; I have no quarrel with them; but I will hear why a man does before I judge him.* They wouldn't condemn a whisper of mutiny until they knew what lay behind it.

It made Lenox feel even more ill at ease than the murder had, in a way. If the worst came would he be strung up? Set adrift in a rowboat with five days' provisions and a map? And what about Teddy?

It didn't help when Evers, McEwan's friend, the one who

thought Lenox was an albatross, passed him without even touching his cap, an angry blank on his face.

Still, as the orders flew back and forth across the maindeck and the *Lucy* bore steadily onwards there was absolutely no outright dissent, and some of the sailors seemed to say their "Yes, sirs!" a bit louder than they had before, as if picking a side. Perhaps all those years afloat together would keep the ship going.

There was another reason that the idea of mutiny bothered him: it reopened the possibility, all but dismissed in his mind, that someone from among the great multitude of common sailors aboard had killed Halifax. Lenox had felt persuaded that it must be someone of the wardroom who had done it, someone with the power to demand a meeting with Halifax in the middle of the night, someone who could have stolen Carrow's medallion and then stolen it again from Lenox's cabin without fear of being observed as far out of place in the wardroom. And then Halifax had been well loved among his men. But what if all that counted for nothing, and it was some madman from below deck who had killed Halifax and now was trying to mount a mutiny?

With a despairing sigh Lenox turned toward the step that led to the main deck. To his surprise—for the man hadn't been there before—he met the ship's redheaded engineer, Quirke.

"How do you do, Mr. Lenox? Taking the air?"

"Yes, and trying to think."

"Please, carry on—I hope I shan't be in your way."

"On the contrary, I wonder if we might have a word."

Quirke nodded. "I thought you might want to speak with me about Halifax."

"I do. Have you any notions of your own?"

"Only that it's a terrible business. Halifax was a good fellow."

"I was just considering in my mind whether it was a sailor who killed him or an officer."

Quirke frowned. "I can scarcely allow in my mind the possibility that it was an officer."

"I confess that I would have expected more grief from his fellow officers."

"Ah, yes. Well, we are at sea—we take death less hard here, I suppose, than they do on land. On a long voyage it's not uncommon to lose several men."

"Not by murder, though."

"No, of course not. But the officers are also private, insular. I doubt they will have expressed their anxieties or their grief to you."

"I see. What were you doing when he was killed?"

"I was dead asleep—excuse me, what a poor phrasing. I was fast asleep, I should say. My man can attest to that. He sleeps directly outside of my cabin. It's unlucky that Halifax's steward strings his hammock below deck, away from the wardroom."

This was a point that Lenox hadn't considered. Several members of the wardroom had stewards, like McEwan, whom they would have had to pass to leave their cabins. Except for the man already on deck: Carrow.

Then again, it was possible that each of these stewards was more loyal to his own master than to the ship or to Halifax.

"Who else besides Halifax has a steward who sleeps away from the wardroom?"

Quirke narrowed his eyes, thinking. At last he said, "Only Lee, I think. I know that you, Mitchell, Billings, Carrow, Tradescant, Pettegree, the chaplain, and I all have servants who sling up outside our doors. Neither Lee's cabin nor Halifax's has the room for it, I believe."

"Tell me, Mr. Quirke—did you hear of the mutiny?"

"Shh . . . not that word. I did, as it happens. I would never have guessed it for the *Lucy*."

"Do you know which officers were on duty during the changeover?"

"Mr. Billings would have been just leaving off, and Mr. Mitchell coming on. Why?"

"Would the captain have been on deck?"

"No—or rather, I wouldn't have thought so. May I ask why?"

"I wonder if this shot—this rolled shot—was directed at one of them."

Quirke's eyes widened. "Do you think they're being targeted by the brute who killed Halifax?"

"It's not impossible. We don't know if Halifax had warning."

"Certainly not any warning of that sort."

"I confess myself puzzled," said Lenox, and in his heart he knew it to be true. He was grasping at straws. He wondered if he might, in his old form, have done better with the facts before him. "At any rate, thank you for your help."

"Of course. If I can do anything further . . ."

Both Mitchell and Billings were on deck now, assisting the captain as he gave order after order to adjust the sails, almost as if he wished he might outsail all of the *Lucy*'s present misfortunes. They were moving along at a brisk pace, and neither man was happy to be interrupted by Lenox. Still, both listened to him.

Billings went pale. "You think I might have been a target, you're saying? The shot wasn't rolled anywhere near toward where I was standing!"

"If it's simply a message, that wouldn't matter a great deal."

"Why would they bother sending a message? They didn't send one to Halifax."

"Not that we know of, you're correct. But who knows what might happen in a deranged mind? At any rate it's only a suggestion. Keep your eyes peeled."

Billings nodded. "I will. Thank you."

Mitchell's reaction was less gracious, and his dark complexion brightened red. "Why on earth would it have been directed at me!" he half shouted.

"I don't say that it was, only that—"

"I'm perfectly capable of looking after myself, Mr. Lenox. Thank you."

He turned away, back toward a group of men awaiting orders.

Lenox decided that he might as well speak to the purser, now that he had spoken to Quirke. Pettegree was in a very small study near the fore of the ship, hunched over a supply list. As Lenox's first impression had suggested, the purser had a slightly embittered air, pinched, ungracious, to go along with a businesslike deportment. It might have been a life spent balancing debits and credits, or it might have been something no speculation could reveal—from childhood, say, or adolescence. Lenox noted it.

"May I ask where you were when Halifax died?" he said after greeting Pettegree.

"Asleep."

"It's inconvenient that everyone was asleep at the time."

"In particular for Lieutenant Halifax, I would have thought."

Lenox grimaced. "Yes, of course. Now, confidentially . . . is there anyone in the wardroom you believe capable of violence?"

"All of them—they're men of the navy, after all. Each one of them, however gentle he might seem, has killed a pirate or an Indian."

"Nobody in particular, however."

Pettegree shrugged. "The code of the navy would suggest I hold my tongue, but since you ask—since there is a murderer loose aboard this ship—I would say that I have seen a great temper in two of the men."

"Who?"

"Mitchell and the captain. For the rest, they are calm enough men."

"The captain has a temper?"

"Oh, yes—a formidable one. But that may be in the usual course of these things, a condition of his position."

"Do you have a temper?"

"No, and what's more I didn't kill Halifax. If I had wanted to I couldn't have done it face-to-face. I'm not a large man."

Almost jokingly, Lenox said, "But the element of surprise—"

Pettegree shook his head. "The point is academic."

"To be sure. And Lieutenant Carrow?"

"He seems to be bearing up under some internal pressure, from time to time—but I have never seen an example of his violence, so I cannot add him to my list, no."

"Tell me, what does your instinct say? Who did it?"

An expansive sigh. "I've been going it over in my mind, in fact. If I had to say I would point to the sailors. They're a brutal species of man, I promise you. They have their own code, their own way of living. They're no closer to civility than the orangutans of Gibraltar, I sometimes think."

It was the opposite of what he had wished to hear, but some truth rang in the statement nonetheless. "Yes. I see. Incidentally, nothing peculiar has happened with regard to the ship's stores?"

Pettegree frowned. "What do you mean?"

"Has anything gone missing? Been stolen? Might Halifax have discovered a theft?"

"I don't think so. The storm washed out a certain percentage of our dry goods, as storms will. Otherwise the stores are intact."

"You're sure."

"I'm planning to check again in the morning—shall I tell you what I find?"

"I would take it most kindly," said Lenox.

"Very well. If there's nothing further, then—"

"No. Have a good afternoon."

"And you."

CHAPTER TWENTY-THREE

Supper that evening was again a somber affair. Only the chaplain drank more than one glass of wine, and the only toast was to the Queen. Martin dined alone.

Lenox returned to his cabin and wrote a letter to Lady Jane, full of misgivings and self-doubt. When he was close to signing it he realized with a start that it was more journal entry than letter, and after ripping the densely scrawled pages in half shoved them through his porthole. When this was done he asked McEwan for a glass of warm brandy—it was cooler than usual, that evening—and took up *The Voyage of the Beagle*, where he lost himself for several hours, long enough for three glasses of the brandy Graham had packed him. He could hear as he read the sound of orders being given and executed, sails being furled and let out, watches changing. The usual business of the ship. None of it sounded like mutiny. But then, he supposed, perhaps it never did.

The next morning he woke with a foggy head. It was his fifth day aboard the *Lucy* now, and he felt helpless. His tin cup of coffee went cold in his hand as he surveyed the rolling ocean from the quarterdeck. At ten or so there was a quick, thin rain, which he waited through before going back down below deck.

He decided to seek out his nephew.

Teddy was still resting in his hammock, strung up outside the gun room, but not quite asleep.

"Oh, hello, Uncle Charles," he said.

"The middle watch?"

"Yes, and it was jolly well cold."

"Why don't you come along to my cabin and have some breakfast? Jane packed a bit of cold bacon for me, and McEwan would be happy to do you some toast."

"Oh, rather!" he said, and nearly upset his hammock for rising out of it so quickly.

They sat in Lenox's cabin, he in his chair, Teddy on a stool dragged in from the galley, the latter munching happily away, pausing only for occasional sips of hot tea.

"Thank you again for inviting me to the gun room. I enjoyed it immensely."

Teddy merely grunted, his mouth rather fuller than would be deemed acceptable in the best society, but his nod was enthusiastic. When he finally swallowed he said, rather hoarsely, "Oh, the other fellows liked you very much."

"You seem to be happy there."

"Yes."

Though Teddy didn't say it Lenox could see that the boy had been worried, and that his worries were now appeased by their days at sea. He fit in well. It was worth writing Edmund with that news alone.

"When your father and I were boys, we once had to go to a great hunt on our own. Just the two of us. I suppose we must have been, oh, twelve and ten, thereabouts. Not much younger than you—or rather, I was quite a bit younger than you are now, but your father was nearly your present age."

"Why did you have to go alone?"

"Our father was in London, an emergency session of Parliament, and our mother was taken poorly."

"Just like my father."

"Yes—just like Edmund, shuttling between the house and the House, if you catch my meaning. At any rate, the hunt was hosted by an older gentleman named Rupert Greville, a minor squire nearby us in Sussex. Very much a roast beef and red face Englishman of the old sort."

"Thomas Greville lives near us. He's my age."

"There you are! Rupert will have been his grandfather, I suppose. I so often forget that you're repeating my childhood in a way, or were till now. Well, but in those days it was rather uncommon for two little boys to show up at a hunt alone, with only their horses and a rather drunk old groomsman. So old Rupert Greville put us in the charge of his sons. Three big, brutish fellows, two of whom were twins, fourteen, and their older brother who was fifteen. Left us all alone to hunt, the five of us."

Teddy had stopped eating and his mouth hung open a little, his attention won. "What happened?"

"They seemed to take it as a personal affront that we had come to bother them during their hunt, and spat a few words at us. We talked back at them, and that was the end of it. Or so we thought."

"What happened?"

"We had to cross a creek to keep on the scent. They convinced us it was too deep to cross on horseback, and so we got off our horses. The second both of our feet were on the ground one of the twins had them by the bridles and they were galloping away. We had a nine-mile walk home."

Teddy's eyes were wide. "Really?"

"Yes. In the end we found them, and fought them. One of the twins bloodied my nose, and your father stepped in and hit him. Then your father had his nose bloodied."

"My father?"

"Ask Edmund about it. He'll laugh. And he'll tell you that one of the twins—who could tell which—won't remember that day so fondly. Which is true. Perhaps it was Thomas Greville's father!"

"Lor."

"I suppose I thought of the story because it's very common, when you find yourself in a group of boys, to discover that they're rotters. You've been lucky. As far as I could gather the *Lucy*'s midshipmen are fine lads."

"They're the best midshipmen in the navy."

Lenox smiled. "I don't doubt it. Look there, have another piece of toast. I don't want any. And some more tea, if it comes to it."

"Thank you."

"Do you have to be in lessons soon?"

"Not for fifteen minutes."

There was a pause.

"We know the midshipmen, then—what of the officers?"

"Who?"

"Any of them? Are they strict? Loose? From good backgrounds, or bad? Who's popular?"

It wasn't an innocent question. He had wanted to check in on his nephew, very naturally, but Lenox also wanted to learn what he might of the officers, from a new ear on the ship other than his own. He felt rather ashamed to be leading Teddy into talking tattle, but weighed against that was the duty he felt to Halifax. It wasn't too great an imposition on the boy, he thought. A normal conversation to be having.

"Everyone loved Lieutenant Halifax, Cresswell said."

"And the others?"

Lenox watched as the midshipman and the nephew wrestled within Teddy, before the nephew won out. He was eager to talk about his new life, it was easy to tell. "Mitchell is a hothead—always yelling—not well liked. Cresswell says he'll never make captain."

"What about Lee?"

"I only know that he has great interest at the admiralty." Teddy took another piece from the steaming stack of toast McEwan had given them. "Pimples likes him. Nobody likes Billings or Carrow."

"How is that?"

"Billings is a lowborn sort, and Carrow awfully strict."

"Are they good officers?"

"Carrow is—you do your work sharply for him, but he's fair. Billings I haven't been on watch with. Cresswell says that Billings belongs in between guns."

With the common sailors. "Is his birth that low?"

"Cresswell thinks him common anyhow. His father was in trade."

"One of the great glories of our navy is that you needn't be born a lord to become a captain."

Teddy nodded without entirely absorbing the point. "And then, they say Billings is peculiar."

"How so?"

"Talks to himself."

"During watch?"

"Yes. Halifax did it too, but nobody seemed to mind that. Pimples does an impression of Billings—well, I shouldn't say."

It still seemed possible to Lenox that the rolled shot had been intended for Billings, then—or, equally plausibly, Mitchell. He was no closer. "You must respect these men, nonetheless," said Lenox.

"Oh, yes," said Teddy, more dutifully than earnestly. "I say, before I go could I have one more cup of tea? We don't get nearly such nice milk, and as for white sugar, I haven't seen a teaspoonful since I went into the gun room."

CHAPTER TWENTY-FOUR

At noon, just before the men received their rations, Martin delivered a short speech to the entire *Lucy*.

"I have sailed with some of you for ten years," he said. "Others of you for six or eight. Nearly all of you were in the Indies with me. I take it as a great compliment that you have all chosen to sail with me again on this voyage.

"Nevertheless, it would appear that one of your number, I doubt more than one, is unhappy. This person is a cancer within us, which I plan to excise as surely as Mr. Tradescant would excise a tumor from any of you. Whatever corrupted soul killed Mr. Halifax, whoever rolled shot down the deck of the *Lucy*— the *Lucy*, gentlemen, our ship!—when we find him he shall be hanged, and that right quick.

"For the rest of you, I won't insult you by believing for a moment that you would ever dream of revolting against me. I know that you know it would be akin to slapping our Queen in the face, may God bless her. And the man who wants to do that doesn't belong on a ship we've worked hard to make the finest in Her Majesty's navy!"

There was a fat moment of silence, and then a slow ripple of applause that with great deliberation mounted and mounted into a full roar of spontaneous approval at the captain's words. Soon the men were whistling and crying out "Three cheers for the *Lucy!*"

Then Martin did something ingenious. "There, quiet, thank you," he said. "I'm glad to see you agree. Now, Mr. Pettegree— please issue a double ration of grog to each man here."

If appealing to their patriotism or their sense of duty had won them over, this announcement made the sailors almost delirious with happiness, and the applause commenced again, sprinkled with ecstatic shouts and yells.

Martin smiled to himself. "And finally," he said, "it's not been a week, but I suppose we should have a game tonight."

The crowd hushed.

"Seven this evening. Each mess to nominate one chap. Follow the Leader," he said.

This roar was the most deafening of all. Lenox looked over to Teddy inquisitively but saw that the boy didn't know what "Follow the Leader" might be either. They would have to wait and see.

Martin, the man of the hour, shook hands with his officers, accepted the measurements they gave him for his log, and went below deck, while all around the main deck long lines formed for rations, the sailors talking excitedly amongst themselves. Pettegree looked red with exertion. The officers themselves seemed happy too, even Mitchell grinning. The ship belonged to them again, it would seem.

He noticed that only Carrow still looked unhappy, unmoved, after witnessing the effect the captain's speech had had on the sailors. It was a small thing, but Lenox filed it in his mind to ponder later.

Now he sought out Pettegree, who was overseeing the bois-
terous reception of double grog by each bluejacket. A small
cupful of his soul seemed to pour out with each extra ration that
was disbursed, and his agonized chatter—"Not so much, that's
easily double, don't give them triple, man!"—made clear the cause
of his turmoil.

Though Lenox had been planning to ask the purser about
his inventory of the stores, and whether anything had been
missing, he decided to wait. Instead he went below deck and
knocked on the captain's door.

Martin was writing in his log again, and once he had offered
Lenox a drink ordered his steward out to begin making him
something to eat.

"Is this about the case?"

"It is, but I can't say that I have anything concrete to tell
you."

Martin threw down his pen. "I don't know why I asked for
food—I've no desire to eat." He sighed. "Well, tell me of your
progress."

Lenox described his various conversations, told the captain
of the medallion and the penknife, and began to wonder aloud
about the plausibility of each officer as the suspect.

Martin cut him off. "You believe an officer did it, then?"

"I think it most likely."

"Hellfire."

"Who would you have suspected among them?'

"That's not a game I like."

Lenox waited, silent.

"I suppose I know Lee the least of them all. Mitchell has the
hottest temper. But honestly I cannot believe it was either of
them. Lee's record in the navy is unimpeachable, and Mitchell
has been a fine lieutenant."

"If it were a sailor—while the men were asleep in their
messes, how easily might one of them have slipped away from

his hammock without drawing attention to himself, do you think?"

"I would call it next to impossible."

"We should speak to the mess captains then, to see if any of their messmates absented themselves for a while without explanation on that first night of the voyage."

"It's a good idea—I should have thought of it myself. The difficulty is that men regularly leave their hammocks to attend to their—well, their various bodily functions, or even just for air. It gets very close, stifling at times, where they sleep."

"You'll speak to the mess captains? For obvious reasons I would prefer that the officers themselves not do it."

Reluctantly, Martin nodded. "Very well. Mind you, a sailor hates nothing more than tattling."

"That might be less of a problem if one of their number doesn't quite fit in—someone perhaps who is even a suspect. They all liked Halifax, I've been told."

"Yes, true."

The steward returned with a plate full of sandwiches. At the captain's prompting Lenox took one. Martin himself took one up and then, having nearly taken a bite, tossed it through an open porthole.

"I keep thinking of that service, for Halifax. He was a fine chap. Would have made a fine captain, if he had a strict first lieutenant to keep the men in line."

"Have you written to his parents?"

"I've tried." He gestured his helplessness. "Difficult to know what to say until you've done your job."

"My job," Lenox said.

"Yes."

He considered this reproach for a moment in silence, then said, "Hopefully it won't be long, anyhow. Some sort of idea is forming in my mind. I just don't know what it is yet."

"Be as quick as you can."

"Nothing you say can hasten me, Captain. I did like Halifax—you'll recall, perhaps, that I met him twice."

"I had forgotten."

Lenox rose. "Incidentally, what is Follow the Leader?"

Martin smiled, some incipient anger gone. "I suggest you be on deck at half-past six, if you want a seat for the start at seven. You'll see then. It's a treat, I can promise you."

CHAPTER TWENTY-FIVE

The sun was still in the sky, though sinking, at around the time Lenox came up on deck. It had been a beautiful day, mild, clear, and warm enough that the gentle breeze had felt welcome upon the skin. Now the sails were slack, the ship all but still, as overhead a calm, whitish blue filled the sky. The constant sound of the water seemed to lessen slightly, and the rock of the ship became gentle.

On the quarterdeck were rows of chairs, brought up from the wardroom. About a dozen in all. McEwan was sitting in one, eating a piece of candied ginger. "Here, Mr. Lenox!" he said, after gulping a bit down. "I've got you a seat, here in the first row!"

Now here was impressive loyalty. "Splendid. Thank you."

"I hoped to make a request, too, sir."

"Go on."

"If you could release me from my duties for the evening, I've been nominated by the other stewards to compete."

"In Follow the Leader?"

"Yes, sir."

So it was some sort of eating contest. "Well, of course."

"Are you quite sure, sir? You might want a glass of wine during the show."

"No, I'd rather keep a clear head. If you could fetch me up a cloak you can be on your own. It's cooler than I had expected here."

"Very good, sir. And, sir, have ten bob on me, if you like a flutter. I reckon you'll get decent odds, too."

"I'll put ten bob on you for each of us," said Lenox. "Who makes the book?"

"Thank you, sir! Just talk to Mr. Mercer, sir."

This was Pimples, who was taking bets from all sides, presumably with the tacit approval of his superiors. Lenox found him and placed the two bets.

The midshipman frowned. "McEwan, Mr. Lenox? Are you sure of that? I don't want you to lose your money, after you treated us to that bread and ham and champagne and all." He said the word *champagne* "shampin," or something that sounded approximately like that.

"My finances can just about stand the loss, should McEwan let me down," Lenox said, trying to keep the corners of his mouth down.

Pimples nodded gravely. "If you feel sure, sir. The odds will be nineteen to three. Already set, wish I could give you better."

"As you please."

Lenox, a full smile on his face now, resumed his seat, the cloak he had asked for laid across it. The deck was filling. A group of men had lofted paper lanterns up along the rigging, which cast a lovely soft yellow color over the whole ship.

"We'll have to pray there aren't pirates, or Frenchies," muttered the person next to Lenox. It was Carrow, he saw.

"Why?"

"Ship all lit up, sails slack, the men saving their second ration of grog for just now . . ."

"Still, the ship looks wonderful with the lanterns."

"To each their own, Mr. Lenox."

Nearly every *Lucy* was on deck now, and to Lenox's surprise a group of them began singing. The melody caught on, and soon more than half the men had joined in. It was a long, flowing ballad called "Don't Forget Your Old Shipmate." Lenox tried to memorize the first verse as the next several proceeded: "We're the boys that fear no noise/Whilst thundering cannons roar, And long/We've toiled on rolling wave, And soon/We'll be safe on shore,/Don't forget your old shipmate, Folde rol . . ."

By the time he had this committed to memory he was in time to hear a verse that gave him a pang for Jane, when the men shouted the word, "Plymouth": "Since we sailed from Plymouth Sound, Four years"—here many shouted "days!"—"gone, or nigh, Jack, Were there ever chummies, now, Such as you and I, Jack? Don't forget your old shipmate, Fal dee ral dee ral dee rye eye doe . . ."

After some two dozen verses of this song a small faction broke out singing a frankly pornographic ditty called "The Mermaid," which was the cause of tremendous merriment and laughter. Then a smaller group, admired by all the others, sang in wonderfully mellow voices a song about Admiral Benbow. This was the leader of a fleet whose subordinates had rebelled against him and refused to fight the French, a refusal for which they had been court-martialed. If anyone other than Lenox saw the irony of the *Lucy*'s crew singing a song about insubordination, they didn't show it. But Lenox reminded himself to bring up Benbow to his nephew. The admiral had been born to a tanner, a birth no doubt lower than Billings's. . . .

Suddenly the song broke off and the master's mate, a fellow with a booming voice, called them to order. All the officers turned forward and watched; for a moment the ship was entirely silent.

"The contestants!" he said.

Up the main hatchway—the passage from the main deck to
below deck—came a parade of two dozen men, all of them grinning fearlessly. (Their bravery in part liquid, Lenox suspected.)
Last among them was McEwan, and though in proportion he
was not dissimilar to an ox, he was the only man in the group
who didn't look to possess that beast's natural strength.

"And now, a game of Follow the Leader! Place your final
bets, sirs!"

"Hey now!" called out Martin, but good-naturedly, and the
sailors laughed.

"The nominee of the first mess, sponger Matthew Tart, to
lead the first round, time to be no more than two minutes and
thirty seconds! Ready, gentlemen? Yes? In that case proceed to
the cathead at the fore of the ship, as per tradition, and keep an
eye on Mr. Tart."

"Christ in the waves," muttered Tradescant, who was behind
Lenox.

"Something the matter?"

"I always have to treat one or two of the buggers."

"I still don't know the game."

Now he learned. Matthew Tart, sponger of the *Lucy*'s first
gun, took his hand off the cathead and with no little speed began to shimmy up the foremast, hiking his haunches up behind
him with his arms and then pushing with his feet. When he was
halfway up, not far from the perch where Halifax had been
murdered, Tart leaped forward into thin air and then, after an
excruciating second or so, grabbed onto a thin rope. He traversed this hand over hand to the mainmast, flung himself onto
the rigging there, and then dropped in a somersault onto the
deck just beside the sunlight of the captain's dining room. From
there he walked on his hands to the aft of the ship, the sailors
congregated on deck respectfully making way for him, all silent, and when he had reached the taffrail launched himself
clear off the ship.

There was a gasp. Lenox half stood, while beside him Carrow emitted a hoarse chuckle.

Then Tart's head popped up. He was evidently perched on the *Bumblebee*, the jolly boat stowed behind the ship's back rail.

It had been a spectacular performance, and the ship cheered Tart with universal admiration.

Each of the two dozen men followed him now, attempting to traverse the *Lucy* exactly as Tart had: for such was the game. One slipped on the foremast, to general groans, and two others failed to walk on their hands. Another refused to jump onto the covered jolly boat. "Which I'll do anything, but I ain't going overboard this ship. I can't swim," he said, and was mocked for his sincerity.

The last man to go was McEwan. From the second his steward's hand left the cat's head Lenox found himself not breathing. But he needn't have worried. McEwan, for all his size, was as nimble and agile as a monkey. He made it through the first course in the quickest time, and rewarded himself with a chicken leg from his pocket, to general good-natured jeering.

The second round began, and Lenox found that he was enjoying himself immensely. So were the other officers, who gasped when a contestant almost fell and cheered when the round's leader did something spectacular.

They went places on the *Lucy* that Lenox hadn't even thought existed: up and down the bowsprit, hanging upside down by their legs, all across every mast and rope that would hold a human's weight, in and out of every boat slung up on deck. They went on their hands, on their legs, on one foot, and holding a flag. They went quickly and slowly—sometimes too slowly, as in the third round two men were ejected for dawdling. A great popular favorite from the eighth gun was disqualified for using his hands to brace himself as he walked along the ship's rail, and attempting the same trick a man came perilously close to falling off the side of the ship.

By the fifth round there were four men left. Easily the best of them, to Lenox's shock, was McEwan. He had earned the crowd's support early on, perhaps because he cut such a rounded, unathletic figure, and despite it moved with the ease of a man taking a Sunday stroll through Hyde Park.

It was McEwan's turn to lead now. With startling quickness he climbed hand over hand up the mainmast. When he was no more than a fattish dot in the sky, it seemed, far up in the crow's nest, he hooked his legs over the ledge of the crow's nest and waved down. Then he let go.

The sound of two hundred and nineteen men gasping at once must have filled McEwan's ears as he fell. One poor soul, a leading seaman named Peter Lee, cried out "No, not McEwan!" in a high-pitched squeal, an utterance that he would find it difficult to live down for the rest of the voyage.

For one horrifying moment Lenox felt sure that his steward was going to crash heavily into the deck, mangled out of all recognition, for the sake of a game. Just when it seemed as if he had been falling for about ten minutes, however, McEwan reached out a hand with almost casual grace and found a length of rope. Having caught on to this he made his way to the mainmast, and then, as something like an encore, climbed down it backwards—that is, with his face pointing toward the deck and his legs toward the sky.

When he achieved the deck there was a moment of breathless silence, followed by overwhelming applause, wave after wave of it, always getting louder just as you thought it might begin to fade. McEwan continued to bow and wave with great grace. When all eyes turned to the other competitors, some moments later, they, in a unanimous gesture, bowed to Lenox's steward, admitting their defeat.

Even Carrow was grinning. "Wish I had bet on him. Couldn't, as an officer, of course."

"I did!" said Lenox.

"He hasn't played for four or five years. Did the same thing last time. Poor Pimples gave terribly long odds, didn't he? Then again memories are short, and two of the other fellows had won it in recent years. Still—such a performance!"

The performer waddled over toward Lenox now, shaking hands distractedly along his way. "There," he said, "aren't you glad of that ten bob now, sir?" he asked.

"I congratulate you, my good man—but here now, why are you a steward? You should be up amongst the tops all the time."

"Oh, no, sir. Much more comfortable below deck, you see. Always a bite to be had when one feels peckish. Speaking of which, sir, could I fetch you a glass of wine or a biscuit?"

CHAPTER TWENTY-SIX

After the singing had gone on for some time longer, and in fact grown quite maudlin, the officers began to go down the hatchway to the wardroom. A group of men, though drunk, cleared the chairs off the quarterdeck with great alacrity and efficiency. Another group rerigged the ship that she might sail steadily through the night. Soon the visible signs of the evening's festivities had been effaced, but their happy mood lingered.

Lenox, for his part, wanted to speak to Pettegree.

He caught the purser in the wardroom and invited him to take the air of the quarterdeck.

"Did you enjoy the game?" Pettegree asked when they were alone. Each man had a glass of port in hand.

"Very much, yes. It determines me to climb to the crow's nest."

"I've been afloat twenty years and I've never ventured that high. Leave it to the sailors, I say."

"You may well be right." Lenox thought of Jane, pregnant

and perhaps, though he hoped not, fretting about his safety. "At any rate, I had hoped for a word with you earlier."

"The inventory."

"Yes. Was there anything missing?"

Pettegree shook his head. "I'm happy to report that there wasn't."

"It was unlikely, I suppose. Thank you for telling me."

"There was *one* thing I noticed, scarcely worth mentioning—"

Lenox laughed. "I wish I had a shilling for every time I heard that preface in the course of my career, only for it to be followed by a decisive piece of information. Pray, go on."

"We're short a bottle of whisky."

"From the spirit room?"

"Yes, precisely."

Just near the gun room was a small closet with a caged metal door and a large, impressive lock. It held the ship's spirits, wine and brandy for the captain and the officers, rum for the men's grog, as well as a bottle or two of harder alcoholic drinks. When ships were foundering or there was mutiny afoot, sailors were occasionally known to break into it, an offense punishable by hanging.

"How many bottles had there been, and how many are there now?"

"The captain keeps them on hand to entertain only," said Pettegree. "We have two bottles of decent whisky at the start of every voyage, and the same at the end of every voyage. The same two bottles for almost a decade. But at the moment there's only one bottle there."

"You don't seem put out that the other one has vanished."

"It's not my place to question the captain's choices."

"The captain's choices, you say? Is he the only one with access to the spirit room?"

"He and I have the two keys. Mine hasn't left my person while we've been at sea, and his—"

"Neither of your assistants has borrowed it?"

"Never. And the only other key is his."

"Did he not have to—to check out the bottle? Keep a record?"

"Oh, no, the whisky is quite his property."

"I see."

"If you like I can ascertain from him that he was the one who took it, though I can't imagine any other possibility."

Lenox's mind flashed back to his visit to the captain's quarters. On his desk had been an ebony ashtray with several cigar ends in it, and next to that a bottle of spirits, half empty. It might well have been whisky.

"If you wouldn't mind keeping it between us, I'd be grateful," said Lenox. "If it comes up I may mention it, but it doesn't seem our place—he's been under a great deal of stress between Halifax and the rolled shot—"

Pettegree nodded vehemently. "Oh, of course, of course. I'll not say a word of it."

Lenox went straight to the wardroom from there in search of Tradescant. The surgeon was absent from the dining table, however, where a few men were playing at cards, and also from his cabin.

Making his way forward to the surgery, Lenox looked at his watch. It was late; he ought to go to sleep. But it was worth speaking to Tradescant as soon as possible.

The surgeon was in a small, leather-backed chair in one corner of the surgery, a candle on a ledge at the level of his snow-white hair, reading a book. He looked up.

"Hello, Mr. Lenox," he said, and from the faint slur in his words Lenox concluded that the surgeon had gone one or two drinks past sober. "Did you enjoy the game?"

"Very much, yes."

"Your steward won! He was terrifically impressive, I thought. I hope he won't need convincing that he's still a steward."

Lenox smiled. "I don't think it's gone to his head."

"How may I help you?"

"Are your patients quite well?"

"Oh, yes. The one long-termer." He gestured toward the back of the room, where the man who had been smacked in the head with a beam not long out of Plymouth Harbor slumbered on. "I believe he'll come out of his sleep sooner or later, though to be honest it's taking longer than I would have liked. Then there are these two chaps, leftover from the storm. Both should be back on duty tomorrow, a few nasty bruises left but not much else."

"I'm pleased to hear it."

"In fact I was just thinking what a quiet trip it had been, and then remembered poor Mr. Halifax. Though it wasn't five days ago it seems like a dream, doesn't it?"

"May I ask you a peculiar question?"

"Yes, but please, sit down, have a glass with me." Tradescant lit another candle and uncorked a dusty, roundish bottle of some richly ruby-colored liquid. He poured two very small glasses of it. "To Halifax!" he said, and drained his glass.

"To Halifax." Lenox drank his off too, and then smacked his lips. "Delicious wine. Where did you come by it?"

Tradescant's eyes flickered in the candlelight and he smiled. "It's an 1842 Burgundy. My father gave me six cases when I first went to sea. They're quite valuable, and I think he intended for me to sell them and live off of the profits. But it was the only present he ever gave me, you see, and so I take two bottles on each voyage. I only drink it with others. It gives me a kind of pleasure."

"Better than money."

"Dissimilar—but yes, perhaps better. I don't mind about money. I suppose he would give me some of that, too, if I needed it especially. He gave me a house in town some years ago, and he's just about alive. I'm a bastard, you see. My father is—" and here Tradescant named one of the great dukes of the realm, of a family second only to the royal family in prestige,

nearly ninety now, who in his day had been one of the few political and social rulers of Europe.

"I didn't know," said Lenox. "A very great man indeed."

"In some respects, yes. My mother was a charwoman, may
she rest in peace, and I think it very likely she had more wis-
dom than he did, and more kindness beside." Tradescant
laughed. "Now I am nearly fifty. It's an age when parents don't
matter as much as they did . . . or they matter more in some
ways, and less in others. I've been happy in my life."

It was a singularly confessional speech, and Lenox smiled—
not too broadly, but encouragingly, grateful for the man's confidence. "If all you had out of your father was that wine, it
wouldn't have been too hard a transaction."

"We agree, Mr. Lenox! Now, your peculiar question?"

"Ah, yes. I wondered about the contents of Halifax's stomach when he died."

"Oh?"

"Not the food, so much as whether—well, it sounds indeli-
cate, but my friend Thomas McConnell, who is a doctor, will
smell the stomach for alcohol, if the body is . . . fresh enough.
I realize it sounds morbid."

"I do quite the same, and in fact I think I'll have made a note
of it . . . yes, here's the book, this little hardbacked one."

Tradescant flipped through the pages. "Well?" said Lenox
when he had stopped.

"Hmm. Whisky, it says here, Scotch whisky. Strange, now
that you've drawn my attention to it—we don't get whisky on
the ship much, the men preferring rum and the officers brandy—
but there was a definite odor of whisky."

CHAPTER TWENTY-SEVEN

Lenox went to sleep not long afterward, his stream of consciousness racing but muddied by drink. The next morning he woke with a single, clarified thought: *Might Jacob Martin have murdered his second lieutenant?*

It would account for the whisky; for Halifax's apparently willing attendance at a midnight meeting halfway up one of the masts; Martin's self-possession the night of the murder; the theft of the medallion and the penknife (presumably to shift blame away from himself) would have been easy, as nobody questions a captain's movements aboard his own ship. And of course, most of all, he was a figure beyond suspicion.

Which meant he was the first person Lenox ought to have considered.

Still, some small part of him rebelled against the idea of Martin as a murderer. It wasn't the man's religious faith; that was so common among murderers as to be mundane. Nor was it his leadership of the *Lucy*. Rather, it was some intrinsic conservatism that seemed to define Martin's character, a deficit of fury. The crime had been at once savage and plotted, and the mind behind it didn't seem to be the mind Lenox thought the captain to have.

Then again, Pettegree had identified Martin as a man of violent temper.

The alternatives that his mind kept circling toward were Lieutenant Lee, despite the man's placid temperament, and Lieutenant Mitchell. Mitchell was the more obvious suspect, because of his temper and because he was new aboard, the only change to the wardroom. For years the *Lucy* had sailed without violent incident, and within a few weeks of Mitchell's arrival on board a man was dead.

As for Lee, there was the matter of his steward, who slept not in front of his door but down below deck amid the guns, with the rest of the sailors. It would have been difficult for the other officers to slip past their sleeping stewards, all situated in the hallways outside of their cabins. It would have been easy for Lee.

Or Martin.

After Lenox had accepted coffee, kippers, and eggs from McEwan, he took one of the last of Lady Jane's oranges and sat down to write her a letter as he ate it. In it he spoke of Follow the Leader, of Teddy, of life aboard the ship. He reassured her that he had yet to succumb to scurvy. The letter ended with a short benediction, not too intrusive he hoped, for her and their child, after writing which he sealed the letter in an envelope and placed it next to the other letter he had written her, which sat in the battered Paul Storr toast rack that had always served as the organizer of his correspondence.

It was a still sort of day, not much wind, and while Lenox strolled the quarterdeck a huge indolent sailmaker's mate named McKendrick played softly on his flute, sitting along the bowsprit. In the empty vastness the sound seemed to carry with special purity, and it lent a magic to the engrossing rhythm of the waves.

Maybe because of the music, or because of the sunny gentleness of the day—and certainly because of McEwan—Lenox decided to climb to the crow's nest. The murder could wait half an hour.

He checked with Mitchell, the officer on bridge watch, who shrugged and sent along a strong forecastleman to keep Lenox safe. The forecastlemen were the best seamen the ship had—by contrast the quarterdeckmen, for example, were of an advanced age that they no longer liked to go aloft, though Old Joe Coffey didn't seem to mind—but evidently Mitchell could spare this one, a short, grinning, towheaded Swede named Andersen. He spoke in a rudimentary dialect of English that was almost wholly naval in origin, and therefore shockingly explicit. His stock of obscenities he seemed to view as ordinary, even courteous, and the rest of the crew found Andersen too funny to disabuse him of that impression.

"Fucking top, here you going!" he said cheerfully, then for the sake of decorum added, "Sir!"

Lenox felt a fool for it, after McEwan's performance, but in his heart he knew from the outset that the ascent was the hardest physical task he had ever essayed. More than once he felt himself slipping and thanked the Lord for the rope looped around his midsection.

After twenty yards or so the muscles in his legs were quivering and tired, and his hands a raw red from clinging desperately to the rope. Andersen, maddeningly, flung himself about the rigging like a monkey, making comments that were supposed to be encouraging, and which after a while Lenox stopped answering.

Don't look down, he exhorted himself over and over, even though looking up was no treat, but after he had gone about halfway toward the crow's nest he nonetheless made the mistake of glancing toward the deck.

His stomach went heavy and hollow, all the air sucked out of his midsection.

"We'd better go back down," he said to Andersen.

"You must attain the crow nest!" replied the Swede with unforgivable jollity.

Lenox gulped and resumed the slow, arduous climb. As one went higher every small wavelet that slapped against the ship seemed greater, resonating through her timbers, until, when he was only twenty feet from the top, a gentle whitecap almost knocked him loose.

"So close!" said Andersen, who was hanging upside down by his legs, evidently having been as inspired by Follow the Leader as Lenox had been.

At last the crow's nest seemed to be within his grasp. It was larger than he had expected, a wide circle of solid oak that could have fit six men snugly around, their legs dangling through the hole in the center. Lenox's knuckles were white with the strength of his grip on the rope, until, almost reluctantly, he accepted Andersen's boost through the center.

"Who's that?" a voice called out as Lenox fell in a lump into the corner of the crow's nest, panting.

The detective, not as young as he had once been, was trembling, sweat-soaked, and shaky; all he had wanted while aloft was a moment of peace. Instead he had found Evers, McEwan's friend. The one who thought he was an albatross.

Andersen's cheerful face popped through the center of the crow's nest. "Rest now, Mr. Parliament! I have brought you reward as well! From Mr. McEwan—he suspects where you need it."

To Lenox's immense gratitude Andersen revealed that he had brought with them a small thermos, which proved to be full of hot, sweet tea, and a napkin wrapped around seven or eight gingerbread biscuits, studded with pieces of rock sugar. Jane had packed them.

Gradually Lenox's breath returned to a steady rate and his

reddened face began to cool. When he had at least some of his composure back he looked at Evers.

"Excuse my intrusion," he said.

"Not at all, sir," said Evers, in a voice that seemed to contradict the graciousness of his words. "They said you was going to try to make it up here. I didn't think it would happen."

"Why have you come up?"

"No reason." As he spoke Evers shifted his hands, and Lenox saw for the first time that he was trying to hide something in his lap, his knees drawn up to his chin.

Lenox's guard went up: was this the murderer? Evers was a large, strong man. Thank goodness for Andersen's presence.

"You're not on watch?"

"No, which it's my time to myself."

"Do you come up here often?"

"Fairly often, sir." Again he said this last word with as much insolence as he could muster. He shifted his hands again and something spilled out onto the bare wood of the crow's nest. Lenox grabbed it just as it seemed to be pitching for the hole at the center.

"Look here, that's mine!" cried Evers.

Lenox held up the object. It was a charcoal pencil, chunky, with black charcoal on one side and white on the other, for shading. "This?"

"Yes!"

"Are you a draughtsman?"

"No," said Evers, but this was plainly a lie; as he reached forward to grab the charcoal from Lenox it was easy to see an open sketchbook.

"May I see?" Lenox asked.

A battle took place in Evers's face: pride and resentment fighting against each other. At last the pride won out, and with a great show of antipathy he handed Lenox the book.

Lenox flipped through it. On almost every page was a different sketch of the same vista, at different times of day—the view from this high perch, sometimes with other masts and even people showing, sometimes with a horizon, and always the sun and clouds and water.

"These are wonderful," said Lenox.

"Oh?" said Evers hoarsely.

"You draw?" Andersen said.

"No!" Evers roared, and snatched the book back.

"Let me see it for myself, this view you draw," said Lenox.

He stood. The crow's nest was high-walled enough that it had concealed the panorama it offered from him while he was sitting, but now as he rose he took it all in.

It was one of the most miraculous moments of his life; he had known the pleasure of rest after exertion, and he had known the heartswell one gets from a sweeping view of the natural world in its beauty. He hadn't known them in combination, however, and together they overwhelmed him. There was the distant deck, populated by miniatures of the men he knew; the masts of the ship, ahead and behind him; there were the cliffs of grayish clouds, and between them, breaking through now and then, the brilliant golden sun.

For five, then ten minutes he gazed out upon the sea and the sky. Raindrops fell on his face. His spirit felt full.

"I don't blame you for drawing it," he said at last, sitting down again. "Will you tell me how you came to start drawing?"

Evers wanted to speak, it was plain, but couldn't with Andersen there. He gulped, and then said, "Some other time, if you don't mind, sir. I need to be on duty."

"Not for hours!" said the Swede cheerfully.

"Bugger," Evers muttered, and set off down through the hole in the crow's nest and back down the rigging, his sketchbook in his teeth.

CHAPTER TWENTY-EIGHT

So absorbing had life on board been that Lenox had half forgotten the reason he was there at all. But it had been nearly a week now. They would make landfall in Egypt after only five or six more days, four if the wind was exceptionally kind.

So that afternoon he went to his cabin and removed the papers Edmund had handed him at the Plymouth docks from their leather satchel. After coming down from the crow's nest he had had a good lunch, of roasted chicken, peas, and potatoes, washed down with a half bottle of claret, and then he had slept for an hour or so, physically exhausted. Now he felt refreshed, his mind sharp. He was prepared to read his orders.

There were three sheets of paper, each a mess of jumbled numbers and letters, none of them ever forming a word, much less a sentence. They had been written in cipher by a cryptographer working for the British government.

Thankfully Lenox knew the key to the cipher. For his sake it was a simple one: the first thirteen letters of the alphabet corresponded to the second thirteen, so that the letter A in fact denoted the letter N, the letter B in fact denoted the letter O, and so on. Meanwhile the cardinal numbers one through thirteen corresponded to the *first* thirteen letters of the alphabet, so that a one denoted an A and a thirteen denoted an M. Numbers more than thirteen were used as line breaks or spaces. The first enciphered word of his brother's letter— 4-5-1-E— therefore translated in plain English into the word *Dear*.

Edmund had told Lenox of this system and made him recite it back several times, until the older brother was satisfied that the younger brother would remember. Now Lenox made a key for himself and set about translating the first of the three documents, his brother's letter. This took half an hour or so of lip-biting effort. In its translated version the letter read:

Dear Charles,
Two documents are enclosed with this letter. We have enciphered both, believing that it would draw attention to have enciphered only one. The first, marked *Alpha* in the upper right-hand corner, details your official responsibilities in Suez, and the second, marked *Omega* in the upper right-hand corner, your covert ones. It is a matter of the highest importance that you should destroy both this letter and the document marked *Omega* as soon as you have committed the simple details of *Omega* to your memory. *Alpha* you may keep, and not bother hiding— should the French find it and decipher it they would discover only your official itinerary, and it might command their attention for long enough to keep their eyes off of you.
Please accept the pistol they offer you at the consulate;

you should carry it as a precaution. Return home safely, please, and know me to be,

Your affectionate and grateful brother,
Edmund

For all his life Lenox had kept files full of the letters he received, dating back to school days and the Lord Chesterfield missives his father sent to Harrow. Now, though, he dutifully shredded Edmund's letter into pieces, did the same with his scrawled translation, and dropped the resultant confetti through his porthole and into the ocean. Now he had only the two letters from the prime minister's office and his quickly drawn-up key on his desk.

There would be time to look over his official activities, and at any rate the resident consulate would no doubt shepherd him through his duties. It was more urgent to memorize the details of his clandestine mission.

Translation of the *Omega* document was more difficult than translation of the letter, because there were more proper names and it was therefore more difficult to guess words after the first few letters. An hour of labor earned him a terse set of directions.

Mr. Lenox:

- Your meeting will take place on May fifteenth at ten minutes before midnight, three days after you are scheduled to arrive. If the *Lucy* has not reached Port Said by the afternoon of the fifteenth, the meeting will be delayed exactly twenty-four hours.

- Near your hotel is a club for the use of European gentlemen, known in English as Scheherazade's. Arrive there early, preferably by an hour or so, and order a (non-alcoholic) drink. In the fourth room on the left is a small door. Behind it is a staircase leading to the establishment's kitchen. Your meeting will take place in the kitchen. A diagram of exits from the kitchen and the Scheherazade are on the back of this sheet. Commit them to memory.

- Your contact, whom you may call Monsieur Sournois, will be at the rear of the kitchen, which at this hour will be empty. He is over six foot, dark-haired, and missing the smallest finger of his left hand. He will say the following phrase to you in English: *"The kitchen is always closed when one is hungriest."* To this you will respond: *"There's never a meal to be had in Port Said after ten."* He will then answer all of the questions your brother has instructed you to ask. He will not ask about payment; it has been arranged.

- When your meeting is concluded, take the exit marked B in the diagram on the reverse of this page. The corridor outside of it will lead to the street. Return to your hotel. Write the answers Sournois gave you in cipher, *without copying down names, dates, or figures.* These you must commit to your memory. Should you be followed, fall in with other people and make your voice and presence conspicuous.

- When you reach Port Said, the consular staff will greet your ship. In all matters other than your meeting accept their guidance.

- Should anything go amiss, you must for your own safety immediately make your way to the consulate, and then with all possible haste to your ship.

- Destroy this document once you have memorized its contents.

As he read this Lenox's nerves began to tense. It had seemed simple in the warmth of his London library: go to Egypt and perform a variety of official functions, and while off duty receive information from a French spy. Now it seemed like a mission fraught with danger.

Mingled with this new anxiety, however, was excitement. He was eager to arrive at their destination: Port Said, a city that lay at the north of the canal, near the top of the continent, just as the city of Suez lay at the canal's southern point. He wondered what it would be like, and a series of images flashed through his mind: the nomadic Bedouins of the desert, almond-eyed women whose mouths were covered with veils, dancing in dimly lit dens, curved swords, camels, tin lanterns carved with Moslem symbols. All the stuff of boyhood books about the great Arabic world.

It was impossible to know whether any of that still existed. Of course the canal had changed Africa drastically, permitting goods from the center of the continent to reach its northern edge, around Port Said, and then to be absorbed into the great trade currents of the Mediterranean and the Atlantic. There would be Europeans crawling all over the city—a concern, now that he came to think of it, though thankfully he and Sournois both had legitimate business to conduct, from all Edmund had said.

Now the implications of this document, the one in his hands, returned with full force to Lenox's mind: conflict between the world's two greatest nations, its two greatest navies, its two greatest armies. A war across the channel. It was within his power to help England, either by avoiding the war or by giving her a head start if the war was inevitable. A daunting thought.

He read through the letter twice more, and then looked out at the waning light and thought for a while.

"McEwan, would you fetch me a cup of tea?" he called out to the hallway at last.

"Yes, sir," McEwan's voice rang back.

"And while you're at it I'll take some toast."

"And cakes, sir?"

"And cakes, why not."

Lenox hid the document marked *Alpha* and then shredded his translation of *Omega*, the original, enciphered document, and his key, and again dumped the confetti out through his porthole. His tea arrived just as the last scraps of torn white paper sank beneath the water. He took a sip and contemplated what they had said, and what the next week of his life might be like.

CHAPTER TWENTY-NINE

Before supper that evening, Lenox took himself to the quarterdeck. Two men were there already, Billings and Quirke, leaned up against one rail and smoking cigars.

"How do you do?" said Quirke, and Billings nodded affably.

"Fairly well—unhappy still about Lieutenant Halifax, but fairly well, I thank you."

"We were just discussing the subject," Billings said.

"What did you conclude?"

"Nothing to merit your consideration—only the anxiety we both feel that his death is somehow linked to this pathetic attempt at mutiny."

"I had wondered about that too," said Lenox. "What puzzles me is that the *Lucy* kept so many of her men, all but two, men who could easily have left the navy forever should they have wished. Now we are to believe that one of them can have had such a change of heart in the past five days that he should murder a man and foment a mutiny? It seems impossible."

"I quite agree," said the engineer, pushing his red hair out of his eyes. "Yet the facts remain."

The wind had picked up now, and above them from the poop deck Lieutenant Lee called out an order. "Reef the topsails, gents! Quickly now!"

"Yes," murmured Lenox in response to Quirke. He lit his own cigar, and tucked a hand into his waistcoat pocket. "They're inconvenient."

Something had occurred to him, and for a moment it engaged his whole attention. The thought was this: the *Lucy's* last two second lieutenants were dead. He recalled dimly Halifax telling him that the man who had held his job previously had been lost at sea.

What if there had been a more subtle variety of foul play in that death, too?

"Tell me, Mr. Billings," he said. "I never heard the details of the death of your previous second lieutenant. Or his name, for that matter."

A look of pain came into the first lieutenant's eyes. "He was a good fellow, named Bethell, born not five miles from Portsmouth Harbor and leaving it only to sail to sea. He died during a storm—was taken overboard."

"Was his death unusual?"

Quirke and Billings recognized at once what the implication of the question was, and in vehement unison shook their heads. It was Billings who spoke. "No, it was the commonest thing in the world, a heavy storm. He had gone fore to instruct the men to lash down the boats, and a great wave thundered us and, as we suppose, sent him overboard."

"Nobody saw it happen, then?"

"No, but several of us saw him go forward, and within not fifteen seconds felt the tremendous wave. I don't think anybody was surprised that he was lost. Saddened, of course, but not surprised."

"Did the captain elevate Lieutenant Carrow to the rank of second lieutenant?"

"Yes," said Quirke, "but he was reckoned too young to keep it. Now he will."

There was motive, if you liked, and Quirke, sensing as much, hastened to add, "But Carrow would never have done it. Bethell was his closest friend aboard the *Lucy.*"

Billings looked less convinced, but said nothing.

"Do you disagree?" asked Lenox.

"No! No, not at all. That is to say, I know Carrow and Bethell had a falling-out, at some point, but I would no more believe Carrow capable of murder than—"

Lenox here forestalled Billings's defense of his friend, interrupting him to say, "Yes, I see. Thank you."

Quirke flung his cigar end into the sea. "Anyhow it's a filthy business, and I shall enjoy seeing the bugger who did it hang," he said. "Until supper, gentlemen."

After he had gone Billings begged off too, leaving Lenox alone with his thoughts and Fizz, the dog of the wardroom, who leaped up onto his lap—being not much bigger than a rugby ball—and snoozed happily there for some while, while Lenox contemplated his duties in Port Said, and, more often, the half-empty bottle of liquor he had seen in Captain Martin's cabin. Impulsively he decided he would go confront the captain now about it. He put an indignant Fizz on the floor and walked toward the captain's cabin.

Martin was sitting in an armchair by his lovely, curved bow window, which looked out upon the ship's wake. In one hand was a small black calfskin Bible. At Lenox's entrance he carefully marked his page in the book and placed it upon the window ledge.

"How are you, Mr. Lenox?" he said. His smile was dry. "I heard of your ascent to the crow's nest."

"I don't envy the fellows who are up and down the rigging all day, anyhow."

"I wish you hadn't gone—it would have been terribly inconvenient for us if you had fallen and died. While you're on board the *Lucy* I would appreciate it if you exercised greater caution."

"There was a rope around my midsection, and Andersen was with me."

"Both ropes and Andersen have been known to fail upon occasion."

"I—" Lenox was about to respond when the image of Jane, pregnant, appeared in his mind's eye. Instead he nodded. "You're quite right. I won't go up again."

"Thank you. Now, what have you come to discuss with me?"

"May I sit?"

"Of course."

Lenox turned to take his seat, stealing a glance at the desk; he saw from the label on the bottle that it was whisky, and from the looks of it no more was gone.

What kind of man drinks half a bottle of whisky in one night and none in the subsequent five? he thought.

He had been planning to ask the captain about the whisky, but decided at the last moment to hold off. Instead he said, "I've just heard a bit about Bethell, your former lieutenant."

"It was a sad loss."

"Did you consider then that he might have been pushed overboard?"

"Never for a second—nor do I accept it as a possibility now. The *Lucy* has been an exceedingly happy ship, Mr. Lenox."

"I'm afraid that doesn't rule out the chance that a single man, whether out of madness or guile, might have killed Mr. Bethell."

Martin shook his head. "No, as I say, I cannot believe it. Deaths of that type are part of naval life, unfortunately. Contrast Bethell's death with Halifax's and you'll see that they cannot be by the same hand—cannot be linked."

"Perhaps," said Lenox.

"And you, are you any closer to finding out who killed Halifax?"

"Not far off now, I think."

"I hope to God not."

With that Lenox returned to his own cabin then, to dress for dinner. As he was fixing his tie McEwan's voice called out to him.

"A note for you, sir," he said.

"Come in."

McEwan entered and handed over a blank envelope, offering along with it an exaggerated wink.

Lenox, puzzled, thanked the steward and took the envelope to open it.

Inside was one of the drawings Evers had made in the crow's nest, a panorama, dated that very day and signed in a surprisingly precise hand. Lenox was touched. Then he noticed that the paper, slightly translucent in the bright sunlight, had something written on its reverse, in small handwriting along the battom. He turned the sheet over.

Butterworth knows something, was all it said.

The instant he read these words—and before he could begin to consider what he knew of Billings's steward—the bell rang for supper.

In the wardroom the men shook hands and sipped sherry, exchanged jokes and the officers' tales of the day's hard sailing. The mood was amiable, and the food smelled wonderful from the galley. Lenox, though distracted, began to feel his tension dissipate.

Just as they were sitting to eat, however, a thin voice cried out from the crow's nest, barely audible below deck: "Ship ahoy! American colors!"

CHAPTER THIRTY

"Fetch me my glass, Butterworth," said Billings to the steward, who was behind his chair.

The captain had been planning to dine alone, but came through to the wardroom now. He was smiling. "An American ship. Come along, anyone who'd like to," he said.

All of the men except one, Pettegree, rose and followed the captain, leaving their bowls of potato and leek soup behind to fall cold; for his part, the purser had a second bowl and then a third, delighted at his good fortune. The American ship wouldn't be near for another quarter of an hour at least.

On the main deck they took turns looking at the ship through Billings's glass (the captain kept his own), while with the captain's approval Mitchell, who was on watch, gave orders for the ship to reverse itself toward the approaching vessel.

Soon Lenox could see her with his bare eye, a one-decked ship of middling size.

Martin spoke. "A sloop of war, clearly."

Lee, when he took the glass, answered the captain almost

immediately, "Yes, she's the USS *Constellation*, I'd bet any sum. We met her once near the African coast, when I was aboard the *Challenger*. She captured a fat little bark with seven-hundred-odd slaves in her, set the slaves free, and imprisoned the slave traders. I would recognize her anywhere."

"A good sailor?" Martin asked.

"Not fast. The *Lucy* could outrun her under jibs and staysails. But she's steady, sir, and because the Americans make their ships of live oak she's tolerably strong. It would be a mighty storm that broke her beams."

There was a tangible buzz of excitement as the *Constellation* drew closer, among the officers and the men alike.

"Prepare the *Bumblebee*," said Martin when they were less than a mile apart. "Cresswell and Lenox, you shall pilot her over there if they invite us on board. Mitchell, you shall stay on watch."

Only now did Lenox see that his nephew was among those lined along the rail, looking out.

At last the American ship was close enough that Martin could cry out "Good evening!" and hear in faint reply from the captain of the *Constellation*, "You're very welcome on board our ship, sir! You're in time for supper!"

It was easy to claim that the French and the British navies were superior to any other in the world. Some fifty years before, however, during the War of 1812, Britain had been shocked at the strength of the American fleet, and now, with that country's civil war receding into the past, the United States Navy was again a formidable force. Fortunately the States and Britain were on excellent terms. In fact their navies had worked jointly to lay the cable for the first Atlantic telegraph, the USS *Niagara* and HMS *Agamemnon* the two vessels chiefly responsible for that achievement, and the comity between the two navies was written on the face of every man on board the *Lucy*: they liked each other.

"Billings, Carrow, and Lee, change into uniform as quickly as possible. Bosun, bring along several men to row us—yes, they may stay on the *Constellation* while we eat, of course"—at this there was a tremendous clamor of men begging for the job. "Mr. Lenox, you may use your own discretion, but you are most welcome to join us."

"Thank you, I shall."

Soon they were across in the *Bumblebee*, Teddy Lenox and Alastair Cresswell rather puffed up with their responsibility and commanding the jolly boat it as if they were carrying Lord Nelson to battle.

As they slipped over the gunwales of the American ship, Lenox saw a half-circle of officers in their best uniform. At their center was an imperious-looking, remarkably thin gentleman, almost Roman in his ascetic good looks, skin tanned and hardened by the sun, with snow-white hair. He looked to be about fifty years of age.

"I am Captain John Collier, of Cohasset, Massachusetts," he said, "and you are exceedingly welcome on board the USS *Constellation*—most heartily welcome."

"I thank you," said Martin, whose demeanor was grave but whose eyes sparkled with happiness.

"Have you dined?"

"No; at least, we began, but didn't finish."

There were introductions all around, now, Martin giving special favor to Lenox, and Captain Collier claiming himself honored to meet a member of Parliament. Lee remembered himself to several of the junior officers. Soon they all went down the hatchway and into the captain's dining room; as he ducked below deck Lenox noticed a furious din of chatter, trade, and tale-telling erupt among the six men who had been permitted to row them over, while Cresswell and Teddy were making themselves at home with the chewing tobacco of the *Constellation*'s midshipmen.

The captain's dining quarters were extremely homey, with candlelight bouncing off of the honey-colored wooden walls and chairs of a deep plush blue color ringed around an oval table. On one wall, over the door, was a large blue and white banner that said "For God, for country, and for Yale," and opposite that was a needlepoint of a large, well-proportioned farmhouse, which Lenox presumed must belong to Collier when he was on land, and which read, "Cohasset Folly," beneath the image. It was a cabin that made the *Lucy*'s own quarters feel frankly starched, unfriendly, by comparison.

As for the officers, they were all exceedingly gracious and excellent listeners—not how one thought of Americans, quite, and yet they wore their good manners naturally. Lenox found himself speaking with the ship's chaplain, who could not have been a figure of greater contrast to the *Lucy*'s: a kindly faced, bespectacled, quiet gentleman, he had been at Yale with Captain Collier, and since then had published several books, apparently of the transcendentalist ethos. He promised to give Lenox a copy of his most recent before the ships parted.

"Now tell me," said Martin, when the table had quieted. "What brings you into these waters?"

"We carried famine relief to Ireland," said Captain Collier.

"God bless you," said Lenox, with more fervor than he had intended; he felt his own country's inaction during Ireland's struggle a point of shame, brought into sharp relief by the Americans' generosity.

"Thank you, sir."

"Was your passage eventful?"

"Not in the least, thank goodness. I feared spring storms, but they never materialized. Now we make our way to the African coast, where we will break up the slave traders for a month or so, and then fill our empty holds with goods for our shores. A routine peacetime voyage, all in all. I suspect we're rather like you; trying to make ourselves useful."

"That is our situation indeed," said Martin. Here he began his familiar disquisition on the lethargy of the British navy, the strange uses to which it was being put. He concluded by saying, almost apologetically, "We understand Mr. Lenox's mission to be of singular importance, but there are ships afloat that are doing—well, what you might call busywork, even."

"What we need, in my opinion," Collier said, "is a return to the age of Banks."

There was an immediate hum of gratified agreement. "Yes, absolutely," said Martin. "Scientific discovery has always been the second-greatest adornment of our navy."

"I know of Banks, of course—a famous figure—but must admit my ignorance of his achievements," Lenox interjected, a statement met with incredulity all around. "I fear it may be a similar black spot for many landsmen. Pray tell me, for what is he most widely known?"

"His voyage with Cook's *Endeavor*, first to Brazil, then to Botany Bay," said Collier. "But, Captain Martin, you are his fellow Englishman; please tell us."

Martin, with great seriousness, said, "He is the greatest figure in our navy's history, barring Drake and Nelson, in my opinion—that is a bold statement but one I stand by, though Banks was never a great seaman himself. There is a whole genus of Australian flowers named after him, nearly two hundred plants in all, *Banksia*, and he was the first to bring the eucalyptus tree, the acacia, the mimosa, back to the Western world."

"The bougainvillea," murmured Carrow. He was smiling, Lenox observed. "Named it after his friend, a Frenchman—and this in the 1780s, when there was a good deal of nerve between the nations."

"Just so, because science exalts our natures," said Collier, "above even national pride, at times. That's why I wish our navies would undertake more voyages of the kind Captain Cook led."

"I'm reading the *Voyage of the Beagle* at the moment," said Lenox, "and—"

"A truly great book," one of the American officers chimed in.

"Unfortunate that Darwin lost his mind subsequently," said Martin. "Apes, indeed."

"We've had that discussion too often in our own wardroom for it to be fruitful any longer," said Collier, smiling. "Mr. Lenox, what were you saying?"

"Only that perhaps science is still alive in the navy. Mr. Darwin is."

"The *Beagle* sailed forty years ago, I'm sorry to say," Martin put in. "There's nothing like it afloat now. More's the pity."

As the discussion wended onward, they ate a wonderful meal, no doubt the best of the *Constellation*'s diminished stores, a tender leg of lamb, creamy mashed potatoes, a dessert of black sugar cake. There was, too, a great deal of excellent wine. Having been at seas slightly longer than the *Lucys*, the men of the *Constellation* eagerly heard the most recent news, and they were into their cigars and port by the time the noise subsided in the faintest degree.

When it did, Collier stood. "Gentlemen," he said, "raise your glasses, please, along with me. I am very happy to welcome you on board, Captain Martin, Mr. Billings, Mr. Carrow, Mr. Lee, the Honorable Mr. Lenox. My family came from England to Massachusetts in the 1630s, and though we have fought against you twice, first in our revolution, then in the war at the start of this century, we have never forgotten that our roots were planted first in English soil. We honor the old country. And it gives me pleasure that our nations have finally understood this special connection, and that we may eat a meal such as this one in the spirit of pure friendship. Your health, gentlemen—oh, and as is your custom, I believe, to the Queen."

"The Queen!"

Martin stood up then, and praised Collier and his ship, her

taut rigging and shipshape sails, and then echoed Collier's delight in the friendship between their nations.

"And now," Collier said, when the toasts were all delivered, "if you can stay a little while longer we have some excellent brandy—American, but good, I promise you—and we would welcome your company for as long as you please to drink it with us."

It was very late at night indeed—nearly morning—when the *Bumblebee* readied herself for her short voyage back to the *Lucy*. Alice Cresswell and Teddy Lenox for their part were shamefully drunk, and the officers, roughly but with a hint of indulgence, piled them into the bottom of the boat; then all of them, including Lenox, turned back to wave goodbye to the Americans as the rowers began to pull. The men of the *Constellation*, among them her own officers, were lined along the rail of the ship, waving back and shouting messages of goodwill, of good sailing, and of good luck.

CHAPTER THIRTY-ONE

Though it was abominably late and he was slightly the worse for drink, when Lenox returned to his cabin he found that he didn't feel like falling straight into bed. He went to his desk and lit a candle there.

"Sir?" said McEwan groggily, from the other side of the door. "D'you need anything?"

"No, no, thank you," said Lenox.

"G'night, sir. Oh! But the Americans, how were they?"

"Most friendly."

"Did they try to boast about the old wars, 1812 and that?"

"Not at all."

"My old granddad fought them then. He was sore about it still, up till he died. Said they were up-jumped ruffians, the Americans."

"On the contrary, I found them most civilized."

"Well, and perhaps they grown up, in all this time."

"Perhaps. Good night, McEwan."

"G'night, sir."

Lenox poured himself a glass of wine and rocked back in his chair, looking out through his porthole. The scent of the still sea blew lightly into the cabin, and above it the sky had just begun to lighten from black to pale purple. In the half-light there was a melancholy to the lightless gray of the water, a solitude in it, and he felt something stir inside him: a feeling that reminded him again of homesickness.

He thought of Jane, sitting on her rose-colored sofa, writing letters at her morning desk, moving through the house, setting small things aright. How did these men tolerate lives at sea, always abroad, always a thousand miles from home! But then, perhaps they weren't as happy by their hearths as he was by his.

It had been only a week after Edmund had asked Charles to go to Egypt that Jane had begun to act strangely. For two days she had spoken very little and spent much time closeted with her close friend the Duchess of Marchmain—Duch, for short—and refusing all invitations.

Lenox had too much delicacy to ask her what was the matter, but he had gone and sat with her at unusual times, running home during breaks from Parliament, hoping to invite her confidence.

It was on the third day that he finally received it. He had been reading on the sofa by the fire—there was still a winter chill in the air, halfway through March—and eating an edge of toast, when Jane spoke.

"Tell me," she said, "how old was your mother when you were born?"

He put his book facedown beside him. "Nearly twenty-four, I think."

"Twenty-one when Edmund was born, then?"

"Yes."

Jane smiled. "I wish she had lived longer. She was such a kind woman."

"Yes," he said, and felt a lump in his throat. It was something he tried never to think about.

"I'm fearfully old," she said.

"You're not!"

"I am, I am. Too old to be a mother."

Since their marriage Lenox had been hoping that she might consent to have a child with him, and now with a start he realized that perhaps the opportunity was being taken from him. "McConnell and every other doctor you've seen have told you you're not," he said.

She laughed, a kind of choked laugh. "I suppose they were right!"

He stood up. "Jane?"

"I'm going to have a child, anyhow," she said, and burst into tears.

What had he felt in that moment? It was impossible to describe the jumble inside him: pride mixed up with fear mixed up with a great surge of excitement mixed up with a million questions mixed up with concern for his wife mixed up with . . . with everything, anything a human could feel.

"My goodness," was all he said. His hands were in his pockets and he rocked back on his feet, staring at a spot on the ground.

"Is that what you have to say?"

His face broke into a great grin, and he went and took her by the hands. "No. I have much more to say. Only I don't know where to begin. At first I thought I would thank you for marrying me, which still surprises me every day, though it happened years ago, and then I thought I would say how happy I felt, but you were crying. So I thought I would stand there and be silent."

She had stopped crying, but her face was still wet with tears. "Oh, Charles," she said.

"When did you know?"

"I've suspected it for some while, but I went to the doctor with Duch yesterday. He confirmed it."

Lenox frowned. "The doctor, there's a point. Do you have

the best man? McConnell knows all of them in Harley Street—
we'll ask him—and of course we must be sure to speak—"

"No, no—this habit you have of solving problems that don't
exist! I have an excellent doctor. Toto used him too."

Lenox sat down beside her and put an arm around her shoulder. In a quick voice he said, "You have made me happy beyond measure, Jane—really, you have."

She tilted her head up and kissed his cheek then. "I'm so
relieved to tell you."

"Were you anxious?"

"I don't know, quite. My head was all in a muddle."

And then she did something that Lenox could almost feel in
his cabin, so far from London: she took his hand and put it in
hers, and they sat, companionably silent for the most part, occasionally bursting into little exchanges about this or that—which
room would the nursery be! If it were a boy he must be put down
for Harrow immediately!—until deep in the morning.

There was a feeling of nervous elation bound up in having
so much happiness, he had found. Every time he thought of his
child, growing strong within Jane, he had a fizzy feeling in his
head and had to remind himself to behave normally, not to run
around telling strangers.

Outside of his cabin the sky was pale white now, and soon,
he knew, it would flash into goldenness. Really he must rest.

But not for twenty minutes, he decided; he would write his
wife first, and tell her how much he missed her, and how very
much he loved her.

CHAPTER THIRTY-TWO

Butterworth knows something, the note from Evers had said.
Lenox woke up late the next morning with a foggy head,
but the phrase popped straight into his thoughts. As he ate breakfast and sipped his coffee, he considered the little he knew of
Billings's valet. Butterworth was jaundiced yellow, some harmless seafarer's disease, Billings had mentioned, and too tall by
several inches for the low ceilings on board a ship, which meant
he always seemed slightly stooped.

Billings himself was in the wardroom, writing a letter,
when Lenox put his head out. Seated alongside him was
Mitchell, who was whittling down a piece of light-colored
spruce into what appeared to be a finely detailed model of the
Lucy.

It was a minor piece of information that Lenox registered
almost automatically: Mitchell must be used to having a knife
in his hands . . .

"D'you know," the detective said in a conversational tone, "I
almost feel guilty, asking McEwan to fetch me more coffee. He

possesses such surpassing grace amidships that it seems he ought to be there."

Billings looked up, smiling; Mitchell looked up too, but without the smile. "Oh, he's landed where he wants to be," said Billings. "It's no bad job."

"Have you had your own stewards long? How were they chosen?"

"Butterworth came to sea with me—my father's servant."

"He must be trustworthy, in that case."

"Oh, very. Mitchell, did your chap come along with you?"

"He and I have been together on several voyages now, but all on the *Lucy*," said Mitchell, still whittling. "We met when I was a midshipman in the *Challenger*, and when I had my step up I brought him along as my steward. Excellent fellow."

"It's common, then, for a steward to follow an officer from assignment to assignment?"

"Oh, yes," said Mitchell. "In fact many of them act as butlers when their gentlemen are ashore. A bit rough, as butlers go, but nobody can keep a house clean like a steward."

"It's true that I have been amazed at the amount of time McEwan spends tidying."

For the first time in their acquaintance, Mitchell smiled at him, albeit thinly. "Such is life afloat, Mr. Lenox."

Billings took a last mouthful of egg and stood up. "I think I'll take a turn on the quarterdeck," he said. "Last night's wine has given me a morning head, I'm afraid."

"I'll come with you," said Mitchell.

"Mr. Lenox?" Billings asked.

"I'll stay here, if it's all the same to you."

After they had gone Lenox rose and went to the closed door behind which lay Billings's cabin, and the tiny nook where Butterworth slept. He knocked on the door, but nobody answered. As he began to push it open, a heavy voice behind him said, "Oy! Who's that?"

Lenox turned. It was Butterworth himself. "Just the man I was looking for."

"Me?"

"Yes. I have a few questions for you."

"About what?" said Butterworth, his face suspicious.

"About Lieutenant Halifax."

"Oh?"

"I was curious where you were during the middle of the night, when Halifax died."

"I was fast asleep, leastways until Mr. Carrow came down to fetch my master."

"You didn't leave this cabin?"

"Not after supper, no."

"Did Mr. Billings?"

"No! And if you're implying—if you think—"

Lenox waved a hand. "Save your outrage, please. I only wanted to know if one of you might have seen something."

Indignantly, Butterworth said, "Which and if we had, don't you think we would have *told?*"

"Sometimes we may see things without seeing them."

"I don't understand riddles, Mr. Lennots, and I won't answer 'em."

"Tell me this, anyway—on the day of the voyage, did you notice anything peculiar?"

"No," said Butterworth stoutly.

"Nothing?"

"Maybe excepting yourself."

"You're dangerously close to rudeness, Mr. Butterworth."

Butterworth rolled his eyes, and then with a sullen bow of his head, said, "Apology."

McEwan came out into the wardroom, munching on what looked as if it might be the toast Lenox had left uneaten on his plate, and, though it didn't sound very good, whistling through the crumbs.

"Will you give us a moment?" said Lenox to him.

"Oh! Sorry, sir. I was coming to ask permission to polish your toast rack, the one with the letters in it?" Then he added, whispering, "It's silver."

"Yes, go on," said Lenox. "But go!"

"I'm vanished, I'm positively vanished already, sir," said Mc-Ewan, and as proof put a finger up to his crumb-covered lips.

When they were alone again, Butterworth said, "If that will be all—"

"No, it won't. I asked you if you saw anything unusual on the day before Mr. Halifax was murdered. You say you didn't. I ask you to consider again—did you see anyone unusual around Mr. Billings's cabin? Anyone who might have stolen something from your master?"

Butterworth looked uneasy now, and Lenox saw he had struck a nerve. "No," was all the man said, however.

"You did—I can see it on your face. Who was in Lieutenant Billings's cabin?"

"Nobody, sir."

"It's 'sir' now, is it? You must tell me—a man is dead."

"But it doesn't mean anything!" said Butterworth.

"What doesn't?"

The steward looked at Lenox for a long moment and then relented. "The captain. He insisted on looking through all the cabins in the wardroom on his own, the day of the trip."

"The captain did? Is that usual?"

Butterworth shook his head. "No."

"Did he give a reason?"

"He's the captain. He don't need no reason. But he wouldn't have killed Halifax—it's not possible." This came out in a low moan. "Please, though, you mustn't think he did anything! Mr. Billings idolizes him."

"Be calm—I agree with you. It's not possible. You may go, now—thank you."

Lenox had told an outright lie. It was certainly possible that Martin had killed Halifax. First the whisky, and now the plain opportunity to have stolen both Carrow's medallion and Billings's pocketknife. The baffling absence of motive was all that held Lenox back from fully believing that Martin was the murderer.

Soon it was noon, and the daily ritual took place again, Lenox on the gleaming, swabbed, and holystoned quarterdeck to observe it. The midshipman called Pimples, under the supervision of Lee and Martin, took a sighting of the sun.

"Our latitude is thirty-five degrees north, and our longitude is six degrees west," he said.

"You'll see African soil soon, then," Lee answered. "We're close to passing through the strait between Morocco and Spain."

All hands were piped to the midday meal, then, and the naval schedule continued apace.

It was two hours later that this routine was interrupted by the unthinkable.

It was Teddy Lenox who rushed to his uncle's cabin, his face pale and his breath short. "It's happened again!" he said. "Again!"

Lenox's stomach fell. "Another murder?"

"Yes!"

"Who? Was it another lieutenant?"

Teddy could barely speak, but he managed to croak it out. "No," he said, "the captain. Captain Martin is dead."

CHAPTER THIRTY-THREE

There was a tremendous lurch somewhere deep in Lenox's spirit. *I failed*, he thought to himself. *What business did I have trying to play detective again?* The contrapuntal voice that rose in his mind—*Who else was there to do it?*—he smothered quickly.

"Where?"

"In his cabin."

"What does the body—are the wounds the same?"

"I don't know."

"Who found him?"

"Lieutenant Carrow."

"I must go to the body."

Lenox rose, and then, about to leave in a rush, stopped himself and looked his nephew in the eye.

He saw a frightened boy.

"Teddy, you'll be safe, I swear," he said.

"Who's doing this, Uncle Charles?"

"I don't know. But it doesn't mean you're in danger, or that I am."

"I remember when I was at school I used to tell my friends about my uncle, the great detective."

Lenox knew the boy wasn't trying to be hurtful. "Listen, stay here in my cabin, would you? If you like, have one of those biscuits. I'll come back in a few moments."

Obediently, Teddy sat at Lenox's desk.

The member of Parliament, feeling every one of his forty-two years, sprinted in the direction of Martin's cabin. Every face he saw along the way was a study in shock and fear. Halifax's death, terrible though it might have been, belonged to a lesser order of magnitude than Martin's. He had been a captain in Her Majesty's navy, a person of mammoth authority and responsibility, at times of crisis nearer a father than an officer to many of the bluejackets.

In Martin's cabin were four men: Billings, who Lenox realized with a shock must be the acting captain, Carrow, the discoverer of the body, Tradescant, and Martin's ancient, white-haired steward, who was seated on the edge of his dead master's bed, weeping.

And a fifth man was also present, of course, when Lenox arrived. Martin himself. As Lenox had dreaded, the captain's abdomen was butterflied open. The corpse was on its back, and the incisions upon it looked just as those upon Halifax had. It was a horrid, bloody mess. Around the neck he observed a red abrasion, a sign perhaps that Martin, unlike Halifax, had been garroted. His eyes were glassy and depthless. Lenox had to take a deep breath to steady his nerves.

Billings was the first to speak. He was pale, his voice tremulous. "A madman is loose on board our ship," he said.

Lenox drew up to his full height. "You are the captain now, Mr. Billings. You must find the strength to face that."

"Yes."

"You are carrying a representative of Her Majesty's government to foreign soil. That is more important than any . . . any fear you might feel."

"Yes," said Billings. "But, what shall we do?"

"First I must look over the body. Mr. Tradescant?"

"Yes?"

"Your assistants should come with a stretcher, that we may lay out Mr. Martin on the same table we did Mr. Halifax. Will you fetch them, or send someone to?"

"I will," said Carrow.

"No, I'd like a word with you," said Lenox. "Mr. Tradescant?"

"I'm on my way." He paused, looking old and bewildered. "It had been such a good day, too, my one long-term patient awoken."

"Has he? Is he well?"

"Sedated and anxious, very anxious, muttering all manner of things, but beyond danger. Ah, poor Mr. Martin."

They all gazed down at the corpse for a moment, and then Tradescant exhaled, nodded, and left them alone.

"Sir, what is your name?" Lenox said to the old steward, seated on the bed, still crying.

"Four and thirty years I known him," the man said, "since he were no more than a boy and pitched out as a midshipman. He took me off his father's farm when he first hoisted his flag."

"What is your name?"

"Slaton."

"Mr. Slaton, look around you. Do you see anything unusual?"

The old man dried his eyes and scanned the large cabin, his eyes rolling over objects he must have tidied and orderered a thousand times out here upon the waves. "No."

"Was he acting strangely?" Lenox said. "The captain?"

"He weren't happy—the shot rolled, Mr. Halifax kilt—but he weren't acting strange, neither."

"I suppose I must look over his cabin later, at greater leisure," said Lenox. "Thank you."

He was surprised to hear a voice say "No." It was Billings.

"Mr. Billings?"

"As you say, I am the captain of this ship now, and I don't want Mr. Martin's belongings disturbed and rooted through, as if he were a twopenny tramp dead of cold outside St. Paul's Cathedral. He was a great man, and it will be his wife who goes through his things. You may look now, but after we leave here and Slaton cleans the blood"—at this the steward emitted a fresh sob—"we will seal this chamber."

Lenox looked to Carrow for help, but there was approval on the younger lieutenant's face. "Very well," he said. "We must be thorough then."

Tradescant appeared at the door, followed by two stout men with a stretcher. After Lenox had carefully walked around the body, inspecting the hands and the face of the dead captain, he permitted them to lift the corpse onto the stretcher and bear it away toward the surgery. Slaton hurried after them, as if he might still attend to his master's orders even now. Lenox didn't bother stopping the old man.

When they had removed Halifax's body there had been left behind an unbloodied spot on the desk, surrounded by dried blood. The same happened now, though on a rich blue carpet.

Lying in the center of this Martin-shaped emptiness was a small, silvery object.

"Not again," said Billings, his voice still weak. "My watch, no doubt, or perhaps Mr. Carrow's."

Lenox stooped and picked the objects up. "A silver tie chain," he said, letting it run through his fingers. The chain was snapped. "Do you recognize it?"

Both men stepped closer, and then, as if in unison, both nodded. "It's Mitchell's," said Carrow. Billings nodded. "He wears it nearly every day."

Billings said, "Look on the reverse and you'll find his initials."

Lenox looked, and saw that Billings was correct. He sighed. What, now, could this mean? The chain was broken: had Martin broken it in the struggle and dropped it as he died? It would be important to discover, from Tradescant, whether Martin had fought back.

Lenox turned and scanned the room with his eyes again, restless for some clue.

His gaze alighted on a piece of paper that stood in a triangle on Martin's desk.

"What is that?" he said.

"What?" Carrow asked.

"That piece of paper." Lenox strode over and picked it up. His heart went into his throat; there was a finger-smudge of blood on the outside. He showed it to the two officers silently.

Their eyes widened. "Shall I look at it?" said Billings. "As captain?"

"It will say the same thing no matter which of us reads it," said Lenox. "Here, we may all look it over together."

The paper, of very coarse stock—the sort that left one's fingers dark—was folded in half, and on the outside at any rate had no markings other than the blood. Lenox flipped it open and all three men looked on the message within at once.

The Lu is ares. Beware.

There was a long moment of disturbed silence.

"It means 'ours' of course," said Carrow at last.

"And the 'Lu' is what men call the *Lucy*," Billings added.

"Christ," Lenox said. "I suppose the mutiny is serious."

CHAPTER THIRTY-FOUR

I ought to go above deck," said Billings. "We must meet this evening to confirm the news, but until then I must be seen. Mr. Carrow, when Mr. Lenox no longer requires your assistance, please pass out the word to your mess captains that we shall gather upon the stroke of six."

"Yes, Captain," said Carrow.

When these two men were alone in the room, blood not far from them on the carpet, Carrow let out a tremendous exhale. Lenox looked at him inquisitively. "Does something trouble you?"

"Only that it is the worst situation I have ever experienced afloat, and that I fear for our lives every moment."

"Yes."

Carrow sat at Martin's desk, his habitual frown etched on his face, and took a bag of tobacco from his jacket sleeve. "Would you like to fill your pipe?" he asked. "It's the worst, blackest sort of shag—only stuff I smoke."

"No, I thank you."

"I'm amazed you don't need it, to steady yourself."

Lenox paced toward a porthole. "You have found both bodies, Mr. Carrow."

"So I have. The first in the company of your nephew, the second not fifteen feet from the captain's galley, where Mr. Slaton was putting tea together. What of it?"

"Mr. Slaton admitted you?"

"No."

"Then he had no way of knowing how long you had been in here."

To Lenox's surprise, Carrow laughed. "That's true enough, sir. But if you think I killed either of these men, you're a bigger fool than I took you for."

"You understand that everyone on board the *Lucy* is a suspect."

"Yes. But I have the good fortune of knowing, infallibly, that I did not murder Faxxie, nor Captain Martin." He lit his pipe. "My god," he muttered, less constrained than Lenox had ever seen him. "Both of them dead. Think of it. I shudder to imagine the newspapers. The navy scarcely needs the negative exposure."

"Yes."

Carrow puffed on his pipe, and blew the smoke through an open porthole. It was a bright, sparkling day now, light shimmering on the quick water. "The worst of it is the manner of the death. The brutality."

It was this that had occupied Lenox's mind, too. "If mutiny is the motive for these murders, I suppose such brutality sends a message. Yet neither man was bludgeoned, which is the sort of death one sees committed in the heat of anger most often."

"No."

Lenox paused, then spoke. "Who do you think murdered them, Mr. Carrow?"

"I wish I could say."

"Do you know anything more than you've told me?"

"A great deal more, I don't doubt. Sadly, I don't know what it is." He rose. "If you don't need me, the ship is badly short-handed of officers now. I'll go."

"As you wish."

But Carrow didn't move. "Mr. Lenox?"

"Yes?"

"The captain—Captain Billings—wants this room sealed. We should leave."

"Ridiculous. I need ten minutes here."

"I don't expect you to understand naval conduct, sir, but I would ask you to leave."

Unhappily, Lenox followed Carrow out of the room, glancing back once, long enough to see that half-empty bottle of whisky that still stood on Martin's desk. With a pang in his heart he thought of the warm, comradely spirit that he had felt upon the American ship—and felt half a traitor for wishing himself in that atmosphere again, rather than this one.

He went on deck now, to think for a moment before he visited Tradescant in the surgery. He had the quarterdeck to himself. From it he could observe the ship's activity, and it was clear to him word had spread. Men were murmuring to each other as they passed; there was a tension, a tangible anxiety, that had flooded the decks.

It reminded him that he had left Teddy, anxious himself, down below deck, and when he remembered Lenox went down.

Teddy was no longer in the cabin. Lenox flew to the gun room and to his immense relief found the boy there, whispering with his friends.

Pimples stood up and smiled wanly. "Is he really gone?" he asked.

"Yes. I'm afraid he is."

"It's the worst damned thing I've ever heard," Cresswell said with an ardent bark to his voice. "Hanging is too good for the bastard who did it."

"Will you find him, Uncle?" said Teddy.

"We're not far now," said Lenox. "Please excuse me."

They weren't far—and yet he couldn't imagine that they were close, either. Which of these men was capable of it? Billings? Carrow? Mitchell? Lee? Perhaps the surgeon, Tradescant—though Lenox wouldn't believe that—or the bitter purser, Pettegree? One of the stewards, perhaps Butterworth? One of the men, bent on mutiny? A midshipman, even. Anything was possible. Which was what made it such a hopeless muddle.

Yet he felt his brain closing in on the answer. If he could just take his eye off of the question, it would come to him. He had answered Teddy honestly. It wasn't far now, the answer to the question of who was responsible for these fearful killings.

The surgery, often one of the dimmest parts of the ship, was brilliant now with a half-dozen hanging lanterns. Lenox saw their light before he turned into the room and saw Martin's corpse, laid out on the table where Halifax's had been.

"Mr. Lenox," said the surgeon coolly, looking to the doorway, "please, come in."

"Thank you, Mr. Tradescant. What have you found?"

"Nothing, yet, I'm afraid. Or rather, I have discovered the means of death, but there was no great mystery to that, sadly."

"Not the same as the last?"

"No. Halifax was stabbed with a penknife, but the captain has been throttled with a thin string, and then sliced open from navel to sternum, and the skin pulled back to reveal a rough rectangle."

"Have you looked for . . . souvenirs?" This word Lenox said with a grimace.

"Among the organs, none, and I have looked very thoroughly."

"As a very great favor to me, might you look once more?"

"Of course."

The body was scrubbed of blood and looked as clean as it

conceivably could, under the circumstances. "Is there anything else? Any odor?"

"As before, an odor of whisky is on the belly."

"Have you looked at his hands? Did he fight?"

Tradescant turned over the hand closest to him and motioned for his assistant to turn the other, so that the palms were faced down toward the table. He leaned over and examined them with a magnifying glass that hung from a gold chain on his neck. But it was an unnecessarily methodical act; Lenox could see with his naked eyes that only old scars were on the back of the captain's hands.

"These white lines are not new, of course," said Tradescant, still leaned over. "I see nothing under the fingernails. No, I don't think he fought."

"It was a surprise again, then," said Lenox, and felt his brain quickening. "And someone he would have admitted to his cabin, in all likelihood, without scruple—an officer."

"A bluejacket might have entered without Captain Martin raising his fists."

"Or his voice? I heard no report of shouting from Mr. Slaton."

The steward, in the corner, shook his old head. "No shouting."

"Call it inconclusive, but leading," said Lenox. "Like everything else in this damnable business."

"A captain murdered on his own vessel," said Tradescant, shaking his head. "It's hard to know what to believe in."

"And mutiny in the bargain," said Lenox.

"Spare my heart and keep that word quiet, Mr. Lenox," said the surgeon, and with careful fingers shut Jacob Martin's eyes forever.

CHAPTER THIRTY-FIVE

A mood of claustrophobia grew now. Men eyed each other as they passed on deck; officers began to snap out their orders more sharply.

The ship would reach Egypt in three or perhaps four days and when she did, no doubt some pressure valve would release, and the tension of this cursed voyage would dissipate. In the meantime they were in open water with a murderer, and possibly with a mutinous gang of sailors.

"The Lu is ares. Beware." That was what the note had said. Lenox wondered whether it was genuine. "Or it might be a red herring," he whispered as he walked the quarterdeck again. His mind flitted to the term's hunting origins, the kennel master at Lenox House training the hounds with pieces of red herring, trying to throw them off the scent.

After all, why would a mutiny declare itself in that way? And the misspelling of the word *ours*—mightn't it be a bit convenient, a bit too directly proletarian?

Weighed against that, however, were the murders, the rolled shot, the guardedness in the eyes of the men on the main deck. Martin had restored the ship's morale when he gave out a double ration of grog and announced the game of Follow the Leader, but it took only one madman, maybe two, to persuade half the sailors on board that a mutiny might be just and proper.

Lenox paced the quarterdeck for a long time, until at last McEwan came to fetch him for some food. He choked down a sandwich of butter and ham, and then made a list for his own benefit of all the case's permutations and potentialities. This took an hour or more, and left him both hopeless and somewhere, in the back of his mind, still convinced that comprehension was close.

At six, the men of the *Lucy* gathered again, and Billings, now the acting captain, watched them assemble.

Pettegree stood next to Lenox on the quarterdeck. He was pale. "What a dreadful day for the navy," he said. "Unthinkable."

"The murder? The mutiny?"

"Both. And poor Mr. Billings—the first to admit he's not ready to be a captain. Halifax would have been better fit to handle her, I think. So Martin thought, too."

"When the men are restless, do you worry for your stores?"

"I do—and my neck, more importantly. Nobody likes a purser. Everyone suspects the purser and the purser's mate are shorting him on beer or grog or beef or pease or any sort of thing. Rope."

"I would never have thought them capable of mutiny."

"And yet here we are. Lord, to have Martin back for three days, to bring us through this—I would offer a king's ransom."

And indeed, Billings looked flushed and anxious when he spoke. But he spoke handsomely.

"As you all now know, your captain, Captain Martin, is

dead. Murdered, by the same cowardly scoundrel who slew Mr. Halifax."

A loud chatter broke out, most of it, or so it seemed to Lenox, sounding of outrage.

"There will be time for a eulogy, but I will say now one thing: Jacob Martin was the soul of the navy, the reason she is the greatest fighting force in mankind's history. He was committed, adventurous, and courageous. A leader of men. His death should have been at battle, or long after his hair had grown white and he had given up the sea. His death was unworthy of his life. Though I shall be your captain, temporarily, no man could step into Captain Martin's place—not Nelson himself—and command the *Lucy* as well as he did, so that she was the finest ship in Her Majesty's navy."

There was a ragged cheer.

"And so I vow that whoever did this shall answer to me— shall answer to all of us—and shall be separated from his head, and that right quick."

There was a louder, more committed cheer now, and Billings shook hands with all the officers, accepting their solemn congratulations on his words.

Lieutenant Lee, Lenox noticed, was the exception.

Back in his cabin, Lenox sent McEwan for Teddy Lenox in the gun room. The lad showed up in what looked like a hastily donned uniform.

"Yes, Uncle Charles? I'm on duty in the first watch," he said, "and must be on deck well before according to Mr. Mitchell."

"Why?"

"Morale."

"I see. Teddy, I want you to be safe. Could you keep this in the small pocket in your sleeve, perhaps?"

Lenox produced a small, stout knife with an ebony handle and a sharp blade.

"Won't I cut myself?"

"No—it has a corked tip, look. Try to stay among other people, and decline any invitations to have conference alone with anyone."

"Even Cresswell, or Pimples?"

"Even them, I'm afraid. You must exercise great caution until we discover the murderer. Your father would never forgive me if I let anything befall you."

"Yes, Uncle Charles."

Lenox took his supper in his cabin that evening, alone. There was a gathering in the wardroom but he wanted no part of it, preferring to be alone with his thoughts. He pored over the list he had written out and tried to find the way in, the door the murderer had left cracked rather than locking. But it was futile. He wrote a letter to Jane, added it to the pile sitting in his toast rack, and fell into an unhappy sleep.

The next morning was cruelly beautiful, the sun-dappled water clear and calm, the wind light but steady enough to push the ship along at a fair three or four knots.

He went to see Billings, the acting captain, who was sitting in his own old cabin, with Butterworth's hammock slung up before the door.

"Have you not thought to move into the captain's cabin?" said Lenox.

"It would be ill-mannered and impudent, I think."

"Yet you must assume Mr. Martin's authority."

"I find myself exceedingly harried by responsibility, in fact, Mr. Lenox. May we come to the point?"

"I wonder if you would reconsider letting me look at the cabin under discussion."

"The captain's? I'm afraid I must say no, still."

"I find it most peculiar, though you and Carrow be in concert on the subject. What must come first, the dignity of this room or the safety of your men?"

"I shall look after the safety of my men, thank you."

"I fear it won't be as easy as that."

"What would you hope to find in the cabin?"

"Anything. A note, a weapon. A clue."

Billings leaned back in his chair and sighed. "I suppose it would be all right, then," he said. "If you consent to let Slaton do the job with you, that he might preserve Captain Martin's things as they have been, for Mrs. Martin."

"Thank you," said Lenox. "It's the wisest course."

"Here, take my note to Slaton." Billings scrawled something on a piece of paper, tore it away, and handed it to Lenox. "And please, keep me apprised of your discovery just as you did Mr. Martin."

"I will, thank you."

"We'll get you to Egypt after all, I hope, Mr. Lenox. It won't be more than another few days."

"I look forward to setting foot on land again. I have grown accustomed to the *Lucy*, but these murders would make the most wonderful ship in the world feel confined."

"Imagine my position: I have attained the object of my life's ambition, my own ship, and these are the circumstances. Still, we must do the work that God puts before us, Mr. Lenox."

"I'll let you know what I find in the cabin."

CHAPTER THIRTY-SIX

One of the most remarkable things Lenox had discovered about life at sea was the near total credulity of the lower deck. On his way to the surgery several days before Lenox had passed by one of the messes, where a short, fattish fellow was barbering his fellow sailors, and telling them with utter certainty that a mermaid had stowed away on board. All of the other men nodded solemnly and said they had heard of similar things on other ships. During the game of Follow the Leader one man had averred with complete confidence in Lenox's hearing that McEwan had royal blood, to which they attributed his unusual grace.

He sought out Evers now in order to discover what tale the man believed of Butterworth, and how he had heard it. Lenox found the man in his mess, face still stern but attitude slightly gentler than it had been before their rendezvous in the crow's nest.

"Mr. Lenox," he said. "Haven't seen you aloft, sir."

"The once was enough."

"The more you go up the less you can do without it, sir."

"Would that I were an albatross, as you think, that I might fly up there without the assistance of ropes or rigging."

Evers roared with laughter. "No, no," he said. "You're no albatross."

"I came to thank you for the drawing you sent me. And the note on the back."

"For the drawing you're very welcome—but what note can you mean?"

"The one you wrote on the back. About Butterworth."

"I didn't write any such thing."

"Are you sure?"

"If I weren't, sir, I could confirm it to myself by telling you that I can't read nor write. Very few of us can, Mr. Lenox."

"I see. Thank you, then, for the drawing alone. You sent that to my cabin?"

"Along with McEwan, yes."

"Thank you."

Somebody must have nipped into his cabin, then, and written on the back. More sneaking around the wardroom.

Then there was the widespread illiteracy of the sailors, which was news to Lenox. "The Lu is ares. Beware." What were the chances a small group of sailors had a man among them to write? Perhaps that was why unwritten forms of mutiny—rolling shot— were more popular.

It was all quite strange.

He made his way now to the captain's cabin. The door to it was open, and within Slaton was scrubbing at the royal blue carpet, attempting to remove the red stain from it. He looked a frail figure, and Lenox knelt down to assist him.

"No, no, I can do it!" cried Slaton, breathless.

"Please, take a moment of rest, then. Would you like a cup of tea? Or there's whisky on the desk."

"The whisky is Captain Martin's."

"I feel sure he would want you to have a glass—here, I shall pour it."

"Well then, I thank you," and Slaton, exhaustion etched on his features, sat down heavily in an armchair near the cabin's broad bow window.

Lenox poured the glass and brought it to the steward. "I have a note here, from Lieutenant Billings—or Captain Billings, I should say. He has granted me permission to look through the cabin."

Lenox held out the note. He had expected a fight, but Slaton merely glanced at it and nodded. "Very well."

"You have read it?"

"I cannot read, sir, but I can see Mr. Billings's mark."

There was a moment of silence as Slaton sipped at the whisky. "May I ask," said Lenox at length, "did Captain Martin regularly drink whisky?"

"Not above once or twice a year."

"Do you know why he had it out now?"

"No."

"Can you think of a reason why he might have?"

Slaton looked up at the ceiling, brow furrowed. "He sometimes asked for it, to celebrate, like, a victory in battle or a promotion. Or when one of Her Majesty's ships was lost, he would take it out for a drink."

"How often?"

"Once every year, or two years, perhaps, sir," said Slaton. "I can't think why he had it now."

"Was anyone promoted recently?"

"Mr. Carrow, I suppose, after Mr. Halifax died."

"Hardly a cause for celebration."

"No, sir."

"Do you know how long it has been on Captain Martin's desk?"

"Now that you mention it, I recall seeing it, full up like, on the first day of the voyage, sitting there."

"I see." What to make of any of that? It didn't click any idea into place; merely another fact to add to the tally. "If you don't mind, then, I will look through this cabin, Mr. Slaton. Perhaps you might rest."

Again Lenox had expected a fight, but Slaton simply nodded, drank off the last of the whisky, and stumbled away, looking for all the world a defeated man.

The cabin smelled strongly of soap, and the scrubbing brush was still sitting on the floor in a small mountain range of studs. Otherwise, however, it looked much as if Captain Martin might step in from the noon sighting at any moment. There was a bookcase, full of battered leather volumes—looking closer Lenox saw that they mostly had naval titles—a desk, which was relatively uncluttered, and that was dominated by the great leather captain's log, a washstand, and a bed, narrow and freshly made. Other than these standard items the cabin had a wide bow window that followed the curve of the ship, with a ledge that would have been at about shoulder height if one sat in one of the armchairs by it. On this ledge was an empty teacup, a silver spoon cradled under it on the saucer, and a book opened facedown, to save the reader's place. A sad final reminder of the interruption of Martin's life.

Lenox started here. He examined the teacup and smelled it for anything strange, without result, and then looked at the book. Perhaps unsurprisingly it was the Book of Common Prayer, bound in red and inscribed on the flyleaf by Martin's wife, Emily, "for comfort at sea." Lenox felt a pang when he read this. Two deaths. The second he might have prevented, and thereby given the world forty further years of service from a good man.

After replacing the book and teacup in their previous positions, he began his customary scan of the room. He started in the back right corner and surveyed it in five-foot-wide segments from floor to ceiling, looking for anything strange. When he reached the bookcase he stooped down and looked beneath, but found only a fallen bit of India rubber.

The contents of the bookcase itself were interesting, but ultimately not helpful. There were a great many books from India, apparently given Martin on his recent voyage to that nation. There were also books of knots, of seamanship, of celestial navigation, all the manuals of which one would expect a captain to be in possession. He turned the books upside down and shook, but none offered any loose paper, and when he glanced through their pages they were all unblemished by handwriting.

He shook the bedclothes loose, but found nothing within them, nor under the thin, heavy mattress Martin had slept on. The desk and bookcase alike held a series of small items he glanced at in turn: a pewter bowl full of seaglass, a fat Bible no longer or wider than Lenox's index finger, with Martin's name on the inside flap, dated ten years before, a marble inkstand and pen, the bottle of whisky, an etching of a pretty, lively looking young woman, perhaps Martin's wife or sister. None of it, save the whisky, indicative.

In all the search took not more than twenty minutes. He looked above the door and beneath the bed, and through the dreary items of Martin's washstand, his soap, his razor. Lenox reminded himself to examine Martin's private dining room and the small galley beside it, as well as the wardrobe outside the door.

But first he turned, rather despairingly, to the captain's log.

CHAPTER THIRTY-SEVEN

It dated back two years, with a red silk marker between the pages that recorded the two distinct voyages the *Lucy* had taken in that time, first to India, now to Egypt. He decided to read entries about the newer journey first, the entries of the last fortnight.

First, however, he flipped through all the pages of the book, to get a sense of its manner. Captain Martin's style, if it ought even to be permitted such a name, was laconic in the extreme. Entry after entry after entry reported simply the date, the latitude, longitude, barometer reading, and so forth, and perhaps two or three words on the conditions, "Squally," for example, or "All clear," or "Exceptionally stiff wind."

Every seven to ten days Martin might write a slightly longer entry. These could be on nearly any subject, though most often they concerned discipline and sightings of other ships. For instance:

Able Seaman Danvers given six strokes for theft and six
strokes for insubordination. Weather clear.

Or there was an entry that was typical of many others,
which read:

Blackwall Frigate Northfleet sighted, flagged, and met.
Exchange of news with Captain Knowles of that ship, bound
for Portsmouth with a cargo of silk. Lunch aboard the Lucy
for the officers of both ships.

This one caught Lenox's notice because of the frigate in question. At the time of Martin's mention it had been another anonymous trade ship going between India, China, and England—the
Blackwall Frigate being a class of ship that had replaced the more
cumbersome Indiaman that had dominated the seas earlier in
the century—but which was now famous throughout the British
Isles. That winter, not many months before, the *Northfleet* had
been in the English Channel when she was forced to drop anchor in bad weather. Almost immediately a Spanish steamer had
run her down, quite by accident, with the loss to the *Northfleet* of
three hundred and twenty men, women, and children. This
Captain Knowles, whom Martin had met in happier times, had
gone down with his ship.

Still Lenox only skimmed these entries, turning before too
long to the pages concerning the ship's present voyage.

Unsurprisingly, perhaps, these were more elaborate. On the
second day, for instance, Martin had recorded the ship's position and condition and then written at length about Halifax's
murder. The last line of the entry was:

Have asked the Honourable Mr. Charles Lenox, formerly a
private detective, to investigate the murder. Hopeful of bringing
this matter to a swift and decisive conclusion.

Subsequently Martin had recorded with dogged precision the hints of a mutiny through which the *Lucy* had suffered, as well as the reports Lenox and Tradescant had given him.

For all this thoroughness, no detail leapt out from the page and grabbed Lenox's attention. He read all of the entries twice, and then, with a great sigh, went back to the front of the book to begin reading about the ship's previous history.

He could pass by whole pages at a glance, because they offered nothing except the noon readings Martin and his first lieutenant, along with the midshipmen, had taken each day. Gradually, however, an accumulation of small details began to present a more complete picture. Both Billings and Lee were repeatedly chastised for mistakes of seamanship or discipline with the men, while, to Lenox's surprise, Mitchell's name almost never appeared. Halifax, it was obvious, had too gentle a hand with the men. Then there were entries that piqued his interest, like this:

Much dismay and disagreement in the wardroom over a game of whist whose stakes and winners have gotten badly confused, such that no man of four can agree with any other about the sums owed to each, etc. Have had a firm word with Billings and Carrow about gambling.

Or there was this one:

Carrow far too violent in his discipline of Forecastleman Bacon.

And then this, several days later:

Forecastleman Bacon given six lashes for insubordination.

Every week church was rigged, storms were survived, men were disciplined, grog and salt beef were disbursed, other ships were met along the water and left behind; there was an almost gentle rhythm to it on the page.

Several men died. There was Topman Starbuck, for example, *killed after falling from the foremast*, whose death Lenox contemplated with a grimace. During a storm one seaman named Sugar had taken a heavy splinter, *longer than nine inches*, in his thigh. *Tradescant having been taken ill, Mr. Billings inspected the wound and recommended amputation.* It hadn't been necessary, however; by the next morning Sugar was gone. Then there was the *rope maker, shoemaker, tinsmith, caulker, painter, and trimmer, Elias, drowned in the bilge, signs of a struggle; Mr. Billings, Mr. Carrow, and Mr. Halifax investigating.* There was no further mention of Elias, however. Whatever man had held him down in the water was likely still aboard the ship.

Might any of these cryptic mortalities have anything to do with the fresher deaths the *Lucy* had suffered? It was impossible to say.

Men survived, too, however. A month later, Martin wrote:

Seaman Wiltshire fell overboard, and, unable to swim, called for help. Sank several times in succession, before at the last possible moment being gaffed through his frock. Upon his recovery on deck, Seaman Wiltshire evinced not the smallest degree of perplexity at the prospect of death, nor any particular exhilaration at his survival. He returned to his place on the spar without any display, in even the slightest degree, of gratitude toward his saviors.

That one made Lenox laugh.

The longest entry in the book recounted a meeting the ship had with pirates, in which she lost four men but won a valuable prize-ship and a great deal of stolen cargo. *Of particular valor were Lieutenants Billings, Carrow, and Mitchell,* the log recorded, *as well as Midshipman Cresswell.* Lenox smiled to himself. Evidently Halifax was more of a fisherman than a soldier.

In India they took on a young midshipman, Mercer, and his saga absorbed Lenox greatly:

Mr. Midshipman Mercer fell ill during watch, and was permitted to go below deck. This morning Mr. Tradescant ruled out seasickness as a potential cause of the illness, but expressed no great anxiety over the boy.

Then, the next day:

Mr. Midshipman Mercer significantly worse, diarrheal and emetic.

Then:

Mr. Midshipman Mercer very close to death, according to Mr. Tradescant. Only human comfort as possible treatment.

Finally, two days later, Lenox read with great joy:

Mr. Midshipman Mercer all but recovered, and, though pale, has taken the air of the quarterdeck. Mr. Tradescant at a loss to explain the recovery.

There was good news! Only after living and dying with the lad in the pages, however, did the truth click into place, and Lenox remembered, slapping his knee at his own stupidity, that Mercer was the proper name of the lad Teddy had introduced him to as Pimples. The poor chap, to have been through that!

Lenox read over all of this carefully, pausing and reading twice wherever he found an entry that he thought might merit attention. When at last he stood up and closed the book the sun was turning orange, occasionally throwing a brilliant flood of light through the bow windows and across Martin's cabin, so that Lenox had to squint. Had he learned anything? Perhaps he had, and perhaps not. The answer must be close, he felt, with a trace of desperation.

Or were his skills rusted and beyond repair, like the *Northfleet* all these months after she had fallen at the bottom of the English Channel? Would more and more people die, because he wasn't sharp enough to see who was killing them? As he had been reading he had grown to like Martin's style; a human hand had written those words, one which would write no more.

CHAPTER THIRTY-EIGHT

He went on deck for a breath of fresh air now, his mind still worrying the same few details. When he reached the quarterdeck he was pleased to see that above, on the poop deck, Lieutenant Lee was pointing toward the sails and talking animatedly with Teddy Lenox. The boy was looking grave and nodding. It was what he needed, thought Lenox, to learn his craft, to take his mind away from Martin and Halifax.

Then he ventured slightly closer, preparing to join the conversation. But as his foot was on the first step the wind died, and he heard Lee's drawl very clearly. The lieutenant said, "I swear her legs must have been taller than you, too, the vixenish little morsel."

"Goodness," said Teddy, his voice rich with trust and interest.

Hastily Lenox stepped back toward the railing. Well, there were all sorts of education, he supposed. Better to leave Teddy alone. If the gun room didn't corrupt the lad, surely Lee wouldn't. And then, they had talked of women, of maids and ladies, when he was a boy at school.

After he had taken several turns on the quarterdeck and filled his lungs with the fresh, saline air, Lenox went down to his cabin. McEwan was seated on his stool, munching on something loud, and polishing Lenox's brown boots with intense concentration.

"Oh, sir," he said, rising, crumbs flying from his mouth.

"Charming," said Lenox.

McEwan smiled. "Sorry, sir."

"Not at all. Could you find me something to eat? A sandwich would do."

"Of course, Mr. Lenox."

"And then I shall need several hours undisturbed."

"Yes, sir. I shall leave your boots till then."

Lenox had decided that he would decode the *Alpha* document that he had received from Edmund on the docks in Plymouth. If he left the case for an hour or two he might find it looked different upon his return.

As he reached for the document, which lay on his desk, Lenox brushed a letter onto the floor. Picking it up he saw that it was one Jane had sent with him, a sweet, short, and loving note. He unfolded it and read it over again, and felt his heart become very full. The air of menace on the *Lucy* hadn't affected him enormously—he was used to it, from his days as a detective—but reading the letter he thought of all he had to live for, his wife, his child, the house on Hampden Lane, the two dogs Jane had given him three years before, Bear and Rabbit, one golden, one black. A domestic life. With a flash of insight he saw that while he thought he had been giving up the drama and danger of detection for his seat in Parliament, perhaps in fact it had been his love, his soon-to-be family, for which he had sacrificed his old life. The thought made him feel homesick.

There was a knock on the door, and McEwan squeezed in with a plate full of roast beef sandwiches with a dollop of Fortnum's horseradish, courtesy of Jane's hamper, and a great pile of cold roasted potatoes, sea salted and studded with twigs of sage and rosemary.

"Do you want a fork for the potatoes, sir?" McEwan asked.

"No, I can eat them with my fingers if you fetch me a napkin. Many a time in my bachelor days I ate worse with my hands."

"Very good, sir."

"I'll take some ketchup, too, from the small white pot. Dickens recommends it with breaded lamb chops, you know, but I prefer it on roasted potatoes."

"Right away, Mr. Lenox. Any wine?"

"A half bottle of the Burgundy—why not?"

He ate happily, and with great care not to spill on the papers began to decipher the list of his official duties in Egypt.

These were both relatively straightforward and, in the customs they involved, inordinately complex. For example, on his first day in the country he was scheduled to take a tour of the Suez Canal. Simple enough, and yet the list of things he could not mention—the slave deaths during its construction, the new and crippling taxes levied on every poor soul in the country, even the word "Ethiopia," for Egypt was engaged in a futile war there—was daunting. The financial situation was so bad that the current Parliament had debated long and hard sending an envoy to the country to inquire into the state of affairs, and many held the opinion that national bankruptcy was inevitable.

The great sultan, whom Lenox would meet once, was called Ismail the Magnificent, and he too was a compromised figure: He lived in unimaginable opulence, and in many ways had made Egypt the most advanced country outside of Europe, and yet his vast public expenditures had made him profoundly reliant on help from France and England, among other countries.

As he read through his instructions, Lenox rather began to wish he had brought a secretary after all. By rights he might have had two, as many men in government did when they traveled, but he had known the *Lucy* to be a small ship, and besides that hadn't wanted to pull his own closest confidant and personal secretary, his former butler Graham, away from London. With good reason, he thought. There was a story Lenox had heard as a boy of the great orator Cicero leaving Rome to administer a colony for several years; when he returned he walked into the Senate and said to the first man he met, "I'm back!" To which the man replied, "Where did you go?" Lenox was out of sight, but Graham might keep him in the minds of the men in Parliament.

If he couldn't have Graham, he decided, he didn't need anyone. The ship would provide a steward. Now, though, faced with this forbidding list of duties, he regretted the decision. Hopefully the English consular staff in Port Said would be competent.

He was reading about one of his final appointments several hours later. Apparently the wali prided himself on his commitment to the scientific methods of Western Europe.

It was then, with the murders far, far from his mind, that the pieces jumbled together once more and fell into their places, as neatly as pegs into holes.

He thought he knew who had killed Halifax and Martin. He stood up.

"McEwan!" he called out excitedly. "Find me Captain Billings!"

"Right away, sir," called out the steward.

Lenox left his cabin and strode toward the hatchway that would take him on deck, hoping he might find Billings sooner than McEwan, and arrange a meeting of the officers. It would take a bit of stagecraft, to be sure. He needed a few hours to plan it. Maybe longer; better make it tomorrow, perhaps, in the forenoon.

McEwan bumped into him coming down the hatchway. "He is working, he says, sir, but will attend you in fifteen minutes in the captain's dining room."

"Excellent. Listen, I may want to go to the crow's nest again. Could you accompany me there, in half an hour, say, after I meet Billings? I trust you more than Andersen."

"Oh, with great pleasure. Will that be all?"

"Yes," said Lenox, suddenly distracted.

"Sir? Are you all right?"

"Fine, fine. Meet me on deck then."

"Yes, sir."

There was one snag that Lenox could see, something from the captain's log. Before he looked into that, though, he took the silence of the wardroom to steal into an officer's cabin.

There he found what he had needed. Verification.

Then, all action, he went to the gun room. Only Pimples was there. (Lenox noticed a faint sallowness to the boy's face that he had not perceived before. A remnant of his illness, perhaps.)

"Do you know where Teddy is?" he asked.

"He should be back any moment."

Indeed, he opened the door to the gun room, his face full of excitement—perhaps to relate Lee's story to Pimples—not a few seconds later.

"Oh! Uncle!"

"Teddy, may I have a private word?"

"Here, you may be alone," said Pimples. "I need to be on deck anyhow."

"Thank you."

When they were alone, Lenox sat down. "Teddy, you told me that on your first night aboard the *Lucy* you were badly ill. Isn't that so?"

Teddy's eyes were hooded with caution. "Yes, I suppose. Why?"

"You must answer me truthfully: Did Mr. Carrow send you below deck to sleep it off?"

"No," said Teddy stoutly.

But his face told a different story. "You never saw Halifax's body, did you? I read in the captain's log that a sick midshipman on his first night was sent below. On a different voyage."

"I never went down!"

"Teddy. It's I, your uncle. Think of your father."

The internal struggle played out on the midshipman's face, but before long he relented. "Well, fine. But Mr. Carrow made me promise not to tell! Said he'd been ill, too, and I could tuck down in the hallway, so the other mids wouldn't laugh at me."

"Mr. Carrow said that?"

"You won't tell, Uncle Charles?"

"Thank you for being honest. I must leave you now."

So. A new fact. He could use it. He left the gun room and went off to meet Billings, his mind racing, adding bits and pieces of what he had seen in the last week—but not truly seen, at the time—all of which confirmed his suspicions.

CHAPTER THIRTY-NINE

Billings was in the captain's dining room when the detective arrived, cutting an apple with a sharp silver knife. Not his penknife, Lenox noted, and didn't blame the switch; it would have been too gruesome.

"Mr. Lenox, I hope that the urgency of Mr. McEwan's request means that you have discovered who murdered our captain?"

"I think I have."

Relief flooded Billings's face. "Oh, thank the Lord. The strain and tension of it—you can't imagine, Mr. Lenox—my first ship. Thank the Lord . . . who did it?"

"If we are to catch him out, it will take tremendous craft on our parts, Mr. Billings. I don't want you flying off half-cocked and confronting him on your own. I suggest we congregate tomorrow morning at ten o'clock. Then you will know."

"Mr. Lenox, I demand that you tell me who killed my captain."

"I cannot, yet, Mr. Billings. I apologize. I fear you would attack him, or arrest him. Please, trust me. We will get a confession from him, I promise you."

"You are aboard my ship, Mr. Lenox. You have my absolute word that I will not confront this . . . this fiend, though I should long to do so. But you must tell me."

Lenox relented. "Very well, then. I will tell you that I have learned in the last ten minutes Mr. Carrow was alone with both corpses—"

"Carrow! I cannot believe it. I cannot."

"The story runs much deeper than him, Mr. Billings. Can you trust me until the morning?"

Now it was Billings's turn to relent. "As you wish, then," he said. "I'll tell everyone at eight bells."

"Excellent. Now, I must be off to the crow's nest."

"I'll send someone with you," said Billings, but his heart wasn't in it. His eyes were cast on the floor, searching for an answer that wouldn't appear there, and he muttered to himself, "Carrow? Carrow of the *Lucy*?"

"No need. I have McEwan. Until supper, Mr. Billings."

He went up to the deck as quickly as he could, and found McEwan waiting for him there, a thermos tied to his belt by a heavy piece of rope.

"Mr. Lenox!" he called out.

"Mr. McEwan. Well, if 'twere done, 'twere well if 'twere done quickly."

"Sir?"

"Let's go up."

He had thought that knowing the way up, its arduousness and its perils, would make the journey easier. In fact he couldn't stop thinking about the remote view of the deck from the crow's nest, and how little he wished to share the fate of the pitiable Topman Starbuck, who had fallen to his death from a similar height—and he more experienced by a lifetime of days than Lenox at this sort of venture.

Still, Lenox had his rope, and he had the unbelievably nimble McEwan. There seemed to be two of him among the rigging, one clearing debris out of the way such that it wouldn't block Lenox's path, one hovering nearby or beneath him, offering quiet, excellent advice and even, very respectfully, moral support. This was a man in his element. Or would have been, had there been a larder halfway up to the nest.

Forty feet from the top he stopped, his muscles quivering in his arms and legs. A beautiful pink sun was in the middle of its descent. That meant there were twenty or thirty minutes before dark. Better conclude his business quickly, or he would have to spend the night up here. Anything was preferable to the idea of a dismount in the darkness of night. He started up again.

"Mr. Evers!" he called out when he was close. "A hand up through the hole?"

A face, seemingly unconnected to any body, popped through the hole. "Mr. Lenox? Can that be you?"

"It's I."

"Come to sketch with me?"

"Ha, ha," said Lenox weakly, and took Evers's proffered hand, and shortly McEwan's as well. "No, I came here looking for conversation with you."

He had observed Evers during the past few days, and knew that this was the hour when he climbed to the crow's nest for solitude. And this was a conversation that demanded they be alone, something that was never easy on a ship of several hundred souls.

"How can I help you?" asked Evers.

"There are two things you may do for me, my dear man. First, I would ask of you another drawing. This one for my wife, Jane, whom I would wish to see what I saw here. Any price you think reasonable—"

Evers, blushing, his face angry, said, "No, no, no payment necessary. I'll leave it off with McEwan."

McEwan smiled gently, and Lenox recalled that the two men, so superficially dissimilar, were friends. "Hey now, go on, Johnny, take a payment. A couple shillings, Mr. Lenox?"

"I would have thought at least a crown or two. Call it two crowns?"

"For a drawing?" said Evers doubtfully.

"For a drawing."

"A fool and his money are soon parted, I suppose."

"Oy! Have some respect!" said McEwan, a drop of genuine anger in his voice.

"'Pologies, 'pologies, 'pologies. Yer can have it for a crown, Mr. Lenox—there, I bargained you down, how do you like that?"

"Very well—a prime sort of transaction."

"What was the other thing you wanted to ask of me?" said Evers.

"Ah. Now that . . . that is trickier by far, I'm afraid . . ."

Fifteen minutes later Lenox began the descent, well pleased with the conversation, and having even given himself a moment to stand in the crow's nest and admire the Mediterranean. He found that they were within sight of land—"Oh, have been for days," McEwan said offhandedly—which meant that he was gazing upon Africa for the first time.

Once, before Jane, really, travel had been a great preoccupation and passion of his, and he had spent hours with mapmakers and travel booksellers, had read of the great Arabian and African and Arctic adventures. Now those wintering roots stirred, life shooting up through them. To be in Africa! The savannahs, sparsely dotted with trees, the great game—lions, zebras, elephants—and of course the natives, so mysterious to him, frightening if he were honest with himself. Were they truly savage?

It was easy, he had always felt, for an Englishman, dotted at the center of a great empire, with London as a heart pumping blood out to the most distant veins, to feel that he too was the center of the empire. Of the world. But it was state of mind that Lenox deplored in his own class; he was happy to hunt fox at Lenox House, and drink tea, and watch the local blacksmith bowl cricket. But he never presumed that these things were all the world could offer, or that they were right. He had very little time for the red-faced squires, convinced of French beastliness and Victoria's place at God's right hand, who did? Unfortunately they populated the benches of Parliament.

With McEwan's encouragement and aid, Lenox made it down the rigging and to deck with only seven or eight moments of utter terror, which was an improvement on his previous rate.

"Thank you, my dear man," he said when they had successfully gained the deck.

"Not at all, not at all," said McEwan, who was rather irritatingly breathing as gently as if he had been out for a spring stroll. "You must be next door to famished though, I reckon. Sir."

"At the moment I would prefer a glass of brandy to a piece of mutton."

McEwan clicked his tongue. "Oh, I'll never understand that, not ever. But here we are, come along."

And so Lenox retired to his cabin, to think over the next morning's assembly.

CHAPTER FORTY

The ship's low morale, its air of suspicion, was still present when Lenox walked the quarterdeck at eight o'clock the next morning. He wondered how the discovery of the murderer would alter that mood. It would come as a shock to the men, he imagined.

He ate a breakfast of mushrooms and eggs, fried together in one of the many scruffy cast-iron pans that McEwan hung on nails near his hammock; he feared that the cook would steal them if they were left in the galley, and swore that their heavy bottoms made food taste better. After Lenox had eaten this breakfast he took, for fortification, a small glass of wine, savoring it as he looked through his porthole. He thought of home.

When it was nearly ten o'clock he had a quick word with McEwan, sent the steward to do a small task, and then went to the wardroom. Soon all the men who ate there every night were gathered around. There was Billings, of course; the grim Carrow; Mitchell, with his temper; Lee, with his drawl; Rogers, the drunken chaplain, a figure of affectionate fun among the bluejackets; quiet Tradescant, Quirke, and Pettegree, who always stood rather apart. Alastair Cresswell had been temporarily elevated to the post of fourth lieutenant, but he was on deck, strutting around and giving his old gun roommates orders. At any rate Lenox had no need of him.

"Gentleman, welcome," he said.

"Who did it?" asked Mitchell without preamble.

"We must go more slowly than that."

"Puffery and showmanship," Mitchell muttered.

"Good lord," said Carrow, "some respect for Her Majesty's representative."

"You will speak with deference, Mr. Mitchell," Billings added.

"Thank you, Mr. Carrow. Mr. Billings. We do need to move slowly, Mr. Mitchell, not to indulge my rather poor sense of showmanship, but because there is a long story to be told."

"Well?" said Mitchell.

"First I wonder whether you would be so kind as to permit me to look outside of the doors. I have no wish to be overheard, even by your stewards." Lenox rose and checked the doors. Nobody lurked behind any of them, though Lee's man was cleaning his cabin.

"Here, follow me into the wardroom. Would you mind stepping up on deck for the half part of an hour or so?" said Lenox.

The steward looked at Lee. "Go on, do it," said the lieutenant, and the man went.

Lenox sat again. "I confess that after Halifax died I suspected all of you, at one time or another. Mr. Tradescant, you have a surgeon's hands; it crossed my mind that you might share the same predilections as some of your less honorable brethren. Please accept my apology."

"Of course," said Tradescant.

"Mr. Mitchell, your anger marked you out. Mr. Billings, your penknife killed Halifax. Mr. Quirke, red hair has been known to indicate a fiery temperament. To all of you I apologize as well."

Mitchell said nothing, and Billings merely inclined his head. Quirke laughed. "A story for my children, me a suspect," he said.

The men who had not been named—Lee, Carrow, Pettegree, Rogers—looked at each other uncomfortably.

"I accept your apology, too," said Lee, and there was a nervous chuckle.

"The first thing to understand, gentlemen, is that the mutiny—the rolled shot, the note on Mr. Martin's desk after we discovered his corpse—is true, a real threat."

There was a knock at the door.

"Come in," Lenox called.

"Are you expecting someone?" Billings asked.

"Yes. You will lay eyes upon the chief mutineer now."

McEwan entered.

"You!" said Carrow.

"Sir?" said McEwan.

"Look for the man behind him, Mr. Carrow," said Lenox.

It was Evers, sporting a red welt on his cheek that hadn't been there the day before.

"What the devil is this about?" he shouted, full of rage.

"Mutiny," said Lenox. "I find that word carries a great deal of weight on this ship."

"Is this true?" said Billings.

"No," said Evers. "Course not, sir."

"What is your evidence, Mr. Lenox?"

"Mr. McEwan, at my behest, infiltrated the gang. This was their leader. I have four other names."

"Mr. McEwan?" said Billings.

"Aye, sir. They meant to take the ship for themselves."

Evers shot a hateful look at McEwan.

"Did you kill Captain Martin?" asked Billings.

"They did not, not directly," Lenox said, "nor Halifax. Yet they were complicit, with an officer of this ship."

A murmur broke out in the room, as the men stared at one another.

"I cannot believe Mr. Evers guilty," said Carrow, standing up. "He serves on my watch, and he is a good man—hard, but good."

"Thank you, Mr. Carrow," said Billings. "Though I wish we might hang him now, we will judge him on Sunday, as we do all criminals on board, and you may speak for him then."

"Captain," said Carrow stiffly, and sat again.

"Mr. Evers, on whose behalf were you working?" said Billings.

"Nobody's, sir. I weren't never no mutineer. I been a *Lucy* eight years."

"Will you say nothing further?"

"I'm innocent, sir."

"Mr. McEwan, bind his hands behind him—yes, there is your rope—and take him to the brig. Mr. Pettegree, you will go with him? I know you have a key."

"Yes, Captain."

This done, and Pettegree returned, all eyes reverted again to Lenox. "How is this related to the murders?" Billings asked.

"First, let me ask a question, if you would permit, Captain."

"Go on."

"Mr. Carrow, you are Evers's watch captain, are you not?"

"I am, but to suggest that I had any role, whatsoever, in—"

"And you discovered both bodies, I know."

"Yes, that was my misfortune. The first time I was in the company of—"

"Of nobody, sir," said Lenox. "My nephew, Teddy, went down to the gun room to rest, ill, on his first night aboard the ship. Nobody else was on the poop deck at that time."

Carrow looked disconcerted. "Well," he began, but Lenox interrupted.

"Do you deny that you were alone?"

Now the second lieutenant's face turned defiant. "I don't deny it. I suppose I am at fault for attempting to protect the reputation of your nephew, Mr. Lenox. The other lads would have been merciless with him."

Lenox stood. "Captain," he said, "the crux of my case is a man's hands. A sailor's hands. Yours, for instance, have all the traits of a sailor's, do they not? Perhaps I might show these gentlemen what I mean."

"Look here," said Carrow, standing again, "if you mean to imply that I killed either Halifax or, the Lord forbid, my own captain, you've lost your senses, Mr. Lenox."

"Let him speak," said Billings. "Hands, you were saying, Mr. Lenox?"

"May I see yours?"

Lenox's heart was beating rapidly. Billings held out his hands, and with a quickness of movement of which he had no longer believed himself capable, Lenox had a pair of shackles out and clasped over the captain's wrists.

Billings's face, at first puzzled, showed an instant of pure, terrifying rage. Then the captain composed himself. "What's the meaning of this?" he said. "What demonstration is this?"

"None at all," said Lenox. "Merely a ruse. Mr. Carrow, I must add you to my list of apologies, and Mr. Billings, I'm afraid I must take yours back. For this man, gentleman, your captain—though I hope not for much longer—is the monster who murdered Mr. Thomas Halifax and Mr. Jacob Martin."

CHAPTER FORTY-ONE

O f all the bloody nerve!" said Billings. "Unlock me at once! I'll hang you for treason, on the same rope as Evers!"

"Mr. Evers is innocent. There was no true mutiny among the men of the *Lucy*. It was never likely, given their loyalty. Mr. Pettegree, perhaps you would fetch Evers up. The welt he gave himself was an excellent touch, I must say, but alas, it was all arranged between us."

Pettegree didn't move, and the other men looked wary, understandably. Mitchell went so far as to say, "He's a madman." It wasn't clear to whom this condemnation referred.

"You had better explain yourself," Carrow said. "How can you possibly be so sure?"

"I wasn't, I confess," said Lenox. "But the relief in your eyes yesterday, Mr. Billings, when I told you I suspected Mr. Carrow— and again I must apologize, sir—was unmistakable. You hid it well, but that was the final piece of evidence I needed. Confirmation."

"This is an outrage," said Billings. "The *Lucy* is my ship— *my ship*, you understand! I've worked too goddamn long to be robbed of her by the likes of you!"

"Watch your language, surely, Captain," said the chaplain, his face anxious.

"To hell with your language," said Billings. "Unshackle me, Lenox, you bastard!"

"You had better start explaining why you suspect our captain, sir," said Lee, more serious than Lenox had seen him look before. "To cuff him like a criminal at the table here, on what is now his own ship—it has been badly done."

"I wanted Mr. Billings under our guard, and shackled. A captain can be a dangerous thing, free on a ship. He could have any of us hanged, or put in brig, if he liked. The men would take his word over his lieutenants'. That was why I led him to believe that his plan had worked, and that I believed Mr. Carrow guilty. I wanted you relaxed, Mr. Billings, and unsuspecting. And I wanted to gauge your face as I spoke to Evers. You'll excuse the charade, gentlemen."

Lenox rose, and took a glass of water from the pitcher that stood on the sideboard.

"Do you remember, Mr. Billings, after we discovered Mr. Martin's body, and you said to me, that I would likely find your watch chain, or Mr. Carrow's, about his body? I began to suspect you then. Nobody other than Mr. Martin, Mr. McEwan, and Mr. Carrow knew about the medallion found beneath Halifax's body."

"Martin told me," said Billings.

"I doubt it. He understood the importance of secrecy. No, I think you put the medallion near Halifax's body, hoping to make it seem as if it had been torn from his breast in the fight. Was that why you stole it back, too? To shift my suspicion onto Carrow?"

"This is preposterous."

"Then there was Mr. Mitchell's tie chain, an object that was closely associated with him. Left by you, to further muddy the waters, I assume?"

"Is that where the damn thing has gone?" Mitchell said. "I'll have it back, thank you."

Lenox waved an impatient hand. "Later, later. Tie chain or no tie chain, Billings, it was always Mr. Carrow you hoped I would arrest, wasn't it? I wonder whether you slipped my nephew something, to make him ill. No? Too far-fetched? At least consider, then, our discussion about Mr. Bethell, who was once the ship's second lieutenant. You saw that I suspected Bethell's death might be related to Halifax's, and pitched me a story about Carrow and Bethell having a falling-out, just before the man's death."

"Did you say that, Billings?" asked Carrow, his voice throaty. "You know he's the closest friend I've ever had at sea."

"I never did," said Billings.

"Mr. Quirke, you were there too, I believe."

"I was," said Quirke. "You did say so, Mr. Billings, I remember. I had never heard of a falling-out between them, but there seemed no reason not to believe it."

There was a silence now, and Lenox began to feel the tide of belief turn, ever so slightly, in his favor.

"What's this business of mutiny, Mr. Lenox?" said Lee at last. "I mislike your use of Evers. Was he involved?"

"He was only an actor, I promise. Mr. Pettegree, I really do think it would be best to free him."

The purser nodded and left.

"No," said Lenox, "the so-called mutiny was another piece of misdirection from you, Mr. Billings. You were on deck when the shot was rolled, were you not?"

"Yes, along with dozens of other men."

"And yet only one other officer. At first I thought perhaps it was directed at you; now I believe you rolled it."

"But how on earth is this anything but a suspicion?" said Carrow, plainly discomfited.

Lenox felt in his breast pocket. "Here's the note that was left in Captain Martin's cabin," he said. "You'll know better than I that few sailors on the ship can write or read."

"Several can," said Mitchell.

"There is a simple expedient I can think of to discover the truth," said Lenox, who suggested it because he had tried it the evening before, when he had stolen into Billings's cabin. "Perhaps you, Mr. Tradescant, might fetch a piece of paper, anything with writing on it, from our captain's cabin."

"I call that an outrageous violation," said Billings, whose tone was almost too cool, too controlled.

Several of the officers looked as if they might agree.

"It's not quite cricket," said Lee.

"If I'm wrong, I'll apologize—grovel—before Mr. Billings. What can be the harm in comparing his handwriting to the note's?"

Tradescant shrugged, rose, and made for Billings's cabin.

Billings shot up then, and shouted, red-faced, "No! You cannot do that!"

"Why not?" said Lenox.

"Lee is right—it's not done!" Billings said.

But the vehemence of his reaction acted against him.

"We may as well see," said Lee, shrugging. "Perhaps the comparison will exonerate you."

Pettegree returned just as Tradescant left for Billings's cabin, and as the door closed behind him Lenox saw Evers and McEwan speaking to each other excitedly.

Tradescant returned, his face grave. "Here is a letter Mr. Billings has written to his sister, Mr. Lenox. I have not read its contents, thinking that an invasion, but perhaps it may be used for comparison?"

Lenox took the note, and then put both it and the mutineer's note out on the table. "As like as twins, you'll see. No attempt to disguise the handwriting. That was foolish, Mr. Billings."

All of the men in the room turned their gaze on the captain, who finally wilted under the inspection. "Well, so what if I wrote the note?" said Billings.

"You confess it?" said Carrow. "What can be your excuse?"

"The captain knew of it—was my accomplice."

"And told you of Carrow's medallion, too? Convenient that he's dead."

"You have no proof."

"And yet there is more," said Lenox. "Your nausea when we stood over Mr. Halifax's body, or Mr. Martin's, seems in retrospect overdone to me. No man has been at sea for more than fifteen years without seeing worse. It was an effective ruse, I'll grant you."

"They were my friend and my captain. I would hate to see the man whom such a sight did not nauseate."

"And yet there is another piece of evidence, Mr. Billings, which suggests to me that you may have a stronger stomach than you let on. The captain's log."

"What of it? More trumpery, I don't doubt."

"Mr. Tradescant, you concluded from the gruesome treatment of both corpses that the hand that cut them had some surgical experience, however rudimentary, didn't you?"

"Not a great deal, necessarily, but some, yes."

"When you are ill, who acts as the surgeon?"

"Why, I have trained my assistant in more recent months. Before that it was Mr."—realization dawned in the surgeon's eyes—"Mr. Billings."

"You toured the sick bay with Captain Martin once, and recommended amputation of a sailor's leg. Would you have carried out the procedure yourself?"

"He would have," Tradescant answered. "After battles he sewed the men up, just as I did. How could I forget?"

"How did you come by that skill?" Lenox asked Billings.

"Go bugger yourself."

"His father was a surgeon in a small town," Carrow said quietly.

"Why would I have, you fools?" said Billings. "Why on earth would I have wanted to do that?"

"Ah," said Lenox. "I have my suspicions on that subject, too. Your motive."

CHAPTER FORTY-TWO

Lenox poured another glass of water, and realized, as he took a deep breath, what a thrill was running through him. He had finally found his old form. It had come too late to save Martin, but there might be justice. That was something.

Again he addressed the room. "When a murderer kills twice, you must ask yourself what unites the two people who have died. What did Mr. Martin and Mr. Halifax have in common?"

"Nothing, except a life on board the *Lucy*," said Billings. "Spare me your speculation."

"And one other thing, Mr. Billings: both stood in the way of your promotion from first lieutenant to captain."

Lee laughed. "There you find yourself using landsman's logic, I expect, Mr. Lenox. Billings outranked Halifax."

"You have the right of it, Mr. Lee—he did. But let me spin you a story."

"Wonderful," said Billings. He jerked at his handcuffs. "I'll have you all up before the admiralty for this. As for you, Lenox, you fool, I'll leave you in Egypt to rot."

"I have wondered since Halifax was murdered why the killer did it on this ship, this contained, unprivate, undepartable vessel, rather than on land. But then I thought yesterday: what if he was only given a motive when he came on board?

"Then several facts came to me. The first was something my brother had told me, that Martin was destined for great things, indeed was rumored to be receiving command of a warship within the next several months. The second was something Martin himself told me in Plymouth, when we dined together. He said that he had to meet with the admiralty the next day, to make or break his lieutenants' careers—a prospect he loathed. Is it possible that he recommended Halifax take the ship after him, 'receive his step,' as a naval man would say? I know Halifax had numerous connections, relations even, within the admiralty. Men who wanted to see him do well. And what did you have? A few surgical tricks you picked up as a child?"

This hit home, Lenox saw; Billings tried not to, but he winced, pained at hearing the truth out loud. The detective wondered if it was as plain to the other men in the wardroom as it was to him.

"That train of thought led me to remember something Halifax told me over the last supper he ate. He said that at sea not all men get their wishes. Not all lieutenants are made captain, however much they may feel they deserve it. I wondered at the time if he was referring to himself, but now I suspect he was referring to you. I think his relations had told him the *Lucy* would be his upon her return from Egypt. By killing Martin and Halifax both, you became captain both now and, perhaps, for the future. An acting captain who does well often retains his command, does he not?"

Heads bobbed all over the room.

"Is that what Martin told you, Mr. Billings, that you would never be captain of the *Lucy*—that Halifax was to have it next, while Martin himself moved on to a new, larger ship? Perhaps he even offered to take you with him? But you wished to be a captain. It's only natural that you would, I know."

"End your squawking, man."

"Over whisky, the first night at sea, was it? Half a bottle was gone—too much for one man, but enough for three. I imagine the three of you meeting together. What was it you told me in our first supper together? That whisky was your favorite drink? Martin was a considerate man; he would have understood that you needed a tipple, to keep yourself together at the bad news. A life at sea, and never a command of your own."

"Absurd."

"Is it? What was it you said earlier? That you had worked too long to get her to be robbed of the *Lucy*?"

"It's true, damn your eyes."

"It is not difficult to imagine that at the conclusion of your drinks together, you might have asked Halifax to join you for a stroll upon the deck. Perhaps even a trip up the rigging. You couldn't have stopped for a knife, so it had to be a penknife. Was it on the spur of the moment, or did you hatch the plan the moment Martin broke the news to you?"

"Why would I have done any of that? Why would I have flayed him open?"

"Ah. There I have dark suspicions of your character, I fear, Mr. Billings. Perhaps we may discuss them later."

Billings looked around the room, and spoke. "All of you—Carrow, Lee, Mitchell, Quirke, my dear chaplain—I have served with you long and short whiles. This man has been aboard the *Lucy* for a fortnight and has accused me of murder. Please, let us all return to our senses."

It was the surgeon who finally spoke. "Why did you write that note? Or roll the shot?"

A look of disdain came into Billings's eyes. "This charlatan's story is true, as far as it goes. The *Lucy* was to be Halifax's. I was trying to send Martin a message."

"Once you've admitted that, haven't you admitted everything?" said Carrow. His eyes were pained, but no longer incredulous.

"No. I never would have raised a hand in violence to either of them. Why would I have killed Mr. Martin?"

"The captain?" said Lenox. "You went back and asked him specifically, after Halifax had died, whether your prospects had changed. A few glasses more of whisky gone from the bottle. When he denied you again, you had to kill him."

"I didn't do it."

Carrow interjected. "But the penknife, your opportunity, my medallion, your surgical training—surely there can be no other answer?"

"I never thought you would betray me."

"I wish you had never betrayed us."

Billings smirked. "Prove it, then. You cannot, because it's not true. The mutiny, yes. But not the murders."

"So this is to be your stratagem?" Lenox said. "Save yourself the gallows?"

"There's no proof that I murdered Halifax or Martin, damn you."

"It was a deuced awkward thing of you to do, Billings, even if it was only the mutiny," said Lee.

"Oh, shut up, Lee, and stow your asinine home county accent."

"Oh, I say!" cried Lee, moved more than he had been at any point heretofore in the proceedings. "I say, you go too far!"

Lenox nearly laughed. "You speak of proof. I wonder, Mr. Tradescant, about your patient."

"Which one?"

"Your long-term patient. What was his name?"

"Costigan."

"You told me several days ago that he was awake?"

"Yes. But fractious, and anxious."

"And muttering all manner of things, you told me? About what?"

"It's nigh on impossible to understand him."

"How long will it be before he could speak, should you stop giving him his sedative now."

"A matter of an hour or two. But why?"

"What was his initial injury?"

"A blunt trauma across the back of the head, from a beam, we presumed."

"I think he may have witnessed our murder, this unfortunate Costigan, or known of Billings's plans. Billings, is that true?"

It was this that finally did Billings in. He sat there insolently, grinning, a dazed look in his eyes. He said nothing.

"When was he brought to your surgery?"

"Not half an hour before we discovered Halifax," said Tradescant wonderingly.

"And Mr. Carrow," said Lenox, "where did Costigan work?"

"He was a flier, a topman."

"Then he might have had cause to go up the—"

"Mizzenmast, yes. Oh, Billings."

They all turned to him, and the same distant grin was fixed on his face.

"We shall have to speak to him," said the surgeon gravely.

"There's only one thing left," said Lenox. "Admit that you killed them, Billings. You, and you alone."

Their eyes were all focused on Billings, and so none of them saw the man who had slipped in. He spoke, and they turned together with a cry of surprise.

"In fact we killed them together," the voice said. "Both of them."

It was Butterworth, Billings's steward. He was carrying a gun.

CHAPTER FORTY-THREE

Known Mr. Billings since he were a boy in trousers, I have," said Butterworth. "And it won't be any of you sees to him. Uncuff him now, Lennots, do it."

Hands raised, Lenox walked over to Billings and uncuffed him.

Billings stood and looked down the wardroom table, a warm, polished red, full of flickering light from the windows, and spat. "None of you is worth a damn. I killed 'em; I'd do it again."

"You helped, Butterworth?" said Lenox quietly.

"Shut up."

"How long have you been helping him?" Lenox asked. "Has he always been . . . this way?"

A pained look appeared on Butterworth's face, but he only said, "Shut up," again, and poked his gun into Lenox's stomach. He looked at Carrow. "Get us up to a jolly boat, hey. We'll take the *Bumblebee*. Else this one gets a bullet through him."

Billings's face was demonic. "Or I could get my penknife, Mr. Lenox. Can we make time for that anyhow, Butterworth?"

"Not now, young master. Now we must go. You come with us, Lennots. You're to be our hostage. The rest of you sit on your bottoms and don't breathe a word, or I'll shoot this great toff."

The walk to the deck seemed to take forever. Butterworth had the gun shoved into Lenox's back, and the detective prayed that the man knew how to use it properly. An accidental shot would mean the end of his life.

"Cut the rudder," whispered Butterworth to Billings. "Order the men away and do it."

"I will. You have the provisions?"

"They're with the *Bumblebee*."

Billings raced ahead.

"You planned for this?" Lenox muttered, as all around them men went on with their work, oblivious.

"Ever since Master Billings rushed in, sleeves covered in blood," whispered Butterworth. "Old Mr. Billings gave me a responsibility. Knew the boy wasn't right."

They were on the quarterdeck, only the two of them, seemingly in conversation, though a few men who passed by, seeing Butterworth in this unaccustomed place, gave him quizzical glances.

"You don't have to protect him. You didn't kill anyone."

"Might as well have. Knew what he was capable of," said Butterworth. He paused, then went on again, as if he felt a compulsion to explain. "The old Mr. Billings was like a father to me, you see." He turned and looked Lenox in the eyes. "You may as well know, in fact. He was my father. I was a bastard born on the local whore. Dovie is my brother."

Lenox's eyes widened. "That's why you were protecting him, then? Is that why you told me Martin was in all the cabins? And wrote on the picture Evers sent? You wanted me to come see you—so that you could mislead me!"

First Tradescant, and now Butterworth; it was the navy, he supposed, a convenient manner of disposition for unwanted children. Friends of his with bastards often put them into the guards, too.

Butterworth didn't say anything. Suddenly the ship gave a great lurch.

"We've lost the rudder!" a voice shouted. "Captain!"

"Captain?" another said.

Billings was hacking off the ropes that lashed the *Bumblebee* to her gunwale, impatient to be off the ship. He turned toward the men on the decks, his eyes wild, breathless from exertion.

"We're leaving now!" he said. "The three of us, aren't we? The *Lucy* won't move, and if any of you follow us in the boats we'll shoot old Lenox here!"

There were gasps all over the deck, and then the *Bumblebee* fell heavily into the water. Lenox saw Carrow edging onto deck, gathering men around him.

"You first, your honourable," said Billings, and shoved Lenox toward the gunwale. "Hope you like to row."

They followed him down the outside of the *Lucy*. He had a terrible, alert feeling in his stomach, a knowledge that he might soon be dead regardless of whether he followed their directions.

They got into the *Bumblebee* and Billings thrust the oars at Lenox, who began to row slowly toward the direction of Africa.

Billings had a manic, wild energy now. His gentle, quiet manner had vanished. He kept looking back at the *Lucy*, whose rail was lined with bluejackets and officers.

It was Carrow who cried out, "Let him go! Bring him back! You can go!"

"*Not likely!*" Billings shouted back. He laughed. "They'll be hours on that rudder, the fools."

Butterworth, less delighted, merely nodded.

"You've been with the family a long time?" Lenox asked as he rowed, trying to keep his voice composed.

"Yes," said Butterworth shortly.

"Why did you cut them open, Mr. Billings?" said Lenox.

"Can I put my penknife in him, Butterworth?"

"No, Master Billings," said the steward quietly.

"Let me."

"No. Your father wouldn't like it."

"Did it start early?" Lenox asked. "Small animals? Then bigger ones?"

Butterworth was silent, but Billings, whose personality had received a kind of electric jolt from his exposure, was happy to speak. "You think you know my history, Mr. Lenox?"

"I cannot think why you cut Martin and Halifax open as you did, unless deliberate cruelty gives you pleasure."

Billings shrugged. "There were animals. I remember when I was five, and my father was trying to make a proper gentleman of me, I saw the fox torn apart. The excitement of it—the thrill of it—there were animals, you could say there were animals. Little buggers. Got them with my penknife, didn't I?" He was jabbering. "Cut them tidily, made them neat. Got them right. My father knew. Tried to beat me for wickedness, oh, ever so hard, when he drank. Sent me to sea, hoping to fix me. I'm still the same, though. You never change."

"Are these the first humans you've killed, Billings?" said Lenox, slowing the pace at which he rowed. The *Lucy* was getting smaller. His heart was hammering in his chest.

"Except in battle. Wasn't any different than the cats and dogs and squirrels," said Billings with another shrug.

"And Butterworth? You can tolerate this?"

"I can tolerate anything in my family, Mr. Lenox," said Butterworth. "Row faster. Master Billings, water?"

"Yes."

"Why must you call him master? He's a man grown."

Nobody spoke, until Butterworth said, "Faster, I told you faster. Here, give me one of the oars."

They sat and rowed, all exchanging looks, for ten, fifteen minutes. Lenox tried to speak and Billings raised the gun. Ten more minutes, fifteen. The *Lucy* was getting farther and farther now, Lenox realized with a surge of panic.

"Was it because they passed you over as captain?" Lenox finally said, increasing his pace slightly.

A transformation took place in Billings. The manic liveliness of the past hour gave way to the self-possession of the first lieutenant Lenox had thought he knew. "It was a damned travesty, I can tell you that."

"Oh?"

"Halifax wasn't a bad sort in the wardroom. Genial enough. He had no place at the helm of a ship, however."

"And yet he had great interest."

Billings laughed bitterly, but he still seemed to be the better Billings, the professional man. "You might say that. His grandmother gave birth to, oh, forty admirals or thereabouts."

"The system is unfair."

Suddenly the mad version of Billings returned. "Let me put my penknife in him," he said to Butterworth. "Let me, Father."

"No," said Butterworth. "You, row."

Lenox rowed on. The *Lucy* continued to recede from view, until he could no longer distinguish between the people on board her deck.

Some part of him wanted to plead for his life now; but another, resistant part forbade it. Foolishness, if it got him killed, but then men lived and died all the time by the peculiarities of their soul, which they could never expect one another to understand.

All he could manage was, "You really ought to let me go."

"We're going to keep you, deal with you on land," said Billings, eyes demonic, purposeful.

Butterworth gave him an appraising glance. "You say that now."

"You have my word, you will not be followed," said Lenox.

"Let me put my penknife in him!" said Billings.

"*No!*" roared Butterworth. "Give us your shoes and your coat, Lenox. They look comfortable."

"Please don't kill me," he managed to choke out.

Butterworth shook his head, and then gave Lenox a tremendous shove into the water.

As he emerged, he heard Butterworth say, "If you can make it back, you can live. It's a fairer bargain than many a sailor I know has had."

CHAPTER FORTY-FOUR

There was the cold, sharp shock of the water, and then the brilliance of the sky and sun. He kept himself afloat and turned, turned, panic in his heart, looking for the *Lucy*, until at last he spotted her.

He started to swim.

His arms were already tired from oaring, and after twenty feet or so of swimming they burned. Should've kept up more regular exercise, he thought, but then Parliament tended to be a sedentary place, full of late-night meals at committee meetings. How many months had it been since he took his scull on the Thames? Now, with the current against him, he wished dearly he had kept in better fitness.

He swam for what felt like an hour, more, and then permitted himself to look up. To his despair the *Lucy* was no closer, although the *Bumblebee* was by now a landward speck. He rested on his back for a while. Thanked God that it was the middle of the day, and warm enough.

He kicked off his socks, his trousers, and swam on.

In the next four hours there were times when he thought he might give up. He had thrown up, had swallowed seawater and thrown that up too. He would have promised to walk from Mayfair to John O'Groats for a drop of fresh water, after two hours. After three the seabed seemed a comforting thought. His friend Halifax was there.

The sun began exert a terrible pressure on his head, in his temples. On he swam, or, more accurately, drifted with some purpose.

The *Lucy* came closer, it seemed, but never very close.

He swam on.

He had never known such fatigue, or for his body to be in such open rebellion against him: actions he had taken for granted once upon a time, in the life before he was in the water, seemed impossible now. He couldn't turn his head more than a fraction of an inch. He couldn't swallow, quite.

It was when he kicked hard for ten yards and looked up to see that the ship seemed farther away than it had, much farther, that he felt certain he would die.

It was just as he was drifting out of consciousness, when even the thought of Jane couldn't make him put one arm in front of the other, that great strong hands pulled him up underneath his arms.

"We've got you, sir," said a voice that in some distant chamber of his mind Lenox recorded as belonging to McEwan.

Then he fainted dead away.

There was a blur of light and hurried voices when he woke, a feeling of being rumbled along over the planks of the deck. A bright light appeared in his eyes, and Tradescant's anxious face, inspecting him.

At last he managed to croak a word, "Water!" and immediately, blessedly, received a small sip of the stuff. Instantly he threw up. He took a little more, then, and finally could bear to have half of a glass tipped into his face.

After that he fell into a sweet, undreaming sleep.

When he woke up it was to a voice saying, "A middling fever. Don't think he'll be delirious." Lenox opened his eyes and saw Tradescant and Carrow standing five feet off, speaking in low voices. They were in Tradescant's surgery. The other beds were all empty.

"Some good news, that," Lenox managed to croak.

Carrow turned at the voice and strode over to Lenox, his face filled with worry. "My dear man," he said, "I can't tell you the pleasure it gives me to see you awake."

"How long has it been?"

"We pulled you on board twenty hours ago," said Tradescant.

"Am I well?"

"You took a bad sunburn unfortunately."

Lenox tried to open his eyes wide and felt his skin fill with fire. Once he had started to feel the sunburn it was impossible to stop feeling it, and maddening. "Balm," he said. "My cabin. Jane sent it."

Tradescant smiled and held it up. "Mr. McEwan found it for you," he said. "And is ready with food, should you need it. Your nephew will be beyond happiness—he has been here every fifteen minutes."

Despite Tradescant's jolliness, Carrow still looked unhappy. "Still, we must apologize, Mr. Lenox, both I and my officers and even Her Majesty's navy."

Of course, Lenox thought stupidly. *He's the captain now.*

"No need," said Lenox. "Glad to be alive. Found Billings?"

Carrow frowned. "No. We have fixed the rudder. At the moment we are on his path, but I shall leave it to your discretion: shall we follow him or take you to Egypt?"

"You're the captain," said Lenox.

To Lenox's surprise Carrow looked as if this were natural enough; he didn't seem overawed. "We shall follow him on for six more hours, then. After that we will be near enough in sight of land to tell whether we may catch him. Frankly I doubt it, but I would sail to the Arctic to catch him, the fiend."

"A dangerous man. I have seen it before." Lenox coughed then, and his lungs and throat burned, but he went on. "Capable of maintaining a professional life and obeying a private devil simultaneously."

"He was always rather peculiar, Billings. Spoke to himself. If anything I would have said he was too gentle for the service, however."

"Criminals are unknowable," said Lenox. "A dissatisfaction I have still yet to learn how to live with."

Tradescant came forward. "We must permit Mr. Lenox a respite from our conversation, Captain," he said.

"Of course, of course."

Lenox thought it foolish—he couldn't sleep again after all that sleep, surely—and yet when they had gone he sank almost instantly into the same profound rest he had taken before. The last thing he remembered was Fizz, the little terrier, jumping up onto the bed and lumping himself companionably against Lenox's leg, happy for the warmth. It was a comfort.

When he woke it was dark out, and Tradescant was leaning over him. "Fever almost gone. All that's wrong with you now is a sunburn and your . . . perhaps less than optimal physical condition."

"Too many parliamentary dinners," said Lenox.

"It was certainly an unaccustomed amount of exercise," said Tradescant, and laughed dryly at his own joke. "But rest again, please. Rest again."

Only in the morning did Lenox at last feel himself. His skin still tingled and prickled with heat, as it might when he over-peppered his food, but he felt clear-eyed.

It was neither Tradescant nor Carrow whose footsteps woke him now, but McEwan's, and, behind him, Evers's.

The small deal table beside Lenox's sickbed had been empty the night before, but since then had become a smaller replica of his desk. There was his Darwin, his letter paper, his pen and ink, his water pitcher, his toast-rack-correspondence stand, even the small picture of Jane.

Lenox was touched. "You did this?" he said to McEwan. "Thank you."

"You must be hungry by now," said McEwan. "Surely, sir." His voice was pained.

"I am, in fact. I have a roaring appetite."

With a great exhale of relief McEwan left, saying not so much as a word.

Evers sidled up to the bed. "Paying my respects, sir," he said.

"I've yet to thank you properly for your acting performance. The stage lost a star when you went to sea I think, Evers."

The bluejacket laughed. "Well, and perhaps the sea lost a sailor when you took up to politicking and detecting and all sorts. You're a proper *Lucy*, now you've half drowned yourself."

"Out of the way!" McEwan bellowed from the doorway, and came past Evers with a heavy tray, laden with every manner of fowl and pastry and vegetable he had been able to conjure. Lenox took a piece of lightly buttered toast and a cup of tea, to see how they would sit with him. Evers touched his cap and left with a promise to be back, but McEwan, rather disconcertingly, watched every bite go down, each of them a small drama to him, full of suspense until Lenox had completed the ritual of mastication and ingestion.

After the tea and toast Lenox made his way through a leg of cold chicken and a half of a new potato.

McEwan took the tray away with a promise to be back soon. Lenox read Darwin and dozed, still physically worn out, pleased to be alive. Occasionally the feeling of the water, or the terror of being at the mercy of Billings, came back to him, but he felt safe on the ship. There was a cool breeze that reached him now and then, and he thought he might almost attain the quarterdeck, if a chair could be placed by the railing there.

When McEwan returned it was with a treat. With great ingenuity he had somehow manufactured a small cup of cool sherbet. It was orange-flavored—"Saved the peels of your oranges," he said with a hint of entirely justifiable arrogance— and Lenox thought he had never tasted anything sweeter or more refreshing. It took all the heat out of his cheeks and soothed him to no end.

The next morning he wrote at length to Lady Jane, a letter he might never send so as not to alarm her, and then, with McEwan's help and Tradescant's permission, began the slow climb to the quarterdeck. It was arduous work, as difficult in its way as attaining the crow's nest, but eventually he reached the hatchway.

When he poked his head through, his breathing labored, he heard all the chatter of the deck stop.

He looked up to see that every pair of eyes was on him, from the foremast to the mizzenmast, the deck to the crow's nest. Then, spontaneously, the men and the officers broke into a long ringing applause.

"Three cheers!" said Andersen, the Swede, and the men gave Lenox three cheers, before clustering around to help him to his chair.

CHAPTER FORTY-FIVE

They reached Port Said two days later. On the final morning of their voyage Lenox felt truly well for perhaps the first time since his long swim, still greatly weakened but now capable of moving about the ship on his own. He spent a great many hours with his nephew Teddy, whom, though the ship was shorthanded for officers, Carrow permitted some degree of latitude in his duties.

The men seemed to bear a philosophical attitude toward Billings's actions, and now his disappearance. Death was not uncommon at sea, perhaps. There were words of sadness for Captain Martin (still unburied) and at first a great deal of gossip on the decks, but even twenty-four hours after Lenox's swim, while Lenox was only just returning to consciousness, the ship had apparently become itself again—albeit with a much reduced wardroom. Evers was back in his crow's nest, Andersen back on the rigging, and Alice Cresswell walking the poop deck as a fourth lieutenant with all the pride and pomp of a king at his coronation.

Lenox watched their approach to the port from the railing at the *Lucy's* spar. It was a marvel, this city. He realized that he had previously thought of the Suez Canal as a modest piece of imperial construction, for all of its expense and fame. Now he saw that it was unlike anything else in the world.

There were ships of every nation, Dutch flags, French ones, a dozen others, crowding the waters of the port. The air was black with steam, the docks frantic with action, and the sheer multitude of small craft on the water was overwhelming. In fact the water seemed more densely populated than the town. Men in skiffs went between all the larger ships, selling fresh fish and Egyptian delicacies. There were pleasure boats with prostitutes crowding their decks, official boats levying taxes and examining goods. Every one of them seemed to linger in the *Lucy's* path until the last possible moment.

When they were quite close to dropping anchor, Carrow came to stand beside Lenox. "And this is what we're hoping to buy into?" he said.

"I believe so."

"It's closer to Gehenna than anything I ever saw."

"Certainly it gives an overpowering impression."

"Filth, children running loose, any manner of ship crowding our boards. The men will love it. Hauling them back onto the *Lucy* at the end of a week's time would be no pleasure, so I fear I must keep them on board. Still, I doubt they'll mind if I permit them the freedom of the pleasure barges—most of them are close to jumping off and swimming every time one passes anyhow."

"How will you spend your time in port?"

"There is a great deal to do about the ship, taking inventory, that sort of thing. I don't doubt there will be congenial company if I do go on land."

"You must come to dine with me, at least," said Lenox.

"I should be honored. And there may well be other officers

I've met, of our nation and others, staying at the officers' club here."

"You're a captain now," said Lenox, half as a question.

Carrow laughed. "Hard to believe, I know, and I never imagined how bitterly I would regret fulfilling my boyhood dream. Martin dead, Halifax gone, Billings a monster living in our midst all this while. Even Butterworth I thought I knew. Not a talkative chap, but not unkind either."

"I think he felt a very great sympathy for Billings," said Lenox. "A sense of protectiveness, even."

"You heard Costigan's tale?"

"Secondhand."

"Billings attacked him. I thank God that someone was in the surgery at all times, per Tradescant's orders, or I don't doubt Billings would have slipped in to finish the job himself. It was lucky Costigan mended at all."

"Will it be difficult to sail back to England with so few officers? Will you recruit here?"

"Oh, no," said Carrow. "If we were near Brazil or India, perhaps. The trip back should be a jaunt. Now, we must see you into the *Bootle* very shortly, and onto land. You have great work to do, I know. I feel honored to help you; truly, I do, Mr. Lenox. Shake my hand, will you, before you go?"

The *Bootle* was the ungraceful little tub, previously a lifeboat, that had replaced the *Bumblebee* as the ship's jolly boat. Lenox and his trunk went aboard with the help of the bosun and McEwan, Carrow at the railing to wave goodbye, Teddy and his fellow midshipmen behind the captain, waving too. (Lenox had left them two bottles of wine, to enjoy during his absence, and rather doubted they would survive the night. "Just keep Teddy off the pleasure barges," he had muttered to Cresswell. "Surely I can count on a vicar's son for that much?")

It was a short journey to the dock; to Lenox's surprise there was a delegation of four waiting for him there, one of them a young Egyptian boy struggling under an enormous flag bearing Saint George's cross, which, seen in a certain light, was no inapt representation of England's presence on the continent.

He stepped out of the *Bootle* and onto the dock, wearing his finest suit, and looked at the three white faces who waited for him there, two men and, to his surprise, a woman.

It was she who greeted him, a young, pale, and sturdy creature, who spoke in a strong Welsh accent. "Mr. Lenox, may I welcome you? We saw the *Lucy*'s color this morning and have been anticipating your arrival since. We have sore need of your authority in dealing with these Egyptians—I count myself very pleased that you have come. My name is Megan Edwards."

"I'm very pleased to meet you. This is my steward, McEwan."

"May I introduce you to my husband, please? Sir Wincombe Chowdery. I didn't fancy being Megan Chowdery, however old a name it might be. I find I like being Megan Edwards better." If this was unconventional talk, even brazen, she didn't seem particularly to care.

Chowdery stepped forward; Lenox knew him to be Her Majesty's consul in Port Said. He had looked at his wife throughout her initial speech with adoring eyes, a very small, stooped gentleman, well past fifty, with a squint and thick glasses. "And quite right," he said, when she had concluded speaking, and then added, "May I welcome you. This is my associate, Mr. Arbuthnot—very promising young gentleman from Cambridge, don't you know—fly-half—terrific hunter."

Arbuthnot was a hale chap of only twenty-five or so, in truth better suited to Chowdery's young wife than Chowdery himself was. For all that Lenox saw Lady Megan grip her husband's hand and shoot him an adoring look while Lenox shook the younger man's hand.

"Most pleased to see you," said Arbuthnot. "Are these your things? Here, boys!"

He clicked his fingers and three boys from a group of fifty or so won the race and picked up the trunks, carrying, it seemed to Lenox, much more than their collective weight. After he had said goodbye to the sailors manning the *Bootle*, he followed his trunks to a carriage, Arbuthnot and the Chowderys alongside him. The shillings he gave the boys were met with almost disbelieving gazes of happiness; Arbuthnot tried to step in and give them a more appropriate tip, but Lenox waved the boys off. They vanished before he had time to see them leaving, back into the great, hot masses moving among the docks. McEwan mounted the seat beside the driver in order to look after the trunks, lashed as they were to the roof of the carriage.

The carriage rode over very rough streets, and in the few blocks close to the port the buildings were shifting sorts of slums, crowded with drying laundry and seemingly overflowed with people. Food sellers and other merchants operated out of small stalls, and shouted over each other. Because Port Said had been truly settled as a major city only fifteen years before, as part of the creation of the canal, everything had an air of shoddy newness.

Gradually, however, the streets cleared and the houses grew slightly larger; then larger still; and finally, as they ascended away from the port, there were villas and manors. All of these were new and sparklingly colored. Some of them had small signs outside with names on them, many more in French than in English, and also in a variety of other languages of Western Europe. It was the most international city Lenox had ever found himself in. The population was only about ten thousand, and yet there must have been two dozen nationalities represented among them.

It was Mrs. Edwards who spoke for most of the journey, informing Lenox of his various duties and reporting to him on recent developments in the competition between the French and English for use of the canal. She also spoke about the wali, Ismail the Magnificent, whose vision had dragged Egypt into modernity and whose spending threatened to ruin all of that progress. In

truth she seemed more competent and informed than her husband, whose few conversational gambits all seemed to involve
books. Lenox thought he understood: Chowdery himself was
more than happy to let his wife hold the reins, while he sat and
sipped cool drinks and read Seneca, Coleridge, Sallust, Carlyle.

It was enlightened, Lenox would acknowledge. But he would
have been mortified to marry a woman like her, however pretty
she might be. So modern!

"Ismail is a strange creature," said the consul's wife. "He
prefers gadgets to all things—I trust you have brought him
gifts of state?"

"Oh, yes," said Lenox, "and the appropriate ministers. There
is English marmalade, an engraved silver tea set for the gentleman who manages the canal's revenues, and who I understand
fancies himself an English gentleman, and for the wali himself
there is a time-saving device, a self-winding desk clock. I can't
imagine it works very well. And a dozen things beside. They are
all in the other trunk, packed tidily by my brother's assistant."

Chowdery spoke. "We have a supper scheduled for this evening," he said. "I trust you are well enough after your voyage to
attend?"

He still felt that swim in every fiber of his body, but said,
"Oh, yes."

"And tomorrow you tour the canal," said Arbuthnot. "A
bother, but they will insist on showing it to everyone."

"I suppose I would too, had I dug it," said Lenox, and everyone in the carriage laughed. "It's an embarrassing question, but
would you tell me the date? One loses track of such things at
sea."

"Not at all," said Chowdery. "It's the fourteenth."

"Ah. Excellent."

Tomorrow, then, he would have his secret meeting with the
Frenchman Sournois. His heart gave a small flutter at the prospect of it.

CHAPTER FORTY-SIX

It was interesting, that evening, to consider the men and women whom the winds of empire had blown to Port Said. There was a naturalist, apparently of some renown, who was raising funds for a trip to the center of the continent. There were half-a-dozen lean, hungry young men, all on the lookout for their fortunes in this fertile land, who variously described themselves as shipping consultants, exporters, or, most commonly and simply, "in business." Many of them were based in Suez, and in town for Lenox's meetings, sensing a chance of advancing their interests on his back, and therefore they were all extremely deferential and welcoming to him. There was a retired colonel from the Coldstream Guards, complete with family, whose continued good health required warm and dry weather. He had just been eight months in Marrakech, and had come to Port Said on a whim.

Perhaps most surprisingly there was a man Lenox had known at Oxford, an earl's son, Cosmo Ashenden, who had killed a member of the House of Lords in a duel and never thereafter returned to English soil. He bore an angry scar over his eye. The woman who had been at issue Lenox still saw in London. She had married an elderly bishop, in the end, and been widowed young and rich.

"We thought there would be plenty of occasion for you to meet the Egyptians," said Lady Megan. "All of us are British here this evening, whatever small expatriate community we can claim."

When he finally reached his bed Lenox was staggeringly fatigued, worn down in body and bone, and he slept almost instantly, a vague thought of Jane passing through a far reach of his mind before he was gone.

As he had with each sunrise since his involuntary swim, Lenox felt better the next morning than he had the day before. His room was a wide, high-ceilinged, light-filled chamber, with an Englishman's essentials—bookshelf, desk, bed—overlaid by an Egyptian's detailing, from the prints on the wall to the perforated geometric patterns in his brass lamps. He ate a positively luxurious breakfast by his window, which was flung open for the breeze and the warmth of the day. As he spread some of Jane's marmalade, still made by her childhood nanny, over buttered toast, he wrote to his wife, a letter to supersede all the others, and which he planned to send first that she might not fret about his condition. He took two or three cups of very strong African coffee, then, and dressed for the day.

"McEwan!" he called.

The steward's face popped around the door. "Yes, sir?"

"You can have the Egyptian boys clear away my breakfast things, but I need you to post this letter."

McEwan nodded. "Of course, sir. You know the *Lucy* will likely beat it home?"

"Never mind that."

"No, sir."

"And I'll take my gray suit, wherever in hell you've secreted it."

"Here in your wardrobe, sir," said McEwan, pulling it out.

Lenox laughed. "I don't know how you expected me to find it there."

"Sir?"

"Only a joke. You'll send that letter? Perhaps their secretary here can tell you how to do it."

"Yes, sir."

Half an hour later Lenox was bouncing over the road to the mouth of the canal, while Chowdery and his wife offered advice on the proper forms of greeting in Egypt.

As it happened he didn't need them; the man who greeted them at their carriage was dressed in a suit that looked as if it might have come from Savile Row, and after greeting Chowdery gave Lenox a firm handshake.

"I am Kafele, emissary of the Magnificent Ismail, khedive of Egypt and Sudan," he said.

"Charles Lenox, member of Parliament."

"It is our profound honor to welcome you, sir."

"And mine to visit your country. I look forward to seeing the canal."

"May I lead you this way?"

They were at the door of the most solid-looking building Lenox had seen in this makeshift city. "Most impressive," he murmured.

"Thank you, sir," said the wali's emissary. "As a man of the world you will appreciate the difficulty of constructing a city from scratch. She had no fresh source of water, Port Said, for the first ten years of her existence, and no stone either. Everything had to be dragged across the desert or floated across the sea. Yet here you stand, in our noblest building."

"What is its official function?"

"It is our customs house, sir."

"Ah, of course."

They walked across a handsome lobby and then down a dark corridor. "Is the canal this way?" said Lenox.

"If you would permit me the pleasure of surprise, sir."

Chowdery, Arbuthnot, and Chowdery's wife were well behind them now, giving the two men space. As they went down still another corridor, the Egyptian said, "Your visit occurs at an excellent moment, sir. We have every hope that the diplomatic and financial relationship between our nations will flourish."

"As do we. The prime minister has instructed me to convey to your wali our pleasure that your relationship with France has not precluded exchange between our nations."

"Indeed, now that the canal is built you are a better friend to us than France, Mr. Lenox, sir. Here, if you will permit me the pleasure—through this door."

Kafele flung a pair of doors open, and the great glittering canal was only steps away, laden with ships bearing goods, just as busy as the port.

Closer at hand was a reception, which Lenox thought for a brief moment he must be interrupting, until he realized it was for him; and yet its splendor was such that he doubted it until the wali's emissary bowed and said, "We welcome you to Egpyt, sir."

A hundred soldiers in military uniform stood at attention in lines of ten, and behind them ten men on horses. A great white pavilion stood to one side, and through an open door Lenox could see tables and men inside. On the water behind the soldiers was a waiting ship.

Standing before them all was a massively fat Egpytian man in traditional dress. This proved to be one of the wali's nephews, who looked as if he would rather be anywhere else, but who went through the forms nicely. He led Lenox to the pavilion, where a dozen men were waiting, some of them government functionaries, others in trade.

With this retinue Lenox reviewed the soldiers, nodding appreciatively at their movements, complimenting their uniforms, their bearing, and their agility.

"They are the sultan's army?" he asked.

"His personal guard," Kafele answered. "The very finest soldiers our nation has ever produced."

From this review of the soldiers the sultan's nephew led Lenox to the waiting ship. It was low in the water, burdened with great crates on its decks. A captain waited, smiling, by a gangway.

"These are the crops that will make both of our nations rich," said Kafele, and led Lenox to a pallet at the ship's edge. "Here you see a bale of cotton and a bag of rice. Please, take them as our gifts, as tokens of our commercial friendship, back to your country."

"Thank you," Lenox said. "I accept them on behalf of Her Majesty Queen Victoria."

The wali's nephew came forward, behind him two men bearing pillows with boxes on them.

"We have these gifts, too, for you," he said. "For your own august personage, an ancient cup of Egyptian marble, held in my family for many generations, and representing the comity of our nations, which share bread and water."

One of the men bearing pillows stepped forward and showed Lenox the cup, whose marble was so thin it was nearly translucent, sand-colored and veined with red. It was beautiful. "I thank you," he said.

"And for your prime minister, we offer this gold dagger, chased with dragons, inlaid with opals, as a representation that our strength belongs to you."

The second pillow-bearer stepped forward, and again Lenox

offered profuse thanks, along with a promise to give the dagger to the prime minister.

"The wali himself will present you with a gift for your queen, Mr. Lenox," said the wali's nephew. "Until then, may I invite you to a feast in our pavilion?"

"With great pleasure," said Lenox.

It had been an interesting morning. The superficialities—the soldiers, the wali's nephew—Lenox could take or leave. But the cotton and the rice were real. The hundreds of ships on the water were real. The economic potential of the canal, already partially realized, was so immense that with any luck Africa might soon be as great, as powerful and rich, as Europe. For the first time Lenox considered the idea that this pretext for this trip might, in the end, be just as important as his true reason for coming to Egypt.

CHAPTER FORTY-SEVEN

That evening as the sun fell, Lenox sat alone at his desk in the consulate, making notes for his colleagues in London about the state of Port Said and the Suez Canal. Following the feast there had been a long, detail-heavy meeting with the wali's emissary, Kafele, and the officials and businessmen who wanted Lenox's ear. These men were surprisingly quick to reveal what the French, the Dutch, and the Spanish had offered them, and what they needed to maximize the revenues the canal could produce. A prudent investment from Victoria's treasury, Lenox argued in his memorandum, might repay itself a hundred times over in the next fifty years. So much of the British Empire—the Indies, parts of Africa, once upon a time the Americas—had been won by brute force. Now intelligence and money might do more to increase England's power than her military could, in this new world that the construction of the Suez had created.

As the hours passed—he skipped dinner, having eaten far too much at midday out of politeness—he could feel his heartbeat

increasing, his nerves growing tauter. The Frenchman, Sournois, was never far from his mind.

Chowdery had invited Lenox to his and his wife's private
apartments for a game of whist, but Lenox had declined, simu-
lating regret and promising to join him for a hand the next evening.

"I thought I might call into Scheherazade's, in fact."

"Oh? I confess myself surprised that you've heard the
name—a rather dingy place, though popular with many Europeans."

"A friend in London recommended it, said the street it was
on had a great deal of local flavor."

"You might say that—certainly it has the balustrades, those
balconies one story off of the ground, you know, that the French
have handed down to the Egyptians. Well, I will be pleased to
accompany you, Mr. Lenox. Membership is relatively informal,
but as far as it goes I am a member."

"Thank you, Sir Wincombe, but I couldn't possibly take you
from your hand of cards—Lady Megan wouldn't like it."

"Heh! Well, I don't deny I like a strong-willed woman. But I
would be more than happy—"

"Please!" said Lenox. "You must indulge me and stay in."

With a look of relief, Chowdery nodded and said, "Oh, well,
if you're sure, if you're sure . . . my carriage is, needless to say,
entirely at your disposal."

"Thank you. And the driver knows where it is, this place?"

"Of course," said Chowdery.

So Lenox's plans were laid. As the minutes ticked on into
hours, and midnight drew closer, he began to feel a certain calm
that he knew to be indistinguishable, in its essentials, from fear,
though rather more useful.

At ten o'clock he asked McEwan to call the carriage round,
and by ten past the hour the horses were warmed and waiting.

"Would you like me to come, sir?" said McEwan.

Yes was the answer, badly. "No, thank you. I say, do you think the *Lucy* is all right?"

McEwan laughed. "In the past she has generally stayed hearty in my absence, sir."

"Carrow, you think, is well enough?"

"Yes, sir. He's a good man, Mr. Carrow."

As the carriage clattered through the streets, the mysterious smells of the city thick in the warm air, Lenox reviewed in his mind what he had to do at Scheherazade's. He could picture the diagram of the building perfectly in his mind, and reminded himself which door he would enter the kitchen by and which he would exit by.

This gentleman's club was housed in an unprepossessing building of three stories, whose ground floor was occupied by a frankly off-putting restaurant. It was popular, however, filled with Africans and Europeans alike.

Lenox instructed his driver to wait, got out, and walked through the restaurant, attracting a number of looks. At the back he found a dim and narrow staircase, at the top of which was a dark door, with MEMBERS ONLY stenciled onto it in gold print.

He opened this door, and found himself in a tiny entryway. A small Egyptian man stood at a table, and when Lenox entered he bowed his head.

"Member number?" he said.

"My name is Charles Lenox, Sir Wincombe Chowdery mentioned—"

"The president of the club is just this way, in the Trafalgar Room. He will see you."

Despite its grandiose name, the Trafalgar Room was nothing much to look at. It held a number of red armchairs, a few chipped tables, and between two great windows, looking out over the street, a small number of books on a shelf. There were also newspapers on a table by the door, in English and other languages, which Lenox saw at a glance were several weeks old.

A single man was sitting in one of the armchairs, pipe in hand, absorbed in some journal. He rose when Lenox entered.

"Mr. Charles Lenox," said the servant, then bowed and left.

"Mr. Lenox!" said the man in heavily accented English. "I had heard you were in town. How delighted we are to see you. My name is Pierre Mainton."

"Pleased to make your acquaintance. You're French, I take it?"

"Well spotted, sir!" said Mainton and laughed.

Lenox switched to his sturdy, unhurried French. "I'm surprised to see you so at ease in a room named for the Battle of Trafalgar!" he said.

"I'm surprised that you speak my language! You are the first Englishman of my acquaintance who has, I assure you." Mainton laughed again. "We have tried here to reflect our membership, which is multinational, by permitting each faction to name a room. There is the Emperor Napoleon the Third room just over your shoulder."

Lenox smiled. "Much more convivial than our nations."

"I hope so. I founded her because I was so bored in this city, and missed the conversation of my home city, Marseille. The storytelling. You understand the name?"

"The thousand and one nights?"

"Exactly! Scheherazade told a different story to her captor each night, never finishing that she might live another day."

"And what brought you to Port Said?"

"Ah, Mr. Lenox, it's a boring tale. My father was a ship broker in Marseille, may he rest in peace, and passed his business on to my older brother. To me he gave a small portion and the advice that I come make my fortune here, after de Lesseps started them off."

"A ship broker?"

"Ah, how to define. A ship needs supplies, yes?"

"To be sure."

"When a ship needs a bit of rope, or a wheel of cheese, or a new sail, I sell it to them. Whatever the ship needs. Coal, for instance, or water. Through no genius of my own—through pure accident and some slight knowledge of my father's business—I became the richest man in Port Said. Now I let my partners worry, and I oversee them. Preferably from this room!" Mainton concluded, and burst into laughter.

Lenox had half forgotten the French habit of frankness about money. "How interesting," he said.

"So you see, I am of humble origins—certainly not fit to greet a member of Parliament—but then Egypt is no great place for our European formalities!"

"On the contrary, I'm extremely pleased to meet you."

"Excellent. Will you take a drink, Mr. Lenox?"

"With pleasure."

Mainton switched back into English. "There are some men who will no doubt wish to meet you, other members?"

"Of course," said Lenox. Inwardly he wondered about his conspicuousness. Would it be possible to decline?

The next room was more sprightly than the Trafalgar Room, and had a row of pen drawings of European leaders along one white wall, Victoria among them. In one corner was a wooden bar with a number of dusty bottles behind it, and Lenox accepted a scotch and soda and took a large gulp of it for his nerves before remembering that his instructions had said: no alcohol. Thereafter he sipped from it sparingly.

There were five or six other men there, two playing cards, another reading, the others in conversation. Lenox met them all, and with good grace asked questions about their homes in Spain, France, Norway, Holland. There were no other Englishmen.

He tried not to check his pocket watch too often, but as the hour grew later he couldn't help it. Twenty minutes till midnight. Ten minutes till midnight. Five. How would he escape?

Then, to his relief and surprise, at three or four minutes before the hour all the men rose and began to say their good-byes.

"Do you close now?" said Lenox, shaking hands and smiling.

"Yes, generally we order our carriages for midnight," said Mainton. "But perhaps you would like to look through the rest of the club rooms, or if you are restless stay and read? I can ask a man to stay."

"Ah, that would be wonderful," said Lenox, wondering how much exactly this French ship broker knew of his plans. Why hadn't his directions included information on that?

The men all said their final good-byes, and lastly Mainton did, too, pressing a coin into the hand of the man at the front desk and shouting a cheerful farewell over his shoulder.

With his heart beating rapidly, Lenox turned. The fourth room on the left. A small door. It was time.

CHAPTER FORTY-EIGHT

The next two rooms were cluttered with, in the first, small card tables, and, in the second, a great number of books. Neither looked particularly lived in. Lenox found his small door and, with a sharp inhale to brace himself, opened it and walked downstairs.

The door to the kitchen was wide open, though the room itself was dim and empty. Apparently the restaurant on the ground floor was closed, too. Still, there was a flickering light in the far corner of the room.

"Hello," Lenox said, staying by the door.

"*Bonjour,*" a voice said.

Lenox waited for the man to go on, but he was silent.

"What brings you here?" he said at last.

The other man paused. "I like spending time in a closed kitchen."

No. The line was: *The kitchen is always closed when one is hungriest.*

"It's easy to get a meal in Port Said after midnight," Lenox said. "Ask anyone."

A long pause. "Ah. So you know the code. Let us speak."

Lenox hesitated for one, nearly fatal second, and then turned and walked through the door and out onto the street.

"Hey!" a voice called out behind him, and there were footsteps.

Lenox turned, saw a short, stubby man bearing down on him—*he is over six feet*, the note had said of Sournois—and began to sprint toward the brightly lit boulevard at the end of the street. He couldn't risk getting in Chowdery's carriage; there wasn't time.

So he ran. He was twenty paces ahead, but his fitness was still terrible, and already he could feel a sear in his lungs and his legs. Judging from the noise of the man's footsteps the distance between them was shortening. Perhaps fifteen paces now. The boulevard was just ahead, and with a lung-busting spurt of effort, Lenox reached it and turned left.

There were men walking hand in hand together, as was the Egyptian custom, and others sitting outside and sipping mint tea. There were still food sellers and beggars, too.

Lenox turned into the second doorway he saw, thanking God that he had kept a hand by his face in the kitchen, just in case. He saw his pursuer sprint breathlessly past, and then, twenty feet on, stop and whirl around.

Lenox retreated farther into the doorway.

A voice behind him said something in an unfamiliar language, and Lenox, his nerves already frayed, now took his turn to whirl around.

It was a young boy. Lenox raised a finger to his lips, to indicate quiet. The boy, with a look of immediate comprehension, nodded, and waved a hand: follow me.

There was no other option, and so Lenox trailed the boy down a mazy corridor, which led into an inner courtyard. From there they found another corridor, and then another. The noise of chatter on the street would get louder and softer as they walked. Finally they took a flight of stairs up, and Lenox, now uneasy, began to wonder what the boy's plan was.

When they reached a balcony he saw. There was a line of donkey-drawn taxis below.

Lenox nearly laughed, and then gave the boy half of the change in his pocket, several shillings. The boy grinned and nodded, then vanished back into the corridor.

Lenox went down to the taxis.

"You know the English consulate?" he asked.

"Yes, sir," said the first one, nodding rapidly.

"Take me there, please."

There was Chowdery's carriage and driver, he reflected; well, it was too bad. He wasn't going back.

What had gone wrong? Suddenly he realized: Mainton. Of course. He had been discovered. He could only hope that Sournois was still alive.

He thought again of his instructions: *Should anything go amiss, you must for your own safety immediately make your way to the consulate, and then with all possible haste to your ship.*

There was nothing he could do for Sournois. He would fetch McEwan and his things and go to the *Lucy*. With the protection of the men and the officers he might still meet with Ismail the Magnificent in two days, but for the rest of the time he would have to cancel all of his other plans and stay aboard the ship.

So he had failed. It was a bitter thought.

He gave the driver who brought him to the consulate a handsome tip, and then pressing an additional coin on him asked the man to drive by Scheherazade's to find the waiting carriage there, and tell its driver to head home.

He walked up to his room with his lungs and the muscles in his legs burning. The house was quiet and dark, but there were servants still awake. The man he had met in the kitchen could not reach him here, he hoped. Still, it begged the question: should he return to the *Lucy* tonight or in the morning?

Tonight, probably; and yet his fatigue was so great that when he went into his room and McEwan appeared, he did not ask the steward even to pack.

"Wake me early," was all he said. "It will be a busy day."

"Yes, sir. Would you like a glass of wine, or perhaps something to eat, before you retire?"

"Perhaps I would like a glass of that red—but no, no, I think not. You filled my water pitcher? Good, then I shall have that. Better for a clear head. Oh, and while I have you—you posted that letter?"

"Yes, sir."

"Thank you."

"Yes, sir. Good night, sir."

"Good night, McEwan."

He sat at his desk for fifteen minutes or so, drinking a glass of water and thinking over the events of the evening. The next morning he would ask Chowdery about any French delegation in Port Said, and perhaps he might hear word of Sournois's official duties in that fashion. Beyond that he saw little that he could do.

He changed into his nightshirt and went to bed then, restless in his mind but also tired, or somewhere beyond tired. Soon he was asleep.

He woke because he felt something sharp at his neck.

He tried to jerk away but a strong hand had him by the shirt.

"Who is that?" he said.

"I knew I'd get my penknife in you," a voice close to his ear said.

A chill coursed through his body. "No," he said. "It cannot be. Billings."

A match struck against the wood along the side of the bed,

and the candle on Lenox's nightstand flared up into light. The knife still to his throat, Lenox saw, in the flickering light, the face of the former first lieutenant of the *Lucy*.

He was dark from the sun now, rather like Lenox. His expression was neutral. There was nothing in it of the fiendish madness the detective had seen on that lifeboat. But this calmness was in itself a fearsome thing.

"How did you get here?"

"We were prepared," said Billings. "Coin, water, food. What sort of fool do you take me for?"

"Where is Butterworth?"

"I left him."

"You killed him."

"If you prefer. He didn't want me to come here."

"He was wise."

The knife pressed into Lenox's throat. It must have been drawing blood, by now. His horror of knives had awakened. "Was he wise? I suppose he may have been. Just like Halifax. Just like Martin. Just like . . . you."

"Me."

"I told you I'd put my penknife in you, didn't I, Lenox?"

"We were friends aboard the *Lucy*, Billings."

A look of bitterness snarled the younger man's lip. "Friends," he said with heavy scorn.

Lenox considered shouting, but knew it would mean his instant death. "You have gone mad. Come back to sanity, I beg of you. Give yourself up."

But Billings was too far gone. His eyes were wild and angry; the sane part of himself, the one that had allowed him to act as a competent naval officer these many years, seemed to have receded once the secret of his other side was out. It was often the way, Lenox knew. When the veneer had fallen away, it was hard to put it back up, for men like Billings.

"I'll give you up," said Billings.

"Did you even mean to carve up Halifax?"

"What?"

"You meant to kill him—but your gruesome little surgery. You couldn't help that, I suppose, but it wasn't part of the plan, was it?"

"Shut up."

"Take your knife from my throat and I'll let you leave."

"Ha."

"Billings, I warn you—"

"You warn me! I ought to—"

And then, to Lenox's very great shock, he discovered that his own warnings were more potent than either he or Billings had imagined. There was an extremely soft footfall, and an instant later something heavy and black swung through the air and knocked Billings in the back of the head.

The murderer stared at Lenox open-eyed for a moment, and then fell, his knife tumbling harmlessly from his hand.

"Who is that?" said Lenox.

"It is I, McEwan, sir." The steward was breathing heavily. "I came because you have a guest."

"At two in the morning?"

"Yes, sir. And if I say so, it couldn't have happened at a better time."

CHAPTER FORTY-NINE

A man came in through the door.

"Mr. Lenox?" he said in a French accent.

Lenox blinked twice and pondered the scene in his room, which now bore a more than passing resemblance to King's Cross Station at the rush hour.

"Who are you?"

But he scarcely needed to ask. "I am Sournois," the man said. "What has happened here? Is this related to . . . to our business?"

"No. It's an old business—an ugly one, I'm sorry to say. McEwan, do you know this man?"

"No, sir. He woke the butler and the butler woke me."

Lenox, still in bed, though now up on his arms, looked at the Frenchman. "How do I know you're . . . Sournois?"

"In front of him?" the Frenchman said, gesturing to McEwan.

"He just saved my life. It's fair to say that he has earned my trust."

"Thankee, sir."

"The kitchen is always closed when one is hungriest," said Sournois.

"There's never a meal to be had in Port Said after ten," Lenox replied. "Show me your hands?"

"Eh?"

"Your finger."

"Ah, of course." Sournois held up his left hand, and it was, as expected, missing a single digit. "That is settled, then."

McEwan, baffled, looked at both of them. "What is it, sir?" he said.

"This man is helping our government, McEwan. He's French."

A pained look flashed across Sournois's face, but he nodded. "It is true. Mr. Lenox, we cannot stay here. I took a great risk in coming, but —"

"Mainton betrayed us."

"Pierre Mainton? No, no, not that amiable buffoon. I am with the French delegation here. It was one of your men who betrayed your plans. He still has connections in the highest parts of your government, apparently. Lord—"

And here Sournois said the name of the earl's son, the one who had fled England after a duel. Cosmo Ashenden. The one Lenox had dined with the night before.

"I never took him for a traitor," said Lenox.

"Use that word more gingerly, please," said Sournois.

"Are you discovered?"

"No. There are presently three hundred and forty Frenchmen in Port Said, and I have a better reason for being here than any of them. As it happens I also am in control of them, at least those who work in government, while I remain here."

"I see. And am I betrayed?"

"Perhaps. We only received information that an Englishman was meeting with a Frenchman in the kitchen below the gentleman's club, but of course it is known that you are freshly arrived in Port Said. Still, two hundred people came with you on the *Lucy*, and the French government would never take action against a member of Parliament. It was their own traitor they wanted."

Just as Edmund had predicted. "I was chased."

"Perhaps incorrectly. We must go, at any rate—every minute I linger here endangers both of our lives. I took a risk in coming."

"Thank God you did." Lenox stood up. "Where would you have us go?"

"Neutral territory."

"Oh?"

"I have an idea—my carriage is outside."

"Should I trust you?" said Lenox.

Sournois glanced around the room, and saw, lying on Lenox's desk, the ornamental dagger that the wali's nephew had gifted to the prime minister. "Please, bring this. You may check my driver and me for weapons."

"Very well."

"But, sir!" said McEwan. "There's Mr. Billings!"

Lenox, dressing now, looked down at Billings's still body. "What do you think we should we do, McEwan?"

"He must be arrested—handed over to Mr. Carrow!"

"I quite agree. Bind his hands and legs and sit over him until I return, please. I'll send word to the *Lucy* tonight."

McEwan nodded. "Yes, sir."

"And have at those ginger biscuits while I'm gone, the ones Jane sent along with me. You've earned them."

McEwan smiled. "Just as you say."

Lenox went to him and looked him in the eyes. "Really, Mr. McEwan; shake my hand. I thank you, as does my family. When we return to England I will think of some way I can properly express my gratitude."

"Thank—"

"But now I have to go." Lenox took the dagger and nodded to Sournois.

A carriage was waiting in the shadows near the consulate, not far from the road. Feeling rather ridiculous, Lenox patted down its driver and then Sournois, and had them turn their pockets inside out.

"Are you satisfied?" said Sournois.

"Yes. Where are we going?"

"The water."

"Can we not speak in the carriage, as we drive?"

"It will take several hours, I expect, our conversation. A carriage at this time of the evening is conspicuous, unless . . ."

"Yes?"

"Well, unless it carries a European gentleman bound for the pleasure boats. The floating brothels."

"And that is where you mean to take us?"

"Yes, Mr. Lenox."

"Very well."

As they drove Lenox kept a hand on the dagger, but his thoughts kept wandering to Billings, to Billings's manic face looming over his own in the half darkness. How close death had come again! If not for Sournois, for McEwan, for Butterworth— his mind was anxious and racing, still convinced of some imminent danger. He felt himself still trembling, every so often.

They came to the water soon, and found it busy and bright, a thousand lanterns from a hundred ships casting a flickering yellow warmth over the water.

There were small messenger boats, and for a few coppers Lenox asked one to take a note to the *Lucy*, which he scrawled out in great haste with pencil and paper bought from the boatman. In fifteen minutes, perhaps twenty, Carrow would receive the message that Billings was alive and in Port Said.

When this business was done Sournois hailed a pleasure bark floating nearby.

"No," murmured Lenox. "Not this one."

"You fear a trap?" asked the Frenchman in an urgent whisper. "Very well. We shall wait for the next one, then. But we wait separately." He walked fifteen paces away from Lenox and lit a small cigar, his hat low and his cloak gathered up around his neck. It was chill out near the water.

The next pleasure bark passed by ten minutes later, and Sournois hailed this one with a flick of his hand in the air.

It pulled up alongside the dock and a gangway was flung out to meet them. A silent Egyptian waited on the deck.

First Sournois and then Lenox crossed onto the ship. Was he being foolish, he wondered? Or daring? He hoped it was daring.

The Egyptian held up a hand to halt them, then held up four fingers and pantomimed payment.

"I am surprised he does not speak English or French," said Lenox, handing over the coin.

"The more expensive boats all call at this dock," said Sournois, "and are all run by illiterate mutes. They cannot ask or answer questions. Many of the wali's family come here, though it is forbidden them."

The Egyptian led them into a small cabin, hung with lanterns and draped with red tapestries that cast a hedonistic crimson glow over the plain chairs and tables. Lenox, distinctly uneasy, took a seat.

After the Egyptian had gone for a few moments, he returned and beckoned them onward, through a small corridor; the ship was rocking unpleasantly, but they followed him. At the end of the hallway he pointed to two doors, then flashed ten fingers three times.

"Half an hour," said Lenox.

Sournois removed a purse and counted out several pieces of silver. Then he pointed out to the sea, and flashed ten fingers ten times. Finally he pointed at the room they had come from, and beyond it the dock, and shook his head firmly.

The Egyptian grinned and nodded, and then left them, apparently, to their own devices.

"The women will be in that room, waiting for us to choose among them," said Sournois. "I will speak to them. Wait in the smoking room, just there. Then we may converse."

CHAPTER FIFTY

When Sournois came back into the room, Lenox asked him a question before he had even closed the door, hoping to catch the Frenchman off guard. "The British spies who died on French soil—does your government have more than a list of eight names?"

Sournois smiled and came to the small table, where he sat down. From an inner pocket of his jacket he produced a gold flask inlaid with three rubies. "My father was a modest man—a *petit fonctionnaire*, yes?—but when I received my offer to join the government, a very prestigious office, you understand, he took several months' salary and commissioned this flask for me, as a present. Before I betray his pride I must have a drink, must I not?"

The dagger was in Lenox's pocket, and he kept a hand around the hilt. He nodded. "Very well."

There were glasses on a stand near the bed, and Sournois poured two glasses of dark liquid. Lenox hesitated until the other man drank his off, and then followed suit. It was a liqueur that tasted of apples, very strong.

"Thank you for drinking with me," said Sournois. "Now, your question."

"The eight names."

Again Sournois reached into his pocket. "Here is the letter I received on the subject. Your officials may inspect the stamps and signatures for authenticity. You see, of course, that I have removed my name and offices from the document."

Lenox took the pages and put them in his own breast pocket. "And?"

"My government killed your men, yes. What's more, we have a list of sixty-five other gentlemen we know to be in the secret employ of Her Majesty, Queen Victoria. Should any of them set foot in France, their lives would be forfeit."

Lenox's eyes opened wide in surprise. "Sixty-five," he repeated. Remarkable news that: It meant that if this trip achieved nothing else, it had protected these men.

"The money you have paid me, perhaps it will buy their safety back. That is some comfort—to spare unnecessary suffering, all the pink-cheeked English girls who would have lost their fathers." Sournois laughed, and took a sip straight from his flask.

"Does this mean war?"

"At the moment my government is fiercely protective of its rights. You fear war, I know, but so do we. What would you do if you discovered French spies in London and Manchester?"

"I cannot say."

"You would not hear, whether or not you are in Parliament, I venture to say."

"Perhaps not. But are your fleets readying themselves? Your armies?"

"Of course. They can scarcely do otherwise, can they? And yet, we may buy peace yet, you and I."

"What do you mean?"

Sournois drank again. "Are you curious about my finger?"

"No."

"Most men are. This same father, who gave me the flask, took my finger away."

"How?"

"When I was nineteen I was a handsome boy, and the daughter of a great merchant in my hometown, Lille, wanted to marry me. But I had a different idea. She was plump and had . . . like this, you see," he said, pulling his mustache. "Hair. So I ran off with my true love, a postman's daughter. Penniless."

"Your father took your finger for it?"

"When we returned to Lille he took me out for a glass of wine. He was already drunk, you understand. Our conversation began amiably enough, but when we began to discuss my marriage he grew angry, very angry. Violent. I stood, and he pushed me back into a bookshelf. There was a sword on the shelf, his father's sword, a man who fought with Napoleon, and the sword took my finger off—*fftt*—just below the knuckle. Cleanly. Do you know why I tell you this story?"

The ship bobbed in the water gently, and from the next room there was a burst of women's laughter. Lenox's grip on the hilt of the dagger tightened again, his unease back. "Why?"

"It is more intelligent to marry for money than love, Mr. Lenox. Our countries must share a financial interest."

Lenox understood. "You mean Egypt. The Suez."

Sournois nodded. "Precisely. Egypt. The Suez."

Neither man spoke for a moment, and then Lenox said. "Very well. There are more questions."

"Of course."

For the next two hours Lenox asked all the questions that his brother had told him to, mixing in some of his own, and Sournois dutifully answered, once even producing another piece of documentary evidence. Troop numbers, strength, movement. France's own spies within England. Information about the men who formed the French government, their martial or pacific inclinations, and private inclinations too, that might be used against them. Sournois told Lenox all of it, in between sips from his gold flask. The price paid to him must have been very steep indeed.

Again and again, however, he stressed that France did not desire war—that *he* did not desire war. Lenox remained impassive in the face of these declarations, though inwardly he agreed.

All of this information Lenox wrote in a shorthand he had used since school, and which he and his brother had both agreed would be relatively difficult to decipher should it be seen by the wrong pair of eyes.

When he had gone through all of Edmund's questions and taken a sheaf of notes for himself, Lenox checked his watch. It was past four in the morning. His attention had been focused so firmly on this task—and on its uncertain execution—that he had pushed Billings almost entirely out of his mind. Yet he could still, if he stopped thinking for a moment, feel the knife at his throat. He took a deep breath.

"All is well?" said Sournois, looking genuinely concerned.

"Oh, quite well, thank you. Is there anything else?"

"You have had it all."

"We will leave, then. Separately I think."

"Of course."

"Where do your men think you are, if they know you're gone?"

Sournois laughed. "Here. I have been making a point of visiting the pleasure boats every evening. I am perhaps later than usual, but not much so."

"Very well."

Sournois stood and offered his hand. "We will not see each other again, Mr. Lenox, and yet I will scarcely be able to forget you."

They shook hands and Sournois left. Lenox spent ten minutes tidying his notes, rewriting them in places, and then felt the boat begin to slow, and finally to stop. There was a voice on deck, and then the boat began to move again.

As he left the room he caught a glimpse of a roomful of six women, garishly painted, sipping mint tea and speaking to each other in bored voices. There were brothels in London, he knew—innumerable ones—and yet he felt shocked, to see these women, and in some measure as if Africa was responsible. Nonsense, and yet he could not persuade himself otherwise. He wanted to be back in Mayfair suddenly, and then laughed at the desire. How much pride the English took in their empire, and how little they understood its alien ways, its strange, disconcerting newness!

On deck the mute Egyptian was smoking a European cigar. He nodded when Lenox appeared and then left him alone, vanishing into one of the boat's many small rooms.

It was still dark but a pale blue light had begun to rise on the edges of the horizon, pure and deep in color, heralding the day. There was a thin rain beating down, and from the deck Lenox caught a glimpse of Sournois, walking down the small dock where they had left him and toward a beach covered with upturned fishing boats. A great swell of some unnameable feeling—melancholy, perhaps, or homesickness, a longing for Jane—filled Lenox's breast. He turned and stared at the lightening sky, his gaze there steady until they were back at the docks.

CHAPTER FIFTY-ONE

Though it was scarcely half past five, the docks were as busy as midday in Portsmouth. Lenox thought of what Sournois had said about the Suez as a possible broker of peace between France and England.

He hired one of the donkey carts that lingered around the wharf to fetch him back to the consul's house.

When he arrived there were lights in every window and the noise of loud conversations within. He knocked at the door and the butler admitted him.

"Sir, your presence is requested in—"

"There you are, Lenox!" said a man behind him. It was Carrow, his face anxious. "Where in Christendom can you have been?"

Lenox froze, trying to think of a reasonable explanation. "I . . . didn't McEwan tell you?"

"He did, and I asked him how could you possibly have been with friends at this hour. Where were you really?"

"McEwan was quite right. With friends."

Carrow threw up his hands in frustration. "So a madman tries to murder you in your sleep and after escaping with your neck intact, just, you decide to visit with friends? At midnight? For five hours? One might question your judgment."

"These friends keep late hours. Egyptians, you see. I was working on behalf of Her Majesty."

These were the magic words apparently. "Oh."

"In my note I asked you to send someone at eight o'clock, to fetch Billings."

Carrow smiled grimly. "Well, you have eighteen of us."

"Where is he?"

The butler, who looked very much like a man who had been woken at irregular intervals throughout the night, answered. "Mr. Billings is secured in the kitchens, under watch."

"Is Sir Wincombe awake?"

"Oh, yes," said Carrow. "He and Lady Megan are interviewing Billings at the moment, along with an Egyptian boy who brought Billings here for a few coins."

Lenox frowned. "Will the boy be punished?"

"Who can say, in this damned strange country."

"I understood Sir Wincombe to mean that he only wished to speak with the boy, Mr. Lenox," said the butler.

"Could you fetch me McEwan?" said Lenox.

"Yes, sir."

When he was gone, Lenox said to Carrow, "What are you planning to do with Billings?"

"Bring him back to England, where they can hang him from a rope by the neck. Is it true he stole into your chambers?"

"Quite true."

"And that you were with Egyptians all night?" Carrow asked doubtfully.

"Yes, quite true."

"Well, I can only thank God you're safe. Halifax, Martin . . . there's been too much bloodshed already."

"Thank you, Mr. Carrow. With your permission I mean to return to the *Lucy* this afternoon, and have the *Bootle* ferry me to the docks when I need to be on land. I would appreciate it if you could spare two men to accompany me on my rounds, as well, strong ones." Sournois might have been sincere when he said that Lenox wasn't in danger, but for his own part Lenox wasn't willing to take the chance.

"But Billings is caught. Do you fear Butterworth?"

"Have you not spoken to Billings?"

"Why?"

"I believe Butterworth is dead. Billings said as much. These precautions are for my personal comfort, Mr. Carrow. The situation here is tense."

"Say no more. Of course you shall have the men."

Lenox put his hands into his pockets. The dagger was still there. "Thank you," he said.

McEwan was coming down the stairs now. "There you are, sir," he said, and he, too, looked as if his night had been sleepless. "I told them you was with your friends, sir."

"Ah, thank you, McEwan. Thank you. I think I shall go on saying that for many years to come. Thank you for saving my life. Was Billings troublesome after I left?"

"He ordered me to unbind him, sir, as my captain. Which I told him he warn't a captain of mine. Then he cursed me, and then he asked for some food, but I didn't dare leave him alone. He got some in the end, though, when Sir Wincombe took him down to the kitchens."

A feeling of unease stole over Lenox. "And he is still bound?"

"No, but there are men with him."

"Let's hope."

Lenox went downstairs, Carrow and McEwan on his heels. To his relief Billings was seated by the broad hearth of the kitchen table. Over his head was a row of pots and pans, and beneath them a row of bells corresponding to the various rooms of the house.

"There he is!" Billings bellowed when Lenox came into view. "The man who assaulted me!"

Carrow laughed. Sir Wincombe looked at Billings and said, "My dear man, it won't do, it won't do."

But Billings had evidently decided on this as a stratagem. "Invited me to his room and assaulted me! He must have killed Halifax and Martin, too, the bastard!"

If Billings was bothered by the incredulous faces ranged around the room, staring at him, he didn't show it. He continued to bellow accusations at Lenox.

"Tell me again, McEwan," said Carrow, "how you found these two men?"

"Mr. Billings had a knife at Mr. Lenox's throat. And Mr. Billings said he wanted to have his penknife in Mr. Lenox."

"What do you say to that, Billings?" asked Carrow in a mild voice.

"Lies! They both did it! I'll get you, McEwan, you great cow!"

Lenox turned to Carrow. "I would feel most comfortable if he were in the brig of the *Lucy*. Sir Wincombe?"

"I see no reason why he shouldn't be transported there."

"Thank you. Now, if nobody minds, I need two or three hundred hours of sleep to feel myself again. Sir Wincombe, I fear I must cancel my appointments this morning."

"Of course, Mr. Lenox, of course."

He slept uneasily, starting out of his rest more than once with a terror. Only when McEwan brought him a glass of sherry at two that afternoon did his nerves settle. He ate ravenously of the lunch McEwan fetched in afterward, quail roasted golden with honey and raisins, cooked in the local fashion, mashed potatoes, and some of the red currant jelly Lady Jane had sent along with him. A cup of tea finally restored him to himself. It had been a harrowing week, and there was more ahead. The next morning he would meet with Ismail the Magnificent.

He went back to the *Lucy* with a feeling of homecoming, her creaking boards and snapping sails. There was a smile from every sailor he saw. His cabin was empty, but McEwan set that straight soon enough, filling his bookshelves and covering his desk.

When he was settled, he asked McEwan to find his nephew.

Teddy came into his cabin with an anxious, distracted air, and though he seemed truly happy about Lenox's survival—word had spread around the ship already, and the sailors held the life of Billings, who was in the brig, very cheap indeed—and enjoyed a cup of tea and a biscuit and spoke with Lenox about his one trip into Port Said, and what he had seen, his mien of distracted worry never left him. Nor could Lenox elicit the mood's cause. Age, perhaps.

After he said good-bye to his nephew Lenox took himself to the quarterdeck, where he said hello to the passing officers, including a curt Mitchell and a chatty Pettegree. Strange to think of how the wardroom had changed in only two weeks.

For the rest of the day he stayed in his cabin and read—first by daylight, and after dusk by candlelight—a memorandum that Chowdery and Arbuthnot had prepared for him on the subject of Ismail the Magnificent.

CHAPTER FIFTY-TWO

In the morning Lenox went across to the docks in the *Bootle* with four of Carrow's heartiest, most impressive men, all dressed in their formal uniforms. At the docks were Chowdery, his wife—"She nearly always runs late, but she would not miss this!"—and Arbuthnot, who was rather graver, and who whispered instructions into Lenox's ear as they stepped into carriages. A detachment of ten British soldiers were with them.

At the wali's palace Lenox met with a series of increasingly important gentlemen, who welcomed him and gave him further instructions about his introduction to Ismail.

As it happened, however, Ismail himself was less formal. He shook Chowdery's hand, waved off everyone else, and invited Lenox to sit on his balcony alone.

It was hard to hear words like *wali* or *khedive* without picturing an exotic, long-bearded ruler, perhaps erratic in temperament and taste. Ismail was different. He had a short beard and, other than the medals pinned to his chest, wore what any gentleman in Hyde Park or the Place des Vosges might have. In fact the person he most resembled was King Henry the Eighth, or at least the portraits of him. Coffee and a tremendous array of foods were waiting on the balcony, which looked out over the port city.

In a heavy accent, he said, "I have been to your country several times, Mr. Lenox—yes, and sat with your Victoria, and been inside your Parliament. They gave me the Order of the Bath. But my heart must belong to France. It was there I studied, and it is the French who have built my canal."

"I love France as well. I took my honeymoon there."

"Ah? Tell me of your wife, sir. She awaits your return in London?"

A vision of Jane's loving, calm face appeared in Lenox's mind. "We were childhood friends, and now we are having a child."

"I congratulate you!" Ismail snapped his fingers and a man appeared from the shadows. "Please see that Mr. Lenox receives a present, for his child."

The man nodded and bowed his way away from them. "Thank you so much," said Lenox. "I have brought you—"

"Wonderful things, I do not doubt. You will have heard I like gadgets. Good. Yet the reason I wished to meet with you— more than a formal meeting, at which we would exchange presents, you understand—is because I know you are on the next ship for London."

"Oh?"

"We need money, Mr. Lenox. Do you see my hands?" He held them out, as if for inspection. "With these hands I have taken my country, ripped it away from Africa, and joined it to Europe. Do you understand the importance of that?"

"Yes, of course."

"Then you will also understand the cost. Opera houses. Industry. The canal, Mr. Lenox. To become European, I had to spend money."

This was unusual frankness, Lenox believed, though the

facts of Egypt's debt were widely known. "Yes," he said cautiously.

"What will you give me, Mr. Lenox?"

It was clear that the customary answer to this question, when Ismail posed it, was "My life," or something close to that. Lenox merely inclined his head. "Certainly I will speak with my colleagues—"

"We need action. Soon."

"Oh?"

"I would never sell my share in the canal. That may go without saying. But it is in your interest as well as our own that Egypt succeed."

A thought dawned on Lenox, then. The wali said that his share in the canal was not for sale—but then, why not? It would take an almost unfathomable amount of money, say three, four, perhaps even five million pounds. But why not spend it? Even from here he could see the canal, crammed with small craft, and then, as Sournois has said, to join England's interests to France's . . .

"You have my word that Great Britain will support your country, khedive."

"Good."

The wali rose, extended his hand, and, after they had shaken, walked away, his coffee still warm and untouched in its cup.

The rest of the day was taken up with meetings with various members of Ismail's retinue, men who offered various ideas, all of which came down to England buying into the canal, somehow and someway. To Lenox, more and more, it seemed that the idea of buying Egypt's share outright would be ideal. That was the idea he would take back to Parliament.

To celebrate the official meeting there was another supper that evening at the consulate, this time with Carrow and his officers in attendance and the traitor, the earl's son, Ashenden, nowhere to be seen. Lenox inquired after him.

"He is bound for the interior of the continent, I understand, on very short notice," said Arbuthnot. "He is a great shooter."

"Indeed," Lenox answered. "I shall have to tell people I have seen him when I'm in London again . . ."

There were men of all nationalities present, Egyptian, French, English, American, Dutch. The noise and the pomp were both at high levels, and Lenox followed Sir Wincombe's speech with a brief address of his own.

In truth, though, he wanted to be back at sea. The glimpse of Jane he had seen in his mind today had made him long for her, for their house on Hampden Lane, for the mingled chaos and order of life in London. He felt a very long way from home.

Over the next several days there were more meetings. For the sake of getting to and from them on time he moved back to the consulate after two nights on board the *Lucy*—the days were too taxing otherwise. At his meetings he heard a great many statistics about customs, about sugar production, about shallow and deep draft vessels. Ismail had been correct: it was, in fact, like Europe here. But when Lenox went back through the streets of Port Said on a tour, he saw that at the same time it was different, and perhaps always would be.

Finally all of his responsibilities were concluded—an amiable supper with several important Frenchmen, Sournois not in their number. It was the morning of the *Lucy*'s departure. She was in fine shape, according to McEwan, having taken provisions on board and made a few minor repairs. The representative of the admiralty in Port Said had charged Carrow with returning the ship to England.

They set out for the *Lucy* early in the morning, seen off by a not very regretful Chowdery, who looked eager to get back to his library, and his imperious wife, who bestowed on Lenox a small parcel of books and letters that she asked Lenox—with more of the air of an order than a request—to deliver to several addresses in London for her.

For his part McEwan was carrying a bundle of packages that were larger than anything he had taken away from the *Lucy*. Food, Lenox suspected. It was gray and cool as the *Bootle* carried them through the water. From a thousand yards away it was obvious that the *Lucy* had been painfully, thoroughly cleaned; she sparkled in her masts and her rigging. An involuntary smile made its way onto Lenox's face.

"Welcome!" said Carrow when they came back on board. "You two, help them with the trunk. Yes, you can put down your cocoa, it will still be here in a moment. Go, go."

(It had been a surprise to Lenox, who associated the navy so strongly with rum, to discover how strongly affectionate the men felt for their breakfast cocoa and biscuits.)

"Your work went well on land, Mr. Lenox?" said Carrow.

"I thank you, Captain, very well."

"Excellent. No more trips to shore?"

"No, thank you."

"In that case, gentlemen, all sail set!" Carrow's voice boomed out, and the men of the *Lucy* burst into action.

As for Lenox, he asked McEwan for a cup of tea, and drank it by the taffrail, where he watched Port Said recede very slowly from view, with that occasional feeling one has in life of leaving a place to which one will likely never return.

CHAPTER FIFTY-THREE

The next two weeks of sailing were full of happy, golden days. It was as if the gods of the sea had decided to offer some small compensation for the benighted journey to Egypt, with its murders, its storms, its threat of mutiny. The wind was steady and the sun warm, and all the men were in excellent spirits, both the sailors and the officers.

Carrow's presence helped enormously. After three or four days Lenox perceived that the young man had the makings not of a good but of a great captain. Martin had been good; Carrow would exceed him. What had seemed dourness in the third lieutenant now seemed like the poise and reserve of a man with responsibility. There was nothing tentative or halting about him. He commanded by instinct.

In turn everyone on ship trusted him instinctively, and with good reason: Carrow knew more about sails than the sailmaker; more about the *Lucy*'s provisions than the purser; could set a mast as well as a forecastleman who had been on the water thirty years; could swab the decks if he had to; could make two provisions of salt beef seem like four; could give a speech; could fight a battle; could set a broken limb; could weather a storm; could laugh with his inferiors without losing their respect; could lead men. The bluejackets no sooner heard his words than they fell to his commands. With a different third lieutenant raised to the captaincy it might have been a different voyage.

Lenox had friends in the upper reaches of the navy, and as each day passed his conviction grew that he must tell them what he knew of Carrow's talent. It was impossible to say with an institution as self-regarding and hidebound as the admiralty, but he hoped that in fact the fate that Billings had assigned himself—to take the *Lucy* in the absence of another leader—would fall instead to Carrow. At least some good might come of the whole foul chain of events.

For his part Lenox spent his afternoons reading and his mornings writing an account, by the end some forty pages, of his impressions of Egypt. This was an accompaniment of his official six-page report, and he planned to circulate it among certain key allies in Parliament, for it argued well, he hoped, for England's greater involvement in Egypt's affairs. There were a select few issues that he had argued passionately about on the floor of the House of Commons—cholera safety, for instance, suffrage, Ireland—and now, almost accidentally, almost by the way, he felt he had found another.

The only blot on Lenox's happiness was Teddy's behavior. He was still in a preoccupied and restless mood, and he seemed to have less to do with his fellows in the gunroom. It was a pity, after they had all seemed to get along so well. When Lenox tried to ask the boy, he met with a definite—if polite—rejection. What would Edmund say, if he found his son this way?

For that matter, he wondered, what would he say, or Jane,

when they learned about the murderer who had been loose aboard the *Lucy*? Lenox thought of this and felt a certain gladness that the world was still a large place; it was getting smaller, to be sure, distances were collapsing—why, the Suez was an example of that! Yet it was a relief to him that he hadn't been able to, say, telegram Jane from the deck of the *Lucy*. Fifty years hence it would be possible, but for now it had saved her, and his brother, a great deal of worry. Then, there was a feeling of majesty to sailing back from Egypt, of wide distances traversed. Though he loved progress, part of him hoped the steamship wouldn't make Egypt a mere two-day voyage away, and take that feeling of majesty with it.

On the sixth day of their voyage he woke to find that they were becalmed. He went on deck and found Lieutenant Lee staring with a look of puzzlement at the water.

"What's down there?" said Lenox.

"I just wonder whether we might give the men a swim. Perhaps I'll ask the Captain."

So it was that Lenox witnessed the men as they dipped a sail into the water and bound it off at the end to form a kind of swimming pool just beside the ship. The sailors—many of whom were appalling swimmers, or couldn't swim at all—spent hours that morning splashing in the water, with great happiness neglecting their duties as the officers looked indulgently on.

Lenox, meanwhile, had another plan for the windless day. After he had spent an hour or two at his desk, he wandered over to what had been Halifax's cabin. Its contents were intact, and in the corner there stood, still, his fishing poles and his tackle box.

Lenox had some experience fishing, in the lakes and ponds of Sussex, where he had grown up. With Carrow's permission he cast off over the rail and spent a happy two hours there. The sun was wonderfully warm without being too hot, and the sky was a clear, cloudless blue. He realized that he would miss being on the water, when the voyage was over.

His luck was indifferent. Two bites in the first hour came to nothing, and it was only when he had nearly given up that he felt a powerful tug on his line. McEwan, who had been fetching up a couple of sandwiches, helped him tug the great fish in.

"What is it?" Lenox said when they caught a glimpse of silver beneath the water. "You, fetch the cook!" he said to a passing sailor.

They had pulled the fish in when the cook came and told them it was a sea bream. "And twelve pounds or I'm a liar," he added.

That night the wardroom ate the fish in white wine and lemon, and toasted many times over to the memory of Halifax.

The next day there was wind again, and the ship sailed upon it again. Lenox felt an urge to see Billings.

The *Lucy's* former first lieutenant was in a brig on the lowest deck, with the rats, the supplies, and the goods for trade that the ship had taken on in Egypt. It was lightless and bleak there, and the brig itself was a very small room, without room for a grown man to lie down fully. When he saw it Lenox felt a pang of sympathy for Billings. Softness, that.

"Lieutenant," he said.

"That you, Lenox?"

"Yesterday I went fishing with Halifax's rod and reel."

"Go and throttle yourself with the reel, if you please."

"Do you feel any remorse?"

There was a pause. "I want to do it again."

"So now you admit that you killed them?"

"It's my word against yours, down here."

Lenox sighed. "You're getting enough to eat and drink?" he said.

"Yes."

"Good day, then."

These were the last words he ever exchanged with Billings. Within eight months the man was hanged, though not before he gained a measure of Fleet Street notoriety as the "Surgeon of the *Lucy*," a sobriquet that seemed terribly unfair to Tradescant. Lurid details emerged of Billings's childhood, of his father, and a report from Egypt indicated that a hastily covered corpse answering to Butterworth's description had been discovered near Port Said.

The episode had one sequel that mitigated the awfulness of the murders in Lenox's mind. Some three months after he was back in London Lenox received a call from Halifax's father, Mr. Bertram Halifax. In person and character he was exactly like his son: gentle, quick to smile, kind-spirited.

"I came to thank you for your letter, Mr. Lenox. It was most thoughtful of you."

"Your son seemed a wonderful fellow."

"Ah, he was! Never cried as a baby, you know. That's rare. Always smiled, from birth on." The father's voice was shaky now. "A splendid lad, I swear it."

"Could I take you to lunch?" Lenox asked. "I'd like to hear more about him."

The elder Halifax recovered his nerve, and answered cheerfully in the affirmative. As they ate they found each other's company congenial, and thereafter the two men met every six weeks or so, perhaps every two months, for lunch, until after a year they had become true and firm friends.

CHAPTER FIFTY-FOUR

When they were three days from London—they were taking Lenox and Billings there, before the *Lucy* went on again to Plymouth—Teddy Lenox knocked on his uncle's cabin door.

"Come in!" called Lenox.

"Hello, Uncle Charles."

"Teddy! How are you?"

"Could I have a crown, Uncle, please?"

"A crown! That's a great deal of money. What do you want to buy?"

"Nothing."

"I can get you that for cheaper than a crown. Come now, tell me what's happened?"

The boy's bottom lip started to tremble, until he screwed it up tight. At last he managed to choke out the words, "I owe it to Pimples."

"You've been gambling?"

"Follow the Leader," Teddy managed to say, and then he burst into tears.

"There, there," he said. "You shall have it, but your father shall hear of it, d'you understand?"

Teddy nodded miserably, but already his face looked a little bit brighter. "Thank you."

"And you must never gamble again."

"Oh, never!"

So that was what had caused the lad's mood. How clearly Lenox remembered the stormy emotions of that age, when anything might seem like the end of the world! What it made him think of most of all was the child growing in Lady Jane, and the thousand such moments that awaited him in the next twenty years, as the child grew into an adult. It filled him partway with fear, but mostly with happiness.

"Well, here you are," he said, and handed over the money. "And in the bargain I'll give you a cup of tea. McEwan!"

"Thank you, Uncle Charles!" said Teddy, the coin in his tightly clenched fest. "I'll pay you back out of my pocket money, I promise."

"Well, and interest begins at nine percent. There, McEwan, fetch us some tea—and some biscuits, why not?" With his own child he would have to be sterner, but that was a father's job, and an uncle might be a gentler touch.

The smile returned to Teddy's face after that, and again he was thick with his fellow midshipmen, all of them somewhere between boyhood and manhood. On the final night of the voyage Carrow had them all to eat in the captain's dining room, and delivered a very fine toast in Lenox's honor. In turn Lenox rose and spoke of the *Lucy* and her men, and how fond he had grown of her.

"She has come to seem like home to me in these few short weeks—"

"You could always join up," said Carrow, and everyone laughed.

"Not just at the moment, thank you," said Lenox, and laughed too. "At any rate, I wanted to thank you all. Thank God the Queen has you all serving in her navy."

"The Queen!" shouted Pimples, and the toast was taken up by everyone else, shouted in high spirits, and then they drank.

The next morning was breezy and wet. They saw land at eight, and by ten they were close indeed to Greenwich, where they would dock. Lenox had packed his trunk, and Teddy, by special dispensation from Carrow, was permitted fifteen minutes on land to see his father, before the *Bootle* returned to fetch Billings.

The last thing Lenox packed was his sheaf of notes from the meeting with Sournois, the first thing he would pass to Edmund.

"McEwan!" he called out when his cabin was bare again.

The steward's head popped around the doorway, its cheeks full. "Sir? A last cup of tea, sir, or a sandwich?"

"Come in here, would you?"

"Of course, sir."

"I don't suppose you want to leave the *Lucy*? Come work for me?"

"Oh, no, sir!"

"Tell me then, what reward I can give you for saving my life—and for tipping me off about Follow the Leader, too."

"None, sir, please."

Lenox went to his desk and found a piece of paper. "Here's what I'll do, then. Have you been to Harrods?"

"No, sir. I've heard of it."

"They've everything you can imagine to eat—ostrich eggs and chocolates from Ghent and cakes and pies, food as far as the eye can see. Next time you're in London, take this note to the food hall, and have twenty pounds of credit as a thank you from me. They'll know my signature. That should keep you in cold chicken and marmalade for a year or so."

McEwan's eyes widened. "Thank you, sir!"

"No, it is you who must accept my thanks. You've been a wonderful steward."

A few moments later the anchor went down. The officers were standing in a ring, offering him a formal good-bye. Lenox shook them each by hand, Tradescant, Carrow, the chaplain, and said his thanks. A moment later he was over the gunwales and into the *Bootle*.

Both he and Teddy looked back at the *Lucy* for a moment, and then turned their gaze toward the docks at Greenwich. This was the day they had been due to return; Edmund would come, he knew, but he had told Lady Jane not to, only to wait at home.

Then he saw with a great lift of his heart that she stood on the docks, staring distractedly in exactly the wrong direction, her hair different than when he had left her, her stomach much larger, their two dogs, Bear and Rabbit, sitting and staring along with her in exactly the wrong direction. With her was his brother.

"Jane!" he called out when they were near. "Edmund!"

"Father!" said Teddy.

Jane whirled and saw them and a great smile appeared on her face. "Charles, Charles!" she said.

"Don't shift yourself, please," he said. "Stay there—your health."

"Bother it!"

He stepped onto the dock and Jane gave him a tight, quick hug, with so many people looking on. "Oh dear, I'll become emotional. Here now, show me your teeth—ah, so the scurvy didn't claim you—excellent, good. Oh, you dear man," she said, and embraced him again.

Meanwhile Edmund and Teddy were meeting, speaking to each other with smiles on their faces.

"How are you?" said Charles, and took her hands in his. "Happy and healthy?"

"Happy, and very healthy indeed. How wonderful to have you back, though! I've planned a supper for this evening—Dallington, of course, McConnell, your brother, Molly, Graham will come, Lord Cabot—how happy we are to have you back!"

"How happy I am to be home!"

He turned and looked back out toward the *Lucy*. As it always did when one traveled, the world felt bigger. But then, in due course, it would shrink back down to its normal size—or perhaps, if he were lucky, seem slightly bigger than it had been before.

"Tell me, did you capsize many times?" Lady Jane asked. "Were they kind to you? What was that sultan fellow like? Tell me everything, all at one time, please."

Lenox laughed. "Well, there's a great deal to tell . . ."

The reunion between father and son was no less happy. As he was reassuring himself that his son had retained all of his limbs on his first sea voyage, Edmund Lenox caught a glimpse of Charles out of the corner of his eye, and it made him glad somewhere deep within to have his brother back on English soil.

"Sophia," he heard Charles whisper to Jane, and she smiled and embraced him. Edmund remembered hearing it very specifically, the whisper, but he did not learn the meaning and import of that stray word until several months later: Only after Charles and Jane had their child, a baby girl.

Turn the page for a sneak peek at
Charles Finch's new novel

A DEATH IN THE SMALL HOURS

Available November 2012

CHAPTER ONE

Charles Lenox sat in the study of his town house in Hampden Lane—that small, shop-lined street just off Grosvenor Place where he had passed most of his adult life—and sifted through the piles of various papers that had accumulated upon his desk, as they would, inevitably, when one became a member of Parliament. In fact now they were like a kind of second soul that inhabited the room with him, always longing for attention. There were outraged letters about the beer tax from his constituents in Durham; confidential notes from members of the other party, inviting his support on their bills; reports on India, anarchism, and the poor laws; and oh, any number of things beside. It hadn't been an easy year so far, 1874. As his stature within the House increased, as he progressed from the backbenches to the front—aided, in part, by the knowledge of international affairs he had gained on a trip to Egypt that spring—the amount of work increased commensurately.

While he organized his correspondence, Lenox's mind worked over each problem the papers presented in turn, going a little ways on one, then turning back to the start, then going slightly farther, like a farmer plowing a furrow, setting out to break still newer ground. If he could get Cholesey and Gover, of the Tories, to agree to vote for the Ireland bill, then he might just permit Gover and Mawer to let it be known that he would stand behind the military bill, in which case Mawer might . . . His thoughts ran on and on, ceaselessly formulating and analyzing.

Eventually he sighed, sat back, and turned his gaze to the thin rain that fell upon the window. Whether he knew it or not he had changed in the past few years, perhaps since his election, and would have looked to someone who hadn't seen him since then indefinably different. His hazel eyes were the same, kind but sharp, and he was still thin, if not positively ascetic, in build. His short brown beard had been clipped only the evening before to its customary length. Perhaps what was different was that he had developed the air of someone with responsibility—of multiple responsibilities, even. Thinking of one of them now, his face changed from discontent to joy, and though his eyes stayed on the street a great beam of a smile appeared on his face.

He stood. "Jane!"

There was no reply, so he went to the door of the study and opened it. This room of his was a long, book-filled rectangle a few feet above street level, with a desk near the windows; at the other end of it, around the hearth, stood a group of comfortable maroon couches and chairs.

"Jane!"

"Keep quiet!" a voice cried back in an urgent whisper from upstairs.

"Is she asleep?"

"She won't be for long, if you bellow about the house like an auctioneer."

He came out to the long hallway that stretched from the

front of the door to the back of the house, rooms on either side of it, and a stairwell near the end of it. His wife came down this now, her face full of exasperation and affection at once.

"May I go up and see her?"

Lady Jane reached the bottom of the stairs and smiled at him. She was a pretty woman, in rather a plain way, dark-haired and at the moment pale, wearing a gray dress with a pale pink ribbon at the waist. The impression she often left on people was of inherent goodness—or perhaps that was the impression she left primarily on Lenox, because he knew her so well, and therefore knew that quality in her. For many long years they had been dear friends, living side by side on Hampden Lane; now, still to his great surprise, they were man and wife. They had been married four years before.

To add to his great happiness and evergreen surprise, at long last they had been blessed with a gift that made him stop and smile to himself at random moments throughout every day, as he just had in his study. A gift that never failed to lift his spirits above the intransigent tedium of politics: a daughter, Sophie.

She had been theirs for three months, and every day her personality developed in new, startling, wonderful directions. Almost every hour he snuck away from his work to glimpse her sleeping, or better yet, awake. Granted, she didn't do much— she was no great hand at arithmetic, as Lady Jane would joke, seldom said anything witty, would prove useless aboard a horse—but he found even her minutest motions enchanting. Babies had always seemed much of a muchness to him, but how wrong he had been! When she wriggled an inch to the left he found himself holding his breath with excitement.

"Hadn't we better let her sleep?"

"Just a glance."

"Go on, then—but quietly, please. Oh, but wait a moment—a letter came for you in the post, from Everley. I thought you would want it straight away." Lady Jane patted the pockets of her dress. "I had it a moment ago . . . yes, here it is." She handed him the small envelope. "Can you have lunch?"

"I had better work through it."

"Shall I have Kirk bring you something, then?"

"Yes, if you would."

"What would you like?"

"Surprise me."

She laughed her cheery, quiet laugh. "I doubt Ellie will surprise you very far." This was their cook, who was excellent but not much given to innovation.

He smiled. "Sandwiches will be fine."

"I'll go out for luncheon, then, if you don't mind. Duch invited me to come around. We're planning her Christmas ball." Lady Jane, rather more than Lenox, was one of the arbiters of Mayfair society, and much sought after.

"I shan't see you for supper, either."

"Dallington?"

"Yes. But we'll put Sophie into bed together?"

She smiled, then stood on her toes to kiss his cheek. "Of course. Good-bye, my dear."

He stopped her with a hand on the arm, and leaned down to give her a kiss in return. "Until this evening," he said, his heart full of happiness, as so often it was these days.

After she had gone downstairs to arrange his lunch with the butler and the cook, Lenox remained in the hall, where he opened his letter. It was from his uncle Frederick, a relation of Lenox's late mother.

Dear Charles,

Please consider this a formal invitation to come down for a week or two, with Jane of course and the new Lenox; I very much want to meet her. The garden is in fine shape and Fripp is very anxious to have you for the cricket, which takes place next Saturday. I haven't seen you in more than a year, you know.

Yours with affection &c,
Frederick Ponsonby

Postscript: To sweeten the pot, shall I mention that in town, recently, there have been a series of strange vandalisms? The police cannot make head or tail of them and so everyone is in great stir. Perhaps you might lend them a hand.

Lenox smiled. He was very fond of his uncle, an eccentric man, retiring and very devoted to his small, ancient country house, which lay just by a small village. Since the age of four or five Lenox had gone there once a year, usually for a fortnight, though it was true that the stretches between visits had gotten longer more recently, as life had gotten busier. Still, there was no way he could leave London just at this moment, with so many political matters hanging in the balance. He tucked the note into his jacket pocket and turned back to his study.

Ah, but he had forgotten: Sophie! With soft steps he bounded up the stairs, past a maid carrying a coal scuttle, and to her room. The child's nursemaid, Miss Taylor, sat in a chair outside the bedroom, reading. She was a brilliant young woman, accomplished in drawing and French—both useless to the infant at the moment, but fine endowments nevertheless—who had a reputation as the most sought-over nursemaid in London. She cared for a new child every year or so, always infants. Jane had acquired this marvel for them—at great expense, to Lenox's derision—and he had to admit that she was wonderful with Sophie, with a gentle comprehension and tolerance for even the child's worst moods. Despite her relative callowness—while she was perhaps two and thirty, her complexion retained to an unusual degree the bloom of youth—Miss Taylor was an imperious figure; they both lived in frank terror of offending her. Still, she was used to Lenox's frequent interruptions and indulged them with less severity now than she had at first.

"Only for a moment, please," she whispered.

"Of course," he said.

He went into the room and crossed the soft carpet as quietly as he could. He leaned over her crib and with a great upsurge of love and joy looked down upon his child. Such a miracle! Her serenely sleeping face, rather pink and sweaty at the moment, her haphazard blond curls, her little balled-up fists, her skin as smooth and pure as still water when you touched it, as he did now, with the back of his fingers—she was absolute perfection.

It was happiness beyond anything he had ever known.

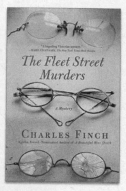

"*Somewhere in detective heaven, Sherlock Holmes and Lord Peter Wimsey are already preparing a glass of hot whiskey for Mr. Charles Lenox.*"

—Louis Bayard

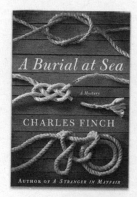

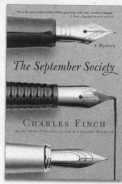

Don't miss *DEATH IN THE SMALL HOURS*
available November 2012